Hugh stared down at the windows of Faith Carson's house.

He'd almost given himself away when he'd let his reaction to seeing Beth's child for the first time get the better of him. Caitlin Carson was Beth's child—he was convinced of it, although he couldn't say how he knew.

But according to the law, Faith was Caitlin's mother. He'd seen a copy of the birth certificate. Everything about it seemed to be in order. Still, he knew his hunch was right. Even though the accident that had killed Jamie and taken Beth's memory had occurred a hundred miles away, he was sure his sister had been in this place. Here she'd given birth and for some reason, left her child behind.

It was the slightest of hunches that had brought him to Painted Lady Farm. A baby born to a woman alone, during a terrible ice storm. A woman who was a nurse and could have delivered a frightened teenager's baby. A woman who was also a widow and had, perhaps, despaired of ever having a child of her own—and who might have been desperate enough to risk keeping another woman's baby.

He didn't know the details, but nothing he'd learned led him to believe that Faith Carson was a baby snatcher. He was determined to find the truth, but he had to proceed carefully. He wasn't the only one searching for Beth's baby.

ABOUT THE AUTHOR

Marisa Carroll is the pen name of the writing team of Carol Wagner and Marian Franz of Deshler, Ohio. The sisters have published over thirty romance novels in the past twenty years and have been the recipients of several industry awards, including *Romantic Times* Career Achievement Award and a B. Dalton Booksellers' Award. They have also been finalists for the RWA RITA® Awards and have appeared on numerous bestseller lists, including the USA TODAY list.

Carol and Marian were born and raised in northwestern Ohio. They pursued careers in nursing, X-ray technology and the business community before entering the writing field in 1982. Marian is employed at Bowling Green State University in Bowling Green, Ohio. Carol is writing full-time.

Books by Marisa Carroll

HARLEQUIN SUPERROMANCE
655—PEACEKEEPER
718—THE MAN WHO SAVED CHRISTMAS
742—MEGAN
811—BEFORE THANKSGIVING
841—WINTER SOLDIER
942—LAST-MINUTE MARRIAGE

Little Girl Lost
Marisa Carroll

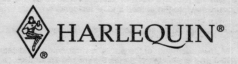

HARLEQUIN®

TORONTO • NEW YORK • LONDON
AMSTERDAM • PARIS • SYDNEY • HAMBURG
STOCKHOLM • ATHENS • TOKYO • MILAN • MADRID
PRAGUE • WARSAW • BUDAPEST • AUCKLAND

ISBN 0-373-71113-1

LITTLE GIRL LOST

Visit us at www.eHarlequin.com

Printed in U.S.A.

Little Girl Lost

CHAPTER ONE

THE CALENDAR SAID it was November, but the scudding gray clouds and lowering sky made it seem as though winter had arrived in southern Ohio. The maples and slippery elms had long ago lost their leaves. The mottled trunks of the sycamores blended into the white and gray of the storm clouds. Only the oaks held stubbornly to their tattered brown leaves, the way she had been holding stubbornly to her grief.

No, not stubbornly, Faith Carson told herself as she trudged along the path that skirted a small lake and ended at a tiny, hidden roadside park bordering her farm. "Surely six months isn't too long to mourn a dead husband?"

She wasn't talking to herself, not really. She'd addressed the question to her two-year-old Shetland sheepdog, Addy, trotting at her heels. She'd found Addy at the local animal shelter a few weeks after she'd moved into the echoing old farmhouse that Mark had inherited from his grandparents, and which, until three weeks after his death, Faith had never set foot in. Addy was the only friend Faith had at the moment. The little dog pricked her ears at the question and gave a yip of sympathetic agreement.

Six months. Not nearly long enough when that sorrow was coupled with the aching loss of a child barely conceived. Surely six months was only a beginning. Faith blinked hard to hold back tears as icy raindrops touched her cheeks. She had nothing left in her but a sense of bereavement so deep and unrelenting she sometimes felt as though she had died, too, on that mountain road in Mexico.

They had been vacationing, their first real vacation since their marriage, looking for the remote area where thousands of monarch butterflies came to spend the winter. Mark was a computer programmer whose passion was butterflies. It was a trip he had wanted to take for as long as she had known him. But a washed-out section of road and a blown tire had caused their rented Jeep to roll over.

Somehow, for some reason, her heart had gone on beating when Mark's had stopped as she held him in her arms and their baby's life drained away between her legs. A loss like that scarred the heart so much the healing might take six years, or sixty—or never come.

She walked out of the trees just behind the rustic two-sided building that, along with a pair of old-fashioned outhouses and a rusty jungle gym, were the park's only amenities. An expensive, sporty blue car was parked in the graveled lot at the edge of the small body of water the county had named Sylvan Lake, but that was still known to the locals of Bartonsville, Ohio, as Carson's Pond. A young couple, the boy's arms wrapped around the girl, her head resting on his shoulder, sat on one of the picnic tables near the blackened fieldstone fireplace that took up the entire north wall of the building. Faith halted, half-hidden by a huge pine whose low branches brushed the ground, and acted as a windbreak on one side of the small picnic shelter.

She hadn't expected anyone to be in the park on a day like this, certainly not a pair of amorous teenagers. She took a quick step back, deeper into the shadow of the pine. They hadn't seen her. She could melt back into the woods, retrace her steps through the frosty grass and be home before the raindrops that were now falling steadily changed to sleet. Addy growled low in her throat.

"Shh." Faith knelt down to fasten the leash she carried in her pocket to the dog's collar before Addy could begin barking in earnest. She scooped the small dog into her arms and prepared to depart. The teenagers were absorbed in each other and didn't look in her direction, but some trick of sound brought their words to her ears.

"Beth, we can't stay here. There must be a town close by. Maybe it's big enough for a hospital."

"If we go to a hospital they'll call your parents." The girl cried out, a moan of pain and fear. These weren't just two moonstruck teenagers making out. Something far more serious than that was going on. Addy whined nervously and squirmed in Faith's arms. The boy turned his head and stared directly into her eyes.

"Help us," he said, his face as gray-white as the

clouds and the sycamore trees. He was blond, broad-shouldered, square-jawed, seventeen or eighteen at most. A good-looking kid, or would be if he weren't half-scared to death. "My girlfriend's having a baby. And I don't know what to do."

Faith couldn't believe her ears, didn't want to. He couldn't have said what she thought she had heard.

"Please," he said, raising his voice so there could be no doubt as he repeated the words. "She's having a baby. I don't know what to do."

Instinctively Faith shook her head. "I don't, either," she murmured, but he couldn't hear her above the moaning of the wind in the trees. And she did know what to do. That was one of the things that made her own loss so hard to bear. She was a nurse. She had the skill and knowledge to help save lives. Once, she had even delivered a baby herself. But that had been five years ago in the hospital emergency room where she'd worked while Mark finished up his graduate studies. She had been young and fearless, then. Now she was not. She hadn't even set foot in a hospital since three days after her miscarriage.

The girl shifted her position, and Faith took a better look at her, her heart sinking. Her arms were wrapped around her swollen middle, which strained against the fabric of her pale-green sweater. She wasn't wearing a coat and shivered in the cold air. She was very, very pregnant. Her face was white, her eyes dark with fear. "I—I hurt so badly. I can't walk."

Feminine instinct and medical training took over,

marching Faith forward on stiff legs. She tied Addy to a sapling at the corner of the shelter and hushed her with a stern warning. The little dog dropped to her belly on the cold ground whimpering with anxiety, sensing the tension in the humans around her, but obedient to Faith's command.

Faith looked from one terrified young face to the other. "She needs to be taken to the hospital." She took off her all-weather coat and draped it around the shivering girl's shoulders. She was wearing the sweatshirt Mark had given her for Christmas the year before, a heavy black one covered front and back with butterflies so she would be warm enough without her coat.

"No!" The girl panted, then bit her lip and groaned, a low, guttural sound. The sound of a woman who was almost ready to give birth. Faith's heart hammered. This couldn't be happening. Not today of all days. The day her own child should have been born.

"Your baby is coming, and it shouldn't be born out here in the cold. I'll give you directions to the hospital in Bartonsville. When you get there the nurses can notify your families—"

Silvery strands of gossamer-fine hair danced in the cold air as the girl shook her head. "I don't have a family," she said defiantly. "Only my brother in Texas."

"What about you?"

"I—I don't have any family, either," he said miserably.

He was lying, but before Faith could call him on it another contraction rippled across the girl's belly. Less than two minutes had passed since the last one. She had to move quickly or the situation would get out of hand. "I'm Faith Carson. I live just down the road at the bottom of the next hill. What's your name, honey?"

"Beth."

"And you are?"

"Jamie." No surnames. Faith let the omission pass. For the moment there were more pressing matters.

"You're the baby's father?"

He nodded, his Adam's apple working up and down in his throat. "Is Beth going to be okay?"

"She needs expert care. You know that, don't you?"

"We were looking for a hospital. We got lost. I'm—I'm not used to driving in the country. The road's go every which way."

"It's okay. You're only a few miles from a good hospital. I'll give you directions, but you must leave now. Your baby's going to be born very soon if I don't miss my guess."

"How do you know it's going to be soon?" Beth was gasping for breath, clutching at Jamie's arm with both hands. He stood beside the table, ramrod straight, breathing almost as hard and fast as the mother-to-be.

Faith sighed. "I'm a nurse," she said. "I know."

"First babies take a long time, I've heard. This—this only started about an hour ago."

"Has your water broken?"

For a moment Beth looked puzzled, then nodded. "Yes," she said. "I didn't know what it was at first, then I remembered from health class. It was this morning. Then the cramps started." She began to sob. "I hurt so bad. I just want to get this thing out of me." The sobs turned to a groan, and she dropped her hands to the tabletop, lifting herself into a crouch, straining against the contraction.

"Don't push," Faith ordered automatically. "Try to breathe through the contraction. Like this." She made an O with her mouth and panted.

Beth tried, but she was too upset and in too much pain for the exercise to do any good. She cried out and her knees buckled.

Jamie had gone from looking scared to terrified. "Help us. I don't know what to do. The doctor at the clinic in...back home...told us the baby probably wasn't due for another three weeks."

"Have you had regular prenatal care?" Faith asked.

"I—I just went twice. I had a test where they rub a wand over your stomach—"

"A sonogram," Faith supplied.

"Yes. My baby's a girl. But they wanted—" Beth broke off what she was about to say. Faith guessed it was that the clinic doctor wanted to notify her family. She was a little thing, and if she wore baggy clothes, like the sweater she had on now, she probably had been able to hide her pregnancy. "If we go to the hospital they'll take my baby away." Beth's eyes sought Faith's. They were blue Faith noted, as blue as a country sky on a cloudless June day.

"No they won't. Not unless you want to give the baby up."

"I want my baby." Beth bit down hard on her lower lip as another contraction began.

"Beth," Jamie said, his tone edged with desperation. "We've gone over this and over this. We don't have any money or jobs or a place to live. How can we take care of a baby?"

"Other girls have. I can, too. You don't have to marry me. You know that, Jamie. Your parents don't want you to, anyway."

"I—I just don't know how we'll manage—" He broke off as she cried out again. "Do something," he pleaded to Faith.

"Do you have a cell phone?" she asked.

Jamie wouldn't quite meet her eyes. "We lost it."

So much for the easy way out.

Faith took one more look at the car. It was a two-seater. Warmer than the open shelter, certainly, and out of the wind, but with little room to maneuver. If there was a problem with the birth she would be at an even greater disadvantage shoehorned inside it than she was now. Beth moaned again, leaning against her young lover, straining.

"Don't push," Faith said sharply. Beth's labor was progressing rapidly. Even if she left Addy behind and they all squeezed into the car, the baby's arrival would probably occur before they reached the hospital. "We're going to have to deliver the baby here," she said with false calm.

Beth started to cry harder. "I think so, too."

Faith reached out and touched her fingertips to Beth's cold cheek. She couldn't think about her own grief, couldn't remember that she should be laboring in the same way as this girl, bringing the baby she had longed for so desperately into the world.

"It's going to be okay." She swallowed against the familiar lump of sorrow in her throat, made her voice as soothing as she could manage. "I'm going to deliver your baby and Jamie's going to help."

"Me?" He swallowed audibly. "I… What can I do?"

"Do you have any blankets in the car? Towels?"

"We have sleeping bags. And I have a couple of clean sweatshirts. Will they do?"

"Yes. We can wrap the baby in them. How about a pair of scissors?"

The last of the color drained out of Jamie's face as he made the connection. He shook his head. "No scissors."

"Not even cuticle scissors? A penknife, then." Faith held on to her composure with both hands. It wouldn't do to let these two terrified kids see that she was almost as afraid as they were.

"I have a penknife." Jamie pulled a small one out of his pocket. "It's sharp."

"Good. That will do."

She'd been burning trash earlier that morning so

she had matches in her pocket. She could sterilize the blade to cut the umbilical cord. But she would need something to clear the baby's nose and mouth, and something to tie off the cord. "Do you have any cotton swabs? Dental floss?"

"In my makeup case," Beth groaned. "I have floss and Q-Tips. Will the baby be all right being born outside like this? It's so cold." She was shivering, but not entirely from the cold. Her legs were shaking hard, another sure sign she was far along in her labor.

"Everything will be fine," Faith assured her, but she had no such assurance for herself. "Give me the knife." She held out her hand. "I'll deal with Beth's clothes while you get the things we talked about."

Jamie took off for the car at a run. Faith looked at the shivering girl on the wooden picnic table. It looked hard and uncomfortable but the only alternative was the stone floor. Thankfully Beth was wearing thin leggings and not jeans. If the penknife was sharp enough Faith thought she could split the crotch and panties and at least protect the girl's legs and feet from more exposure to the cold.

She told Beth her plan and the girl nodded, lifting her hips off the table. Faith said a little prayer of thanks that Jamie's knife was indeed sharp. The baby had not yet crowned but Faith was certain that one more contraction would bring the top of its head into view. She couldn't risk examining Beth anymore closely for fear of infection later; she had no way to sterilize her hands. Washing them in the icy water of the old-fashioned pump outside the shelter house would have to do. But she couldn't leave the laboring girl exposed on the table. She would have to wait on Jamie's return to do even that much.

"Try to relax," she said.

"Are you really a nurse?" Beth was half sitting, half reclining against Faith's arm. But her weight was slight.

"Yes."

"And you've delivered babies before?"

"Yes," Faith assured her. That it was long ago and far away needn't be said.

"You're wearing a wedding ring. Do you have children?"

"No. I'm a widow." The words came out tight and hard. There was no way she could stop them.

"I'm sorry for your loss," Beth said politely.

"So am I."

"I have to push again." The sounds Beth made deep in her throat were no longer quite human.

"Jamie, hurry!" Faith called over the rising wind and the sharp tattoo of sleet on the metal roof. Tiny icicles were already forming along the eaves, and the pine tree's needles had begun to chime slightly whenever the wind set the branches swaying. Addy turned her back to the wind and dropped her head on her paws.

Jamie started the car and left it idling. He ran up the slope to the shelter, slipping a little on the icy crust forming on the brown grass. His arms were full of two down sleeping bags, a couple of red sweat-

shirts and a small plastic case, pink and sparkling—
the kind of case teenage girls used to keep their trea-
sures safe, emphasizing again how young they both
were.

"Good thinking to start the car," Faith praised
him. "We'll move Beth and the baby inside as soon
as we can." The baby was crowning and there was
only time to lift Beth enough to slide one of the
sleeping bags beneath her and to wrap the other
around her as best they could. Faith murmured en-
couragement, forcing her breathing into a normal pattern, steeling herself not to show any of her own fear
and uncertainty.

Another contraction, another long unearthly moan,
and the head emerged. No one saw but Faith. Beth
was staring fixedly at the butterflies on Faith's sweatshirt, and Jamie was watching Faith, too, not wanting
to look between his girlfriend's legs.

Faith's cracked and bruised heart began bleeding
anew as she cradled the baby's head in her hands.
*Oh, God, why did you have to ask this of me today
of all days?*

Aloud she said only, "Okay, honey. You're doing
fine. Just rest now, wait for the next contraction."

Beth groaned. "When will it be over? It hurts too
much. I can't stand it any longer."

"Yes, you can," Faith said soothingly. "This will
do it. Her shoulders will come out and the rest of her
body will just slide along. I promise. Just push
slowly and steadily so you don't tear. You can do it,
come on."

"Please make it—" The word ended in a long drawn out moan as the baby's shoulders came free and the rest of her small body slipped into Faith's hands.

"You have a daughter," Faith said. *Mark had wanted their first child to be a girl.*

"The baby's not breathing," Jamie whispered.

At the words, Beth—who'd dropped her head against his shoulder—jerked upright. "She's not breathing. She's all blue. What's wrong?"

"Nothing's wrong. She's cold, that's all." Faith said another silent prayer that she was speaking the truth. She wiped the baby's face and head with one of the clean sweatshirts, then bundled her into a second, careful not to entangle the umbilical cord. She took a cotton swab and cleaned out her mouth and nostrils as gently, but as thoroughly as she could. It wasn't ideal, she really needed a suction bulb, but it would have to do. She tapped her middle fingernail against the soles of the infant's feet, then a second time a little harder. The baby's eyes popped open and she looked directly at Faith. She blinked once, then opened her mouth, took a deep breath and began to wail. The cry was weak and thready but the most beautiful sound Faith had ever heard.

"Look. She's turning pink," Beth murmured. "May I hold her?"

"Of course you can."

Faith placed the baby in her mother's arms, pulling the edges of the sleeping bag more closely around them both.

"She's awfully tiny." Jamie's voice cracked as he spoke.

"She's perfect," Beth murmured. "Just perfect."

Faith handed the matches to Jamie, who couldn't seem to take his eyes off his daughter. "Here, sterilize the knife blade with these. The afterbirth will be coming soon and we'll need to get the cord cut and tied. Do you want to do it?"

He shook his head. "You do it." His expression was suddenly grim.

Faith didn't press the matter. Beth was already beginning to breathe heavily with the beginning of another contraction. "This won't be as bad," Faith promised. "It's the afterbirth, the placenta."

Beth shook her head, smiling down at the tiny infant in her arms. "It's okay. I can handle it. Now that she's here, it's worth it. Oh, Jamie," she whispered, looking up at the boy with love shining from her sky blue eyes. "She's beautiful, isn't she?"

Jamie didn't smile back. He looked as if the entire weight of the world had shifted onto his shoulders. "She's so tiny. How will we take care of her?"

"We'll manage," Beth declared.

Jamie didn't speak again.

Faith delivered the placenta a few minutes later. It appeared to be intact and there was little bleeding. She recited a silent prayer of thanks. With any luck she would have her charges safely in the hands of the competent staff at Bartonsville Medical Center in a very short while.

She bundled the afterbirth into the oldest looking

of the sweatshirts Jamie had brought from the car. "We should take this along to the hospital for the doctor to check. You do realize that Beth and the baby need to be seen by a doctor? Your daughter is very tiny," she said quietly, so that only Jamie could hear. "She seems to be healthy but she might have some difficulty with her breathing, or regulating her temperature. Newborns sometimes do. She should be where she can be monitored."

"Problems breathing?" His nostrils flared and he swallowed hard. "Like needing oxygen and everything?"

Beth had overheard. "No. She's fine. We don't need to go to the hospital."

"Even if she is okay, we don't have any bottles or milk or diapers—"

"We can get them. And I'll nurse her," Beth said defiantly.

"You don't even know if you can. What if she gets too hungry? Or something like Mrs. Carson just said happens? We wouldn't know what to do."

"We'll learn."

"I've never even held a baby. She's so tiny." There was real panic in his voice. "We only have about sixty dollars left."

"It will have to do," Beth said, her eyes glued to the baby.

"That's barely enough for gas. No way can we stretch it to buy food and formula and diapers. I don't even know what else we need. I can't use the credit card—" He broke off realizing that he'd probably said too much. He glanced at Faith and his eyes were desperate, the reality of responsibility overwhelming any joy he felt at his child's birth. "Maybe it would be better if we—"

"No!" Beth's refusal cut off what he meant to say.

Faith interrupted. "We can work everything out when Beth and the baby are safe at the medical center." The ice storm had hit in earnest while Faith had been preoccupied with the baby's birth. Already a silvery sheet of ice covered everything in sight. It was going to be tricky walking home for her car, but there was no way she and Addy could fit into the sports car for the ride to the hospital.

Beth looked up from the baby to the car in the parking lot. "I don't know if I can carry her that far," she said. "I feel all wobbly."

"Give the baby to Mrs. Carson. I'll carry you."

"Please be careful with her, Jamie. If you should slip on the ice…" Faith let her voice trail off.

"I'll be careful," he promised. His face was chalk white. Once more he refused to meet her eyes.

She ought to press him for some answers now that the immediate danger to mother and child was past. Where had they come from? Where were they going? The infant cried out again, and it sounded weaker than before. She had waited this long to ask those questions, surely a few minutes more wouldn't make any difference. When Beth and the baby were safely in the small, but up-to-date maternity ward of the hospital there would be time for answers.

Beth had eyes only for the baby held tightly against her breast. Faith brushed her hand softly against the infant's cheek. Her baby's skin would have been this soft and rosy if she'd lived. There was dried blood under her fingernails just as there had been that awful day six months before. She dropped her hand quickly.

"It's time to go."

Beth's blue eyes darkened to the color of a twilight sky. "Couldn't we stay with you? You must live nearby. Just for a few hours…"

Faith shook her head. She couldn't have a baby in her house. Not today. "We might get trapped there by the storm. There's a bad one coming." She gestured to the icy scene beyond them. "It's already here. I promise you I'll come to the hospital as soon as I can get back to my home and get my car. There's no room in yours."

"We'd better get going," Jamie said. "I'm going to carry you, and Faith will bring the baby."

Beth's mouth tightened but she didn't protest again. "Okay." She lifted the small bundle toward Faith as though offering her the most precious gift in the world.

Faith swallowed hard again, but this time against the tears she could not let fall. How wonderful the fragile little body felt cradled against her breast. A tiny hand worked its way out of the folds of the sweatshirt and clamped onto Faith's cold finger. The baby was a fighter, stronger than she looked. She could feel the baby nuzzling, searching for nourishment. Warmth pooled in her womb and her heart, melting a bit of the ice that sealed her emotions away.

Jamie scooped Beth into his arms, sleeping bags and all, and started down the slope at a quick pace. Faith looked down at the baby she held. ''I wish you were my baby,'' she whispered very, very softly. ''I would love you and care for you as best I could if you were.''

But she was not. Faith's baby was dead. Her husband was dead and she was alone.

That was the reality of her life.

Addy began bouncing up and down, straining at her leash, barking in short, frantic yips. Shelties were herd dogs, bred for centuries to protect their flocks. And when they didn't have sheep to watch over they transferred those instincts to their human companions. She did not want to be left behind by her mistress, and she wasn't shy about letting Faith know. ''Sh, Addy. It's okay. I'm not leaving you. I'm just taking the baby to the car. Then we'll take the shortcut home through the woods.''

Faith turned her back on the indignant dog and stepped out from under the shelter into the stinging sleet just in time to watch Jamie open the driver's door and look back at her over the roof of the car. ''We can't take her with us, Mrs. Carson. Not all the way to Texas. I know you'll take good care of her. Keep her for us. We'll be back. I—'' His voice broke. ''I promise.''

What happened next would stay in Faith's memory

until the day she died. The sleek blue car sprayed ice and gravel from its back wheels as Jamie roared out of the parking lot and fishtailed down the steep, narrow drive toward the county road that led to the state highway. For a split second Faith saw Beth's face, her hands pressed against the window as if she were trying to escape, her mouth open in a soundless scream of anguish and protest.

"Don't go! Don't leave the baby."

But they were already gone.

Faith was alone in the storm.

But not really alone.

For she held in her arms the one thing she wanted most.

CHAPTER TWO

Two and a half years later.

HUGH DAMON RESTED his forearms on the steering wheel of his much traveled Blazer and looked out on the tapestry of farm fields that stretched toward the low hills on the horizon. In the shallow valley below him a century-old brick house sat squarely in the middle of a grove of massive oaks and maples.

Painted Lady Butterfly Farm and Guest Lodging, stated a tasteful white-and-gold-lettered sign on the grass verge of the sleepy county highway he'd been driving since he'd left Cincinnati an hour ago. He hadn't expected his search to bring him this far east, but it had.

The house itself was a monstrosity of Victorian overindulgence that made the engineer in him cringe. Elaborate gingerbread gables and bay windows abounded. There was even a widow's walk on the roof. But the native red brick had mellowed with the years, allowing the building to blend into its surroundings, and the ornate trim was painted a pale cream instead of white, softening the effect still more.

On the other hand the red, clapboard barn behind the house was a masterpiece of function and design. Set on a native stone base, it was large and imposing, with a high-pitched slate roof and the same cream paint on the doors and windows. A working barn from the looks of it. Through the open double doors Hugh could see a big green tractor and what looked like an even bigger combine, dwarfing a minivan. Farmers didn't build barns like that anymore. They couldn't afford to, and it was to the owner's credit that she spent the necessary money for its upkeep.

Beyond the barn were fields of soybeans and corn, the beans barely higher than the lush green carpet of lawn that abutted them, and the corn knee-high only to a small child at this stage of growth. There was also a pond complete with a small dock and an angled telephone pole with a long rope attached, just perfect for swinging out over the water on a hot summer's day.

A large fenced-in area several acres in size directly behind the big house wasn't planted in any cash crop, as far as Hugh could tell, but seemed to be left as meadow. Spindly, dried pods of milkweed provided sentinel posts for red-winged blackbirds. Red, pink and yellow flowers bloomed among the waving grasses. At the very edge of what he now recognized as a naturalized garden, there was a greenhouse-type building.

The butterfly house he'd read about on the Internet, he supposed. Along with the three small, fifties-era tourist cabins to his left, it gave Painted Lady Farm and Guest Lodging its claim to fame.

Butterflies.

Beautiful, ethereal, innocent. And in many cultures said to represent the souls of lost children.

The stuff of his sister's nightmares.

They were what had drawn him to this place.

Did it hold the answers he sought? Or was it just another dead end?

He'd find out soon enough. He turned his attention to the vintage cabins, one of which, the largest, he'd already reserved. They were painted the same cream color that highlighted the house and barn, but were accented in pine-green with window boxes filled with red geraniums, just coming into bloom. Round-backed, metal lawn chairs flanked the front doors inviting weary travelers to sit a spell and watch the sun set behind the hills.

The cabins, a reminder of times when travel cross-country was an adventure, not a blur of fast-food restaurants and strip malls glimpsed from a super-highway, were as carefully preserved and maintained as the barn and house. It was just good business to keep the place in top-notch shape, Hugh reminded himself. It was no indication whatsoever that the owner was a good and caring person who loved the land and its buildings. None at all.

A small sign, hanging beneath the larger one, proclaimed the farm and cottages the property of one Faith Carson and directed guests to the butterfly house for check-in, or to the back door of the main house if the butterflies weren't in season. But butterflies were very obviously in season this late May afternoon. A big yellow school bus was parked in the gravel lot beside the barn. Small children raced around the yard, some brandishing what appeared to be large, colorful foam butterflies attached to sticks, the boys attempting to fight duels, the girls swirling around like ballerinas. It seemed he had arrived in the midst of an elementary school outing to see the butterflies that Faith Carson raised.

Now was probably not the best time to announce his arrival. He wanted to meet the object of his search alone. If he had to wait until nightfall to gain that advantage he would.

He put the Blazer in gear and drove up the gentle rise to the top of the hill. An old but well-maintained cemetery occupied the crest, weathered marble stones warming in the sunshine. The lettering on most of the markers was so faded he couldn't read them from the road except for the newest one. The name engraved on the granite stone was Mark Carson and the date of death, just days short of three years before. It was the grave of Faith Carson's husband.

Hugh pulled the Blazer onto the grass and opened the door. The air was humid, filled with the scents of newly turned earth and the sound of birds. A gigantic red pine shaded the oldest of the stones. As he walked, he realized many of the graves belonged to Carsons, some predating the Civil War if he was reading the faded numerals correctly. Probably all related to the dead man whose headstone drew him closer almost against his will. Hugh had no idea what it was like to have roots this deep.

He'd left home at seventeen. And after their mother had died in a car accident five years ago he'd had no one but his half sister, Beth, in his life. To his eternal regret he hadn't returned to Texas to take care of her then. Instead he'd sent her off to the father she'd barely known in Boston. She'd been miserable and lonely, and like many miserable, lonely teenage girls she'd gotten pregnant. And run away. The flight had ended in a terrible accident that had killed her boyfriend and robbed Beth of her memory and almost her life.

And had sent him in search of a child she didn't remember.

A newborn baby that had disappeared without a trace.

Hugh hunkered down on the balls of his feet and peered more closely at the lettering on the stone.

Mark Carson
Beloved Husband of Faith
and
Father of Caitlin

The question that had driven him to this place wasn't whether the dead man was the father of Faith Carson's two-and-a-half-year-old daughter. But whether Faith Carson was actually her mother.

Or was the child she called hers, really his sister's baby?

That was what he'd come to Painted Lady Farm to find out.

Faith waved the Bartonsville Elementary School bus out of the yard. Having 35 eight-year-olds underfoot for an hour and a half was exhausting. She wondered how teachers could do it all day, every day. Still, she enjoyed having the school groups come to the butterfly house. It was the kind of thing Mark would have loved to see happen.

She turned back to the T-shaped glass-and-metal building that had been specially designed by an entomologist friend of her late husband. The top portion of the T was a greenhouse, open-sided now that the weather was warm. It contained a small gift shop where she sold butterfly and hummingbird feeders and figurines along with gardening books and paraphernalia. It also contained tables of colorful bedding plants and shrubs that especially appealed to butterflies and hummingbirds, along with vegetable plants and kitchen herbs.

The butterflies themselves were housed in the back half of the building in a gardenlike setting that Faith had spent the entire winter after Caitlin's birth creating on paper, and the summer after bringing to reality with hours and hours of backbreaking work.

It had taken a sizable portion of Mark's life insurance settlement to build the greenhouse and butterfly habitat. Perhaps too much, but it had been for the best that part of her comfortable nest egg had been spent, since that had forced her back into working two days a week at the Bartonsville Medical Center. And being back at work had forced her back into society, which was important for Caitlin if not for herself.

At first she had avoided anything to do with the small farming community where members of her husband's family had lived for four generations before his grandparents had moved to Cincinnati after the end of World War II. Now she was the only Carson who shopped along Main Street, belonged to the garden club and attended the church where one of the stained-glass windows had been dedicated in the family name, but she felt at home. She had put down roots. No more crisscrossing the country as Mark moved from one troubleshooting systems project to the next for the huge software conglomerate he'd worked for. Next year she'd enroll Caitlin in Sing, Giggle and Grin Preschool two mornings a week. Her daughter was bright and quick for her age. A slender, elfin-faced bundle of energy with silver-gilt hair and her own green-gold eyes.

The center of her universe appeared at the back door of the house. ''Hi, Momma,'' Caitlin called in her piping, toddler's voice.

''Hi, Kitty Cat,'' Faith called back, lifting her hand to shade her eyes from the bright spring sun. On the western horizon storm clouds had begun to form, not an unusual occurrence for this time of year, but it wouldn't hurt to check the weather forecast when she got back into the house. It was tornado season after all. But for now the spring afternoon was perfect, warm and only a little humid.

"I awake," Caitlin announced unnecessarily.

"I can see you are."

"She did take a nice nap." Faith's older sister, Peg, appeared behind Caitlin and hooked her finger inside the collar of the child's pink Winnie the Pooh embroidered sweatshirt to keep her from tumbling headfirst down the porch steps. "And she went potty like a big girl, too."

"You did?" Faith clapped her hands, making her tone excited and incredulous.

Caitlin nodded vigorously. "Big girl."

"You are a big girl. Mommy's so proud of you." Faith opened the wrought-iron gate that separated the old herb garden she was slowly restoring and Caitlin's play area on the other side of the brick walkway, from the rest of the yard.

Faith gathered the little girl into her arms and hugged her tight. Caitlin was the most precious thing on earth to her. Her whole life revolved around her daughter. Having her to love was nothing short of a miracle.

Caitlin hugged her back then wriggled to be free. "Cookie," she said emphatically. "I want a cookie."

"I could go for a cookie myself. How about you, Aunt Peg?"

Peg glanced at her watch. "No cookies for me. I'm dieting as usual." Peg was two inches taller than

Faith and full-figured. She had their mother's dark-brown eyes and rich auburn hair. She was five years older than Faith's thirty-one, and had dropped out of college to raise her younger sister when their mother had died of kidney failure when Faith was fifteen. Their quiet, hardworking father had died just a few years later—of a broken heart, Faith often thought.

A year and a half earlier Peg and her two boys had moved to Ohio from upstate New York to be closer to Faith and Caitlin. At Christmas she'd married Steve Baden, who farmed Faith's acreage for her, and whose large and close-knit family had taken all three of them under their wing.

Peg was also the only other person who knew that Caitlin was not Faith's biological daughter.

They walked back into the kitchen, and Faith went to the cookie jar.

"Two cookies," Caitlin demanded.

"I think I'm raising a Cookie Monster here," Faith lamented, handing over the demanded treats.

"Are you kidding? She's an angel compared to Jack and Guy at that age." Peg rolled her eyes. Her boys were seven and nine and every bit as ornery as their mother proclaimed them to be.

Peg looked at her watch again. "I'd better be going. Steve's cutting alfalfa at his uncle's place, and I should be home when the boys get off the school bus, or they'll trash the kitchen making snacks."

"I really appreciate your watching Caitlin this afternoon."

"I love watching my adorable niece." Peg had

never once let slip by word or action that Caitlin wasn't Faith's daughter. Despite her profound misgivings over Faith's actions, she'd accepted Caitlin completely. ''What's on your agenda for the rest of the afternoon?''

''Caitlin and I are going to gather up the feeding dishes in the butterfly house to wash them for tomorrow, and then we're going to walk up the lane to make sure the big cottage is ready for our new guest. He's supposed to be checking in this evening.''

Peg's eyebrows went up a fraction. ''Is he by himself?''

''I haven't the slightest idea. Why do you ask?'' But Faith thought she already knew the answer to that question. Peg worried about her.

''Just curious. You're so isolated out here.''

''I'm not isolated. You spend too much time watching those women-in-jeopardy movies on the Lifetime channel. I'm as safe here as you are a mile down the road.''

''I have a husband. You're alone.''

''But not lonely,'' Faith said, firmly, if not altogether truthfully. She had loved Mark, and with that love she had given him faith and trust and honesty. She couldn't envision a relationship that didn't contain all those elements, and she could never be honest with a man again, not completely. She had a secret to keep. Now that Peg was married again it added another layer to Faith's burden. Because of what she had done two and a half years ago, Peg could never be totally honest with her new husband—for her sister's sake.

"Okay, I know when to change the subject."

Faith shook off her heavy thoughts. "And if my guest puts one foot wrong I have a vicious watchdog to protect me don't I, Addy?" At the mention of her name, the sheltie pricked up her ears and wagged her tail. She'd been pouting a little all afternoon because Faith had made her stay in the house while the schoolchildren were visiting. Not all of them appreciated being herded around the yard by a wet nose.

"Watchdog, my fanny. She'd let the devil himself inside if he called her a pretty girl," Peg snorted. "Well, I'm off. I need to run into the IGA and pick up some bread and milk to feed the horde. Anything you need I can drop off on my way back out of town?"

"Not at the moment, but thanks for asking."

"Bye-bye." Caitlin, her mouth still full of cookie, hugged Peg's plump thigh.

"Bye, sweetie. See you Friday."

Caitlin ran to the breakfast nook's bay window and watched Peg get in her pickup and drive off. "Watch *Blue's Clues* now," she announced as the sound of the rough-running engine faded away.

"I have a better idea. Want to go see the butterflies?"

"Yes." Caitlin clapped her hands and nodded so hard one of the little butterfly-shaped clips in her hair came loose and the silken strands floated around her face. Faith sold the clips in the gift shop in a myriad of sparkling colors. They were very popular with the little girls who visited. "See 'flies."

Faith smoothed Caitlin's hair back from her face and secured it with the retrieved clip. "Come on, then. We'll go before any more customers drive up the lane. We'll have them all to ourselves." She carried Caitlin outside and into the greenhouse, then placed her in the lightweight folding stroller she kept just for this purpose. Caitlin loved the butterflies, but the insects were far too fragile for the toddler to be let loose among them.

They crossed through the greenhouse and Faith opened the first door to the butterfly sanctuary, automatically glancing to the left into her tiny cubbyhole of a breeding room. An array of gray-and-brown chrysalises hung from a foam board in an alcove, carefully suspended from a pin with a head color coded to the species waiting to emerge. To a casual observer they appeared wizened and dead, but inside they pulsed with life and in a few days a new batch of jewel-winged butterflies would be ready to release into the habitat.

This was her second shipment of tropical and ornamental butterflies this season. Their life spans were short, and she needed to restock the habitat every few weeks with specimens she ordered from a breeder in New Jersey. Someday she would like to raise the exotic forms of the species herself, but she would need a much larger operation and more disposable income to house and winter over the specific plants each species needed to breed.

Caitlin chuckled as the gentle puff of air from the specially designed door—which blew air back into the habitat so that the butterflies couldn't escape— lifted the fine strands of her hair. It was very warm in the glass house, more humid than the outside air, at least for the time being. Faith turned on the exhaust fan in the far gable of the building. The opening was covered with fine netting so none of the butterflies could be sucked outside.

"Pretty!" Caitlin squealed, reaching for a huge blue morpho as it glided swiftly by. The spectacularly colored tropical butterfly was one of the visitor's favorites.

"Daddy liked them, too," Faith said. To everyone else, Mark was Caitlin's father, just as Faith was her mother, and it wouldn't be natural not to talk to her about him. Above all else Faith wanted everything she did for Caitlin to seem natural.

She glanced through the chrysalis-room window that gave a view of the parking lot. It was empty. She'd probably have a spate of customers again in the early evening if it didn't rain, but now the two of them were alone.

She picked Caitlin up and sat down on one of the rustic wooden benches that were scattered throughout the habitat. She'd made the butterfly house as near to a tropical garden as she could manage. There were paving stone pathways, raised beds of verbena, impatiens, butterflyweed, rudbeckia. The plants all in shades of pink and blue, purple and yellow that butterflies loved. She'd added large specimen plants, ferns, small trees and host plants like dill and parsley, Queen Anne's lace and African milkweed, to encourage the laying of eggs and as food for emerging caterpillars.

Steve and Peg had helped her build two waterfalls of lightweight landscaping rock—it was how they'd first met—a small one directly across from the door, and a much larger one that climbed almost to the ceiling in the farthest corner of the house so that the sound of falling water was everywhere. She loved this place, and Mark would have loved it, too. If he'd lived.

But if Mark had lived she would not have Caitlin. She seldom let herself think of the dark days after Mark had died anymore. She preferred to believe her life had started the day Caitlin was born. It was a task she was mostly able to accomplish.

The sun disappeared behind a cloud and the butterflies disappeared from the air almost as swiftly, settling on leaves and flowers and feeding dishes to await the sun's return. Faith stood up, deciding to come back for the dishes later, and set Caitlin back into the stroller, then checked her backside in the long mirror beside the door. Butterflies often landed on visitors unawares and had to be carefully removed before anyone left. Today no colorful hitchhikers had attached themselves to her.

A rumble of thunder came rolling across the fields, so faint and far away it was felt more than heard. The wind had shifted while she was inside the butterfly room and the big baskets of red and white impatiens and trailing blue lobelia were swinging wildly from their hangers.

"Darn, I should have asked Steve to take them down for the afternoon when he was here earlier," Faith muttered half to herself, half to Caitlin. The hanging baskets were some of her best sellers and she didn't want to see them ruined by a storm. Her brother-in-law was six foot five and he'd hung the baskets high enough so they weren't a hazard to the skulls of customers, but they were out of Faith's reach, even standing on her tiptoes.

"Stay put like a good girl and I'll take them down," Faith told Caitlin, wishing she'd remembered to bring a cookie along with her. Caitlin had been an inquisitive baby and now, in the midst of the terrible twos, she was always on the go, poking her little snub nose in every nook and cranny the moment Faith's back was turned.

Faith retrieved the big stepladder that she used to open the vents in the roof of the greenhouse and set it up under the hanging baskets. But she'd positioned the ladder just a little too far from her objective and had to lean precariously to reach the first basket. To make matters worse the chain refused to come free of the hook. "Drat," Faith muttered, wishing she could give voice to something a little more stress-relieving, but she'd learned the hard way that Caitlin was a perfect mimic when it came to swear words.

She wrestled the first basket free, making a mental note to get Steve to lengthen the chains, customer liability or no, and reached over to take down the second. A flicker of movement from the direction of Caitlin's stroller caught her eye at the same moment a dusty black Blazer turned off the road and started down the lane. A last-minute customer stopping in on the way home from work, or the man who had rented the cottage? It didn't really matter who it was, she'd rather not be seen struggling down off the ladder with the two heavy baskets swinging from each hand.

"Caitlin, honey," she said over her shoulder. "Are you being a good girl and sitting still for mommy?"

A tremor of movement and a piping voice directly below her sent Faith's heart into her throat. "I help you." A small hand tugged on the leg of her slacks. Caitlin had crawled out of her stroller and climbed up the ladder. Now she was perched a good four feet off the ground, and blocking Faith's way.

"'Fraid," Caitlin mumbled suddenly, clinging like a limpet. Faith would have to lower the heavy baskets by their chains as far as she could, let them drop the rest of the way to the floor, then twist around and pull Caitlin into her arms. But as she shifted her weight one of the ladder's legs began to sink into the soft earth. Faith let out a gasp as she pitched forward.

"Can I help you with those?" a male voice asked.

Faith looked toward the source of the voice. The occupant of the black Blazer was standing just inside the greenhouse entrance. He wasn't a tall man, but solidly built with broad shoulders that tapered to a narrow waist, and long blue-jean clad legs.

"No, don't bother." Faith swallowed to ease the lump of anxiety that had lodged itself in her throat. She could feel Caitlin wobbling on the step behind her as she attempted to look around at the stranger. "It's...it's what's behind me I'm worried about." She was going to have to drop the heavy baskets, there was no help for it. The ladder was sinking more deeply into the soft earth each time she shifted her weight. In another few seconds it would tumble over taking both of them with it.

The stranger in the doorway took two long steps forward to see what she was talking about. His eyes widened a moment at the sight of Caitlin clinging to Faith's pant leg.

"So that's what has you treed. Come here, little one," he said, his voice slightly rough around the edges, but with a Southern lilt underneath. "Time to get down."

"Hi," Caitlin said, brightly and to Faith's surprise she held out her arms to the stranger.

"Hi, yourself." He lifted her up into one arm and steadied the ladder with the other.

"I climb high," Caitlin informed him smugly.

"Too high." Faith started down the ladder. It was still tilted at an awkward angle, but she made it without making a fool of herself by falling, even when he reached out and laid a steadying hand on her elbow.

A strange shiver went up and down her spine. Not because his hand was cold or his touch too personal. It wasn't. His hand was warm, slightly rough against her skin and he let go of her the moment she was steady on her feet. But still his touch unsettled her.

"I go high. I big girl."

"You are a very brave girl," he said in a wondering tone. He had a strong face, stern looking, all masculine lines and angles. Not a handsome face, but an intriguing one. As she watched, it softened and relaxed as Caitlin's laughing giggle coaxed a smile to his lips.

"I Caitlin."

"Hello—" he hesitated for a brief moment, "—Caitlin."

Caitlin wrapped her arms around the stranger's neck. She was a loving child, but she was usually reserved around people she didn't know, especially men. Caitlin planted a kiss on his cheek. "I like you," she said.

Faith dropped the heavy baskets and held out her arms. A rush of protectiveness coursed through her. The instant connection between her child and this stranger unsettled her even more than his touch. "Thank you. I'll take her now."

He placed Caitlin in her waiting arms. "I don't think she's suffered any harm from her climb."

Faith's sudden anxiety attack faded away once she held her daughter. She tried to summon a smile and thought she mostly succeeded. "She climbs like a monkey."

"And you're all right, too?" he asked, fixing his dark gaze on her directly for the first time. His eyes were blue, like dark, still water, or the color of the sky at twilight. "You look a little pale." Once more Faith's breath caught in her throat. Whatever had made her think he wasn't a handsome man? When he smiled it took her breath away. She would have to be a dead woman not to respond to that smile. "No strains or sprains? Those baskets look heavy."

"I'm fine, really," Faith insisted, although her left shoulder was aching a little. She fell back on formality to hide her continuing confusion. "Thank you for your help. I'm Faith Carson." She shifted Caitlin's slight weight and held out her hand.

He gave her his. "Hugh Damon. I've reserved one of your cottages for the week."

"Yes, Mr. Damon. Please wait a moment. I'll get you the key." She attempted a smile of her own. "Let me thank you for your rescue of me and my daughter one more time. And, of course, welcome to Painted Lady Farm."

THE STORM ROLLED through quickly leaving the air fragrant with the scent of wet grass. Twilight lingered a long time, the sky shading from red to orange to dusky pink and purple-gray, before the stars twinkled to life in the east. Hugh stood beneath the shelter of the high-pitched overhang at the back of the cottage. Beneath his feet were fieldstones that formed a small patio edged by a low stone wall and flowering plants, fragrant with scents that were heady but unfamiliar. He stared down at the lighted windows of Faith Carson's house.

He'd almost given himself away earlier, when he'd

let his reaction to seeing Beth's child for the first time get the better of him. She was Beth's child; he was convinced of it, although he couldn't say how he knew.

Caitlin Carson looked a great deal like his sister had at that age, the same elfin shape to her face, the gossamer fine hair. But Caitlin's eyes were not blue, like Beth's, like his. They were green-gold and changeable, exactly the same color as the woman who called herself her mother. Otherwise there was little resemblance between them. Faith Carson's hair was brown, her face more rounded. Her figure, too, was rounded. In all the right places he had to admit, but her body type was not the same as Caitlin's, who would grow up as slender and petite as Beth. But if he commented on that fact Faith Carson would say her daughter took after her dead father, not her mother, and her suspicions would be aroused.

She was Caitlin's mother according to all the laws of the land. He'd seen a copy of the child's birth certificate. Everything about it seemed to be in order. But still he knew his hunch was right. Even though the accident that had killed Jamie Sheldon and taken Beth's memory, had occurred a hundred miles away in another state, he was convinced she had been in this place. Here she'd given birth. And for some reason she'd left her child behind. Despite all the damage to her body and her mind, that memory had not been completely erased. She remembered the baby crying in the snow. And she remembered butterflies.

It was the slightest of hunches that had brought

him here. A baby born to a woman alone, during a terrible ice storm. A woman who was a nurse. A woman who could have delivered a frightened teenager's baby. A woman who raised butterflies. A young widow who, perhaps, despaired of ever having a child of her own and who would take the desperate risk of keeping another woman's baby.

He didn't know the details, but nothing he had learned led him to believe that Faith Carson was a cold-blooded baby snatcher. He was determined to find the truth for Beth's sake but he had to proceed carefully. He didn't want to bring the law down on his sister for abandoning her baby, anymore than he wanted to see Faith Carson jailed for kidnapping— at least not yet. The whole situation was a minefield. One misstep on his part could spell disaster for all of them.

Faith Carson was wary of him, and he would have to be careful to earn her trust before he brought Beth here. He was convinced his sister's well-being, and certainly her happiness, depended on learning the truth of the events that were the basis of her nightmares.

But he wasn't the only one searching for Beth's baby. Jamie's parents were determined to learn the fate of their lost grandchild. And they would not stop with merely learning that truth. They wanted the baby. And they were rich and powerful enough to take her from Beth, from Faith Carson. From him. If they discovered where she was.

CHAPTER THREE

"CAITLIN SEEMS TAKEN with your renter," Peg said, peering out the window above the kitchen sink. Hugh Damon had been staying in the cottage for several days now, over the long Memorial Day weekend, and the third anniversary of Mark's death.

"She's taken with anyone who spends time swinging her." Faith was standing in front of the open refrigerator, enjoying the blast of cool air as much as searching for juice for Caitlin's afternoon snack. It was 85 degrees, and the still air was heavy with humidity and the threat of approaching storms.

Faith snared the plastic bottle of apple juice from behind the milk where it had been hidden and shut the refrigerator door, coming to stand beside her sister. She had made up her mind to ignore her first disquieting reaction to Hugh Damon, but it didn't mean she was comfortable talking about him.

Faith watched him push Caitlin in her tire swing, as Addy lolled in the shade beneath the picnic table. The muscles in his back and shoulders moved smoothly beneath the light fabric of his shirt. His thick, dark-gold hair lay heavy and straight against his forehead. He wore no jewelry except a service-able-looking wristwatch. That was another direction she didn't want her thoughts to take. He was a good-looking man, who didn't wear a wedding ring.

"She's usually a little shy around strangers," Peg observed, running cold water into a glass she'd taken from the cupboard. Peg had started a wallpapering and painting business when she'd moved to Bartonsville and it was doing well. She was on her way home from a job and was wearing paint-splattered jeans and an old, long-sleeved white shirt of her husband's. Her hair was tucked up under a ball cap and the smell of solvent and paint scented the air around her.

"She likes him," Faith admitted. She rubbed the back of her neck with her hand. A storm coming always affected her that way, a tightness in her muscles, pressure behind her eyes.

"She's female. Even a two-year-old woman can spot a stud like that one."

Faith laughed. "Hey, you've only been married five months. You aren't supposed to be ogling other men already."

"I'm married, not blind. Steve's a dear but not fantasy material. Put a leather kilt on that guy, give him a sword and he'd give Russell Crowe a run for his money any day."

"Does this mean you're taking back your warning about renting the cabins to single men?"

Peg drained her glass and shook her head as she set it in the sink. "Nope." She tilted her head in Hugh's direction. "Men as good-looking as that one are trouble. I ought to know—I married one the first time around, remember.''

''Men like that one are engineers,'' Faith said, putting two Oreos on a paper plate for Caitlin.

''Engineer? I admit that sounds respectable enough.'' If Peg had been a grasshopper her antennae would be quivering. ''What kind of engineer?''

''The kind who build shopping malls, I guess. He's working on that fancy new complex they did a feature on in the *Cincinnati Enquirer* a couple of months ago. You know, the one with all the high-end stores.'' He'd told her that much the afternoon he'd inquired about continuing to rent the cottage for the month of June, since his work on the project would last several weeks.

''Has he asked you out yet?''

''No. Of course not.''

Her sister didn't look convinced but she didn't say any more. Faith had perfected the talent of sounding very sincere when she lied. And this was just a little white lie, not a universe-size one, like taking another woman's child to raise as your own. Hugh Damon hadn't asked her out on a date. Not officially, so her conscience was clear.

But he had offered to take her and Caitlin out to eat. It was while he was helping to rehang the baskets the day after he'd arrived. They had talked as he worked and she tallied the day's receipts. She was alone in the greenhouse and it would have seemed churlish to refuse his offer of help. Or so she told herself.

He'd been wearing an old University of Texas T-shirt that stretched tight across his chest and shoulders, she remembered, and faded jeans that hugged his long legs. "Where do you find a good meal in Bartonsville?" he had asked. She brought out muffins and bagels, orange and grapefruit juice, and made coffee in the greenhouse every morning for herself and Steve and Peg, or whoever was around. Guests at the cabins were welcome to them, as well. Painted Lady Farm was as close to a bed-and-breakfast as you got in Bartonsville.

She had replied without hesitation. "The Golden Sheaf. It's run by a family of old order Mennonites who make everything from scratch. The mashed potatoes are my daughter's favorite. I'm surprised you haven't found it already. All you have to do is follow your nose down Main Street."

Caitlin had been sitting at the small table Faith kept for her behind the counter coloring in a *SpongeBob SquarePants* book. "Eat," she'd said at the mention of food.

"Maybe the two of you could join me for dinner there this evening?" Hugh had said as he tested the strength of the chain extension before rehanging the planters. The invitation was offhand, but it caught Faith by surprise and she immediately said no. The refusal hung harsh and unfriendly in the air between them and she hurried to soften its uncompromising sound. "I mean, thanks, but I already have dinner started."

"Some other time then. Do you recommend the meat loaf?"

"It's the specialty of the house."

He'd looked pleased. "Homemade meat loaf. Nothing better."

"Don't forget to try the pies. The coconut cream is to die for."

"I'm a banana cream man myself," he'd answered with a smile.

Faith had managed a smile in return. Her eyes had been drawn to the hard muscles of his thighs as he worked, and suddenly, from out of nowhere, she remembered the feel of legs and bodies tangled together in lovemaking, and she nearly dropped the stack of receipts she held in her hand. The flash of eroticism had come and gone in a heartbeat, but the aftereffect left her shaken. In her vision the arms holding her hadn't been Mark's. They'd belonged to this man.

She'd mumbled something about liking banana cream, too, and made some excuse to leave the greenhouse. Her legs were wobbly as she picked Caitlin up to carry her to the house, her breath coming in quick little gasps that couldn't be blamed on the heat or the slight weight of the child in her arms. It was lust. Something that for three years had been completely absent from her thoughts.

That incident wasn't the last erotic thought she'd had about Hugh Damon, but it was the last one she had let get the best of her. Perhaps because she also couldn't quite forget the disquieting certainty that he was here, not just to avoid spending several weeks at an interstate off-ramp motel, but for some secret reason of his own.

A rumble of thunder announced the arrival of the storms that had been predicted all day. Peg angled her head to check the sky visible between the branches of the big maple outside the kitchen window. "Nasty-looking clouds," she said, forgetting, at least for the moment, her fixation with Hugh Damon. "I have a feeling we're going to get a real bad storm out of this cold front."

"I think you're right," Faith agreed.

"You're sure you don't need me to watch Caitlin Wednesday and Thursday?"

Those were the days Faith was scheduled to work at the hospital. It was going to be her last week of duty until the fall. She would be busy with her own businesses from now on and had taken a leave of absence until September. "No, thanks. Martha's going to watch her." Martha Baden was Peg's mother-in-law.

"Well, then she'll probably end up at my house part of the day anyway."

"Probably." Faith laughed as they headed outside.

"Introduce me to your engineer," Peg said under her breath as she held the screen door open for Faith.

Faith continued on into the yard, setting the paper plate of cookies and the sippy cup on the picnic table. She introduced her sister to Hugh Damon and then followed her to her truck to say goodbye.

"My Lord, he's even better looking up close than

he was from the kitchen window," Peg said fanning her cheeks with her fingertips. "If he asks you out while he's here, you go. You've been alone for three years, that's long enough."

"I don't want another man—"

"That's what I said, too, until I met Steve." Peg switched on the engine and drove off. She loved having the last word.

Faith walked slowly back to the big maple. Caitlin dragged her little sneakered feet in the wood chips layered under the tire swing to slow its movement. She was wearing a pink top and darker pink shorts. Her fine silvery hair was in pigtails, and she looked like a spun sugar angel to Faith. An angel, but a mischievous one.

"Juice," she squealed as Hugh stopped the swing so that she could hop out and come dancing across the grass to Faith. "I want juice. I'm hot."

Faith bent down and gathered her daughter against her heart. "That's because it's hot outside and you've been swinging and laughing and talking real hard."

"Hugh's hot, too." *That went without saying.* Faith was glad she had her face buried in Caitlin's neck. She was having more and more trouble controlling such unsuitable thoughts. "He needs a juicy," Caitlin declared.

"I'll settle for a drink of water." Hugh moved toward the old-fashioned hand pump that stood by the gate. Once there he took the antique ladle off the hook and began working the long handle up and

down. The well was as old as the house, but the
water was pure and spring fresh. Faith had it chan-
neled into the greenhouse to water the plants and
keep the waterfalls topped off.

As soon as a steady stream of water began to rush
out of the pump into the shallow stone trough that
had once held chicken feed a century before, Caitlin
wiggled out of Faith's arms and darted over to Hugh.
''Swim,'' she said loudly. ''Let's swim.'' She squat-
ted down and started to untie her shoes to wade in
the trough.

''No way, Kitty Cat. The water's too cold and I'm
too big for the basin.''

Faith followed Caitlin to the pump. She wondered
when Hugh had started using her pet names for Caitlin. The endearment came so naturally to his lips she
felt churlish in mentioning anything about it. ''No
playing in the water now. It's going to storm and you
have to help Mommy bring in the plants and shut up
the greenhouse.'' Peg had offered to help before she
left but Faith knew she was anxious to get home
before the rain so had assured her she could manage
on her own. Besides, she didn't want to answer any
more questions about Hugh Damon. Since she'd re-
married, her sister's mind was focused entirely too
much on sex, especially Faith's lack of it.

''Would you like a drink of water?'' He rinsed and
refilled the ladle and held it out to her.

She took it gratefully. It was hot and she was
thirsty for something that wasn't full of sugar or caf-
feine. Her hand brushed his knuckles and she felt a

tremor like a tiny earthquake rattle her bones, just as another long rumble of thunder boomed overhead.

"It's getting close," Hugh said, raising his eyes to the sky.

"I have a feeling the cold front is going to get here ahead of the weatherman's prediction." She handed the ladle back to him. "Please excuse me, Mr. Damon. I think I'd better batten down the hatches in the greenhouse."

"I'll help. And I think we've known each other long enough to drop the honorifics. My name's Hugh."

"Thank you, Hugh." She liked the way his name sounded on her tongue. "And please, call me Faith."

Addy grabbed her much chewed Frisbee in her teeth and trotted along at Hugh's heels as they walked toward the greenhouse, obviously hoping for a game of catch. So Faith could add her faithful sheltie to the list of females at Painted Lady Farm who had fallen for her guest.

"I can manage," she started to say, but he was already moving the remaining flats of bedding plants off the old farm wagon she used to display them. It had grown noticeably darker in the ten minutes they'd been standing in the yard. And the clouds were moving fast, roiling like water in a saucepan. The green cast to their undersides was more pronounced than ever, a sure sign of hail.

Faith deposited Caitlin at her table behind the counter and went to help Hugh. They were both soaked by the time all the bedding plants were inside.

She struggled to close the wide panels that were usually folded back against the side of the greenhouse. Hugh reached a hand over her shoulder and unhooked the panel, then tugged them into place. He had just closed the final one when the hail came pelting down.

The roof of the greenhouse was made of the same industrial weight plastic as the sides and the hailstones, small ones thankfully, bounced off harmlessly. But the roof of the butterfly habitat was made of glass. It was reinforced and supposedly shatterproof, but so far it hadn't been put to the test. Faith picked up Caitlin and hurried into the chrysalis room. The sound of hailstones on glass was deafening. She'd reached for the handle of the pressurized door when Hugh spoke from behind her.

"It might be better if we get back to the house in case there's a tornado."

"Oh, God, don't say that." Ohio wasn't technically a part of Tornado Alley, but they still had their share of the deadly storms.

"Back in Texas this is the kind of weather that has us heading for the nearest storm cellar. You do have a cellar, don't you?" His tone was ordinary, for Caitlin's sake, Faith realized. There was even a tinge of laughter beneath the faint drawl, but his eyes were grim.

"Yes, there's a cellar. Have you always lived in Texas?" Faith kept her tone as light as his. She was determined not to allow her own fear to be transmitted to Caitlin.

"From time to time," Hugh said. He turned to go back into the greenhouse. "My dad was in the military. We lived in a lot of places, but Texas was where I went to high school and college. My mom and my half sister stayed on there after I left home. When I got back to the States last time it seemed as good a place as any to hang my hat."

"Back to the States? You build malls overseas then?"

His laugh was short and held little amusement. "I've only been building malls the past couple of years. Before that I worked all over the world. Dams in China, bridges in South America. Never more than a year or two in one place, and most of them were pretty far off the beaten track."

Faith wanted to ask him more about what sounded like a fascinating life, but a blinding flash of lightning and the earsplitting crack of thunder that accompanied it brought her back to the situation at hand. This was no time for conversation, fascinating or otherwise. She gave one more troubled glance through the chrysalis room window into the habitat. The insects were on their own now. She couldn't risk injury to Caitlin staying where they were. But how was she going to get her daughter safely back into the house?

The hailstones weren't that large but they were coming down so thickly she had to shout to be heard. And the wind was picking up, too. There would be blowing leaves and twigs, perhaps even falling tree branches to contend with between here and the house. She didn't even dare to consider what damage the storm was doing to the crops in the fields. "I can't take Caitlin out into the storm." She indicated the sleeveless top and shorts her daughter was wearing. Caitlin had her face buried in Faith's shoulder. She didn't like thunder and lightning, but she wasn't unduly afraid of them. That might change if she had to go out in it unprotected.

"No umbrella or raincoat in the greenhouse?"

"Nothing like that." The radio on the counter began to vibrate with the sirenlike alert that signaled a weather update. A disembodied voice announced a funnel cloud had been spotted about ten miles west of Bartonsville. It was moving northeast at thirty miles an hour. Everyone in the area was to take immediate cover.

"If it stays on course it will probably miss us but we need to get into the cellar," Hugh said. She didn't for a moment question the accuracy of his pronouncement. It had taken Faith weeks to orient herself to the land around Bartonsville after she'd moved to the farm, but it appeared Hugh had had no such difficulty.

She racked her brain for something to use to cover Caitlin. "I suppose we could wrap her up in one of the those nylon garden flags. They're heavy enough to give her some protection."

"It's better than nothing." Hugh reached out to slide the nearest off its pole, a springlike design of pink and yellow tulips on a green background. Faith's eyes flicked past the display to the shelf of hummingbird and butterfly statues.

"Wait a minute. I have a better idea." Faith darted around the counter. She pulled out a roll of packing material. "Bubble wrap! I keep it around to pack the figurines. We can wrap her in it."

She was rewarded with one of his heart-stopping grins. "Great idea. Here, give her to me."

Faith didn't let herself hesitate. She couldn't hold on to Caitlin and wrap her head and shoulders at the same time. Hugh held out his arms and Caitlin tumbled into his embrace. "Bubbles," she giggled. "Poke the bubbles."

"You can poke all the bubbles you want in the house, Kitty Cat," Faith promised. "Just hold still now like a good girl." Thirty seconds later Caitlin grinned out at her from a cocoon of packing material.

"Hey, you're Cocoon Girl now," Hugh said admiringly.

Faith laughed despite the anxiety that made her hands shake and her throat close. "Not Cocoon Girl. She...she needs to be Chrysalis Girl. We don't want to take the chance that she'll hatch into a plain old moth. We want her to be a beautiful butterfly, don't we, sweetie?" She leaned forward and touched noses with her daughter. The spontaneous movement brought her close enough to feel the heat of Hugh's body and the evocative smell of his soap and aftershave. She straightened quickly, taking a step back.

Hugh didn't seem to notice her awkward movement. "Okay, Chrysalis Girl it is. Up, up and away!"

Faith tugged open the main door, the swirling wind working just as hard to keep it closed. Addy started barking, backing away, stiff-legged, as hail-stones clattered on the paving stones just inside the door. "C'mon, dog. Move," Faith ordered, but Addy was too excited and too frightened of the storm to be her usual tractable self. Faith made a dive for the sheltie but Addy bounced out of range. "Addy! Come. Or you're going to get blown to Oz." This time Addy obeyed the stern command and Faith lifted the little dog into her arms.

Hugh motioned her through the open door first and then pulled it shut with one hard jerk. The sting of hailstones against her cheek and head made Faith gasp. She took off across the gravel parking lot at a run, the dog squirming and whimpering in her arms. Hugh's Blazer was parked under the big maple that shaded the back yard. Faith hoped a limb didn't come down on it. Thank heaven, her own dependable Car-avan was parked in the barn.

The ground was an inch deep with marble-sized hailstones. The footing was treacherous, almost as bad as it had been the day Caitlin was born. What a terrifying trip home that had been, the tiny newborn clutched tight to her chest, nothing to protect her from the sleet and wind but the sweatshirt she was wrapped in.

Faith didn't dare look back to see how her daugh-ter was faring in Hugh's arms for fear of turning an ankle and ending up on her bottom with an armload of indignant sheltie. She shoved open the wrought-iron gate to the yard and went directly to the house. Inside the kitchen she motioned Hugh to follow her down the steep, narrow cellar steps. The big white-washed room contained her washer and dryer, the hot water heater and a huge old boiler that she was hoping would provide heat for one more winter before it died. Otherwise, the low-ceilinged, stone-floored room was empty except for some of Caitlin's toys, an old castoff sofa and a small TV and VCR. She often brought Caitlin down here to run around and let off steam on rainy days. Faith hit the light switch inside the door. Thankfully the two overhead lights came on.

She kept a powerful flashlight and some candles and a lighter on a shelf by the stairs for an emergency such as this, but she hoped they didn't have to use them. She turned on the TV, and muted the sound so that Caitlin wouldn't become alarmed by storm bulletins. A map of the county filled the screen, and a dark red blotch, the indication of the strongest storm cell, was superimposed over Bartonsville, but it had begun to move off to the east. "I think the worst of the storm's passed, thank goodness." She glanced out one of the small windows, placed high in the thick, stone walls of the cellar. The hail had stopped; now it was only raindrops hitting the wavy glass.

She turned back to find that Hugh had set Caitlin on her feet and hunkered down beside her to unwind the bubble wrap cocoon.

As soon as she was free Caitlin bolted for the stairs. "Need Barbie."

"Oh, no, you don't." Hugh's long arm shot out

and his fingers curled around the child's wrist. Faith's heart leapt to her throat. Caitlin was such a tiny thing, her bones so delicate he could easily hurt her and not even realize it. She almost cried out, but she needn't have worried. His grip on Caitlin's wrist was so light it scarcely touched her skin.

"I think I see Barbie over there." He pointed to the seat of the old couch and let Caitlin go skipping off to retrieve the doll.

"She's smart and fearless, isn't she?" he said with a note of wonder—*and love?*—in his voice that sent shivers through Faith.

"She was born in the middle of a terrible ice storm." Faith hadn't meant to let that slip. She had perfected her story of Caitlin's birth, but she never volunteered details. His actions had thrown her off balance, and it was too late to take back the words.

"Tell me about it," he said, standing up, towering over her it seemed, although there was no more than three or four inches difference in their heights. The tone of his voice didn't change, nor the look in his eyes, but Faith felt compelled to answer as though bidden by some unspoken command.

Suddenly she was afraid, completely and unreasoningly afraid, and the fear had nothing to do with the storm, but was caused by the man before her. She felt for a moment that he could see right through her and that he knew what she would say next was a lie. Her throat closed and the litany of carefully constructed half truths and fabrications that was her fortress, as well as her prison, wouldn't come.

CHAPTER FOUR

FAITH OPENED HER MOUTH but no sound came out. She was suddenly thrust into the midst of her worst nightmare. In it, she was standing in a huge echoing chamber. Stern, shadowy figures sat in judgment of her, demanding to know why she had taken another woman's baby. No matter how eloquently she tried to explain her actions, her motivations, no matter how she many tears she shed, slowly, inexorably, one of the shadowy figures would pluck Caitlin from her arms and melt away, leaving her alone. She would wake in terror, tears running down her cheeks and only a trip to Caitlin's room and the warmth of her baby's skin could dispel the dread.

It was the middle of a late May day, and she was wide-awake. This was not her dream. This was reality, and she had told the story many times before. Today would be no different, unless she allowed it to be. "There was no one to help me when Caitlin was born," she said as lightly as she could manage. "My husband had died six months earlier. I…I was here alone."

Raindrops glistened in Hugh's dark-blond hair, the harsh light catching steaks of lighter gold that she hadn't noticed before. He didn't seem menacing anymore, although his dark gaze held hers. ''You must have been very frightened.''

''It was terrifying.'' The words were heartfelt. She had woven as much of the truth into her story as possible. She had become a very good liar, but she did it only when necessary.

''Did you try to contact the emergency squad? Bartonsville has one, I imagine.''

''There wasn't time.'' She forced herself to keep eye contact. She was back in stride now, back on script. ''Contrary to conventional wisdom about first babies, labor went very quickly. The ice storm hit and a broken tree limb brought down the phone line. Thank God, the electricity stayed on.'' That was true, too, but it had happened *after* she made her nightmarish trek across the ice-slick fields to the house, with the tiny infant barely clinging to life in her arms.

Faith couldn't help herself, her eyes sought her daughter across the room. She was seated in front of the old TV, oblivious to their conversation and the dying storm, engrossed in an episode of *Rugrats*. ''We were cut off from the outside world for the first three days of Caitlin's life.''

She had made diapers from an old flannel blanket she'd found in a back bedroom. Then she'd taken a plastic sandwich bag and poked a hole in one corner with a pin. She'd dissolved a little sugar in warm water and put the glucose solution in the bag, twisting it into a cone, as though she were a chef preparing to frost a fairy cake. She had coaxed Caitlin's tiny mouth open with the tip of her little finger and pushed the makeshift nipple inside. Fortunately, Caitlin's sucking reflex was strong and Faith was patient. Eventually the baby swallowed an ounce of the liquid.

After she'd held the newborn close to her breast and wrapped them both in blankets until the worrisome blue cast to the baby's skin had been replaced by warm pink. They'd stayed snug and warm in their isolated cocoon as the storm raged, and when they'd emerged a transformation had taken place that was as complete and life-altering as that of a caterpillar changing into a butterfly.

Caitlin had become Faith's child as surely as if she had given birth to the infant. She had labored to bring her to safety through the storm. She had fed her and bathed her and held her close so that she slept against the beating of Faith's heart.

She'd loved her.

But she'd known she couldn't keep her.

The ice melted the fourth morning after the storm, and life began to return to normal, but Faith remained closeted in her big, old house.

She knew Beth and Jamie would lose custody of the infant the moment Faith stepped into the sheriff's office and told her story. The baby would go into the system, into foster care. If she was lucky it would be to a loving home. But it could be months, even years, until all the technicalities were sorted out. Sometimes bad things happened to children caught up in the system. Faith didn't want to think of that. So she stayed put, telling herself it was still too dangerous to drive. She would wait for the phone to be repaired and to give Jamie and Beth time to change their minds. For a little longer she could make believe she had what she wanted most—a child of her own.

And then the newspaper had come.

Faith closed her eyes and could see as clearly as if it were still in front of her—the headline about the ice storm. Below it was a sidebar of storm-related deaths in Ohio and surrounding states. In Indiana, the story read, a hundred miles from Bartonsville, there had been a pileup on the interstate during the height of the storm. Eleven cars had been involved, but as of press time there was only one death, a seventeen-year-old male from Massachusetts. His companion, a teenage girl, was not expected to live. The couple was identified as Jamie Sheldon of Boston, and Beth Harden of Houston.

Jamie and Beth.

Was it only a coincidence that the first names were the same? Or was the child in her arms an orphan?

There were no further details of the accident that she could find. No mention of Beth having recently given birth, or any indication that a search for the infant had been started. Faith waited all that day and the next for someone to come and claim the child. With each passing hour it became evident that it was not going to happen. The young parents had died without telling anyone about their baby.

It was as if she didn't exist.

It was as if she were really Faith's.

And in the end it had been remarkably easy to make Caitlin legally hers.

In Ohio, she learned from the Internet, either parent could register the home birth of a child simply by appearing, within ten days, at the records office of the county in which the birth had taken place. No other witnesses were required, no medical records were needed. Only her own declaration of parenthood. That was her first lie, but one she told gladly. Within fifteen minutes of arriving at the courthouse she'd left with a birth certificate that declared Caitlin Hope Carson was her daughter.

She became aware she had been silent a long time, too long. As it sometimes did the guilt at what she had done burst out of the locked corner of her mind. She didn't want to talk about Caitlin's birth anymore. She didn't want to lie to Hugh anymore. "The storm's passing. I think it's safe to go back upstairs."

He made no objection so she turned off the TV and took Caitlin in her arms. Once back in the familiar surroundings of her yellow-and-white kitchen she felt her confidence returning and the guilt retreating.

"Do you have other family in the area in addition to your sister?" Hugh asked, leaning back against the granite countertop, arms folded across his chest. His shirt was still damp from the soaking they'd gotten. It pulled tight across his chest with the movement and Faith's mouth went dry with need and wanting. She carried Caitlin to the bay window that faced the fields and watched as the dark menace of the retreating storm clouds broke into tatters of gray smoke.

"My husband has a few distant cousins in the area, but otherwise, no. Peg and her boys are my only living relatives."

Caitlin wriggled to be free, so Faith set the little girl on her feet. Caitlin then bounced over to Hugh where she began to tug on his pant leg. "Cookie, please."

"She wants an Oreo. They're behind you."

Hugh swiveled his head and shoulders and spotted the big plastic jar filled with cookies. "May I?" he asked.

Faith nodded. He didn't look out of place at all in her kitchen. He leaned down and lifted Caitlin into his arms, letting her open the cookie jar and extract two of them all by herself. "Bite for you," Caitlin said and pressed the cookie to Hugh's lips for him to take a bite. Hugh went very still for a moment, then opened his mouth to nibble on the cookie. Caitlin shoved the rest of the cookie into her mouth. "Good?"

"Very good." He lifted one hand and smoothed it gently over her hair. "Thank you, Caitlin." Faith went all shaky inside. It looked so right somehow, Hugh holding her daughter in his strong, tanned arms.

He put Caitlin down and she raced through the archway into the dining room, where they never ate, but where she kept many of her larger toys.

Silence stretched between them, and it made her nervous. She returned to the subject of family because she couldn't think of anything else to say. "You mentioned a half sister, I remember. Do you come from a large family?"

He grew very still. "My parents are dead."

"I'm sorry."

He nodded shortly. "Beth is my only sibling. She's twenty."

"Beth? Is it short for Elizabeth?"

"No, just Beth."

A little shiver skittered across her nerve endings. She could never hear that name without associating it with Caitlin's sad and pretty mother, especially when she had just been thinking of her such a short time ago. "It's…it's a pretty name. Are you close?"

"As close as she'll let me get." This time she didn't imagine the pain in his voice. It was raw and real. "She's got a lot of problems right now, both physical and emotional. She was in a bad accident some time ago. It's been a long road back. I wasn't there for her when I should have been and now…"

"And now she won't let you be there for her?" Another Beth. Another accident. Another stinging memory evoked.

"Not as much as I want to be."

"I'm sorry." Impulsively she laid her hand on his arm and immediately wished she hadn't. His skin was warm as sunlight. The feel of rough hair and the solidity of bone beneath her fingers reminded her that she was a woman who had been alone for three years. "I know it's none of my business but perhaps, it would be better if you spent the next few weeks with her instead of remaining here."

"She's in Texas. I need to be available to the architect in Cincy on two hours' notice, or I would go home."

"She has no one else?"

"Her father." His brows drew together in a scowl. "My stepfather is living, but he and Beth are estranged."

"I see." His expression warned her not to inquire further. "You could bring her here." She spoke the words without thinking.

He looked down at her hand, then lifted his gaze to hers. He watched her for a long moment, his eyes as shadowed as the stormy sky had been. "You mean that, don't you?"

"Of course I do. This place brought me comfort and peace after Mark died. It might do the same for your sister."

"Comfort and peace. She could use both of those."

"She would be most welcome."

He leaned closer and Faith felt herself drawn to him as though by an invisible magnet. He reached out and she held her breath certain that he meant to touch her cheek or even to take her in his arms. But she was mistaken. Hugh let his arm fall and took a step backward, leaving Faith feeling chilled. He was silent a long time, then his jaw tightened and he gave a short, sharp nod, as though coming to a decision that had been difficult to make. "You're right, Faith. I think it's time I brought Beth to Painted Lady Farm."

HUGH PROPPED HIS FEET on the knee-high, stone wall that bordered the tiny patio behind his cabin and leaned back in the red metal lawn chair, slouching down far enough in the seat to rest his head against the round back. It was getting to be a habit sitting out here at twilight. The only other guests, a middle-aged couple in a car with Michigan plates staying in the unit next to his, seemed settled in for the evening, and he had the place to himself. He looked up at the faint scattering of summer stars. Off in the west the last of a glorious orange-gold sunset had faded into purple and gray. The storms of the afternoon had passed off to the north and east, taking some of the humidity from the air.

He'd been sitting in the same spot for the past hour observing Faith go about the business of closing the greenhouse. He'd watched as a tall, dark-haired man and two small boys in a pickup had driven down the lane and walked to the edge of the cornfield with her. He could hear the boys whooping and hollering in the backyard, running up to the pond to throw something into the water, then scurrying back down the bank. Caitlin had followed close on their heels, her small legs pumping to keep up.

Faith had called out a warning to the boys and obediently they had each taken Caitlin's hand and led her back to her mother. Faith gathered the toddler into her arms. She'd waited, cuddling her daughter, as the boys ran off again, and the man waded into the rows of new corn to check for damage. Steve, the brother-in-law, Hugh had decided, and the boys would be his stepsons, Faith's sister's children.

When the man left, driving slowly back up the lane in a gray pickup that had seen better days, he stopped and got out. The boys, both towheads with dark eyes and noses too big for their faces, hung out the open window as the older man approached.

"I'm Steve Baden," he said. "Faith's brother-in-law."

"Hugh Damon." Hugh held out his hand.

Steve took it. His palm was callused, his grip strong. He gave Hugh the same once-over he'd gotten from Faith's sister. "Thought I'd introduce myself since Faith says you're going to be around the place for a few weeks."

"A few weeks," Hugh agreed. "I'm working on the Spring Meadow Mall project north of the city."

Steve nodded, frowning. "I've read about it. Supposed to bring a lot of business into the area. The outfit that's developing it bought out three family farms to put it up, I heard."

"I don't know the details," Hugh said carefully. Steve Baden was a farmer. It was obvious he didn't like the idea of all that farmland being paved over. To tell the truth Hugh didn't much, either, but he kept his opinion to himself. If developers didn't build malls Hugh would be out of a job.

"Well, I can see why you'd prefer staying here

than at one of those highway motels. Nice country around here. Quiet. Peaceful. I see to the cabins for Faith. If you need anything done she can give me a holler. My place's only a mile down the road.''

''Thanks, I'll remember that.''

The boys had begun to wrestle in the pickup. ''Jack. Guy. Settle down,'' Steve called, without even turning his head. The boys untangled themselves, but continued to bounce up and down on the seat.

''Jack tried to wipe a booger on me,'' the youngest shouted out the window.

''Did not.''

''Did too.''

Steve shook his head and grinned. He pointed his finger at his stepsons. ''I said settle down.'' Tranquility followed, but the youngest folded his arms across his chest and stuck out his lower lip in a pout. ''Time to get these two hellions home to their mother.'' He held out his hand again. ''Good meeting you, Hugh.''

''You, too.''

As the sound of the truck's engine died away Hugh returned to his chair. Faith's brother-in-law hadn't stopped to introduce himself just to be neighborly. It was obvious Steve Baden felt responsible for Faith and Caitlin. He was checking Hugh out, but he didn't mind. He'd have done the same thing in Steve's position.

He wished there had been someone to perform that service for his mother. Instead, after his Green Beret father had died in a training accident she'd married Beth's father. There was nothing really wrong with Trace Harden. He just wasn't Tyler Damon. The marriage had lasted only long enough to produce Beth, then Trace had taken off and mostly stayed out of the picture, until their mother's death in a car accident when Beth was fourteen.

Thinking it was for the best Hugh had sent her to Boston to live with her likable, but weak-willed father and his third wife. He'd thought Beth needed two parents to raise her, not one brother who was out of the country, and sometimes out of touch, for months at a time. It was a decision he'd regret until his dying day.

Hugh surged from the chair and stepped over the low wall into the wet grass. Mosquitoes rose up in swarms around him. He batted them away and walked out onto the gravel lane and headed up the hill.

The stars were bright and he stared upward, looking for the Big Dipper, but he was really seeing Faith. She had beautiful hair that brushed her shoulders, a rich mixture of gold and brown that defied description. The closest he could come was likening it to sunlight shining through a glass jar of honey. Her skin was honey-colored, too, and as soft as thistledown. He'd damn near made a fool of himself when she'd touched him. He'd wanted to pull her into his arms and learn for himself if her lips and skin tasted as sweet as they looked.

He couldn't think of any better way of making the

whole situation even more complicated—except to take her to bed.

By the time he reached the old cemetery, the moon had risen, dimming the stars. He wasn't afraid of the dead, but he didn't go inside the intricately patterned wrought-iron fence that marked its boundaries. The Carsons and the Bartons and the Badens buried there had earned their rest, and he had no intention of disturbing it. Instead, he leaned on the gate and looked past the burying ground to the lights winking in Faith's upstairs windows. He already knew which was her room, the second on the right. And Caitlin's was beside hers.

Caitlin. Once more he felt her slight weight in his arms. Her skin was even softer than Faith's, her bones more delicately wrought. Only her eyes were the same as Faith's.

He no longer believed that Faith Carson had kidnapped Beth's child, if he ever had. For reasons he might never know, he now believed his sister and her boyfriend had left the child behind. And whatever justifications Faith Carson had made to herself to keep the baby, it had been a good decision for the child. She was a loved and loving little girl. His niece? If she was, he could never claim her. Even making the attempt could cause more problems than he could ever solve.

What if he brought Beth to this place? Would it help her to remember what had happened those hours before the accident? Would she somehow recognize

Caitlin as her child? Or was he only indulging his own obsession?

Perhaps he should leave well enough alone. Caitlin was healthy, happy and loved. Beth was working on building a new life for herself. She was young. He had every hope she would find someone to love and have more children one day. He had no business playing God.

Hugh turned away from the moon-shadowed cemetery and walked back down the hill to his cabin. As he opened the old-fashioned screen door and stepped inside, his cell phone rang.

He picked it up off the table and put it to his ear. "Damon," he said.

"Hugh?" Beth's voice sounded lost and faraway, but not because of the connection. Hugh felt his gut tighten. She always seemed glad to hear his voice, but she almost never initiated a call.

"Hi, Beth. What's up?" He tried to keep his tone from reflecting his uneasiness.

"I'm okay, I guess."

"You don't sound okay. Bad news on your finals?" Beth had been taking courses at Baylor. Her first semester. She still required physical therapy on her leg. She had had to learn to walk and talk all over again, but she was getting better.

That is until a few months earlier when the dreams had begun.

"No, I did great on my finals."

"You don't sound great."

There was silence on the other end of the line.

"Beth? Tell me what's wrong."

"You're doing the big brother thing again." She gave a tiny little laugh, that was half giggle, half sob. Hugh balled his left hand into a fist.

"I am your big brother. Tell me what's wrong."

Beth took a shaky breath. "Jamie's mother called me again today. She...she wants to pay for me to start seeing a hypnotherapist."

Damn the woman. Harold and Lorraine Sheldon had all the money in the world. They could buy and sell him a hundred and fifty times over. And they weren't averse to using that money to get what they wanted. What they wanted was their grandchild, no matter what the cost to Beth. They'd been playing on her guilt and uncertainties almost since the moment she'd regained consciousness three weeks after the accident.

"They say this woman is incredible. They say she can help me remember everything that happened those last weeks. They don't believe I'll never remember everything. What should I do, Hugh? I have a child somewhere. A little girl. And I wouldn't even know that fact if it wasn't for my diary. I—I don't even really remember being pregnant. I just don't know..." She was crying now, quietly, hopelessly, and heartache for his sad little sister warred with Hugh's desire to throttle Harold and Lorraine Sheldon.

"You're not going to do anything you don't want to do, Beth. Remember the doctors told you that making yourself ill trying to recall what happened before the accident will not help.'' Her brain had been damaged from trauma and loss of blood. Her amnesia was complete and irreversible.

"But maybe they're wrong.'' Her tone was a blend of wistfulness and fear. Although the doctors had said miracles did happen, that there were no absolutes when dealing with the human brain, they didn't hold out much hope Beth would regain the lost portions of her life. That knowledge haunted her day and night, and her sadness and guilt fueled Hugh's remorse and frustration. "If I do as she asks we might learn what happened. If we find the baby alive they would have something left of Jamie. And if we don't, at least they will have a body to bury alongside Jamie—'' Her voice broke and Hugh gritted his teeth against a sudden urge to howl along with her.

"God damn that bitch.'' Hugh usually kept his low opinion of Lorraine Sheldon to himself but he felt goaded beyond endurance. The investigation after the accident had turned up no leads, no clues to the baby's fate. Beth had never been charged with a crime, but the case was still open. It was another burden she carried.

Beth's voice was weary. "Hugh, we both know the baby must be dead. Why else would I dream of crying babies and blood and butterflies in the snow, unless some part of me remembers...hurting my baby?''

"That's enough, Beth.'' She would spend the night huddled on the couch in his apartment torturing herself with doubts and fears if he didn't stop this. "Put it out of your mind," he commanded.

"I can't." He could hear her sniffle back her tears and he suddenly remembered her at four, doing the same when she'd scraped her knee and had come running to her big brother because he could fix everything. God, how he wished that was true.

"Yes, you can. Remember the relaxation techniques Dr. Webster taught you." Beth's therapist was a jewel of a woman, but she'd told Hugh the last time they'd talked that there was not much more she could do for Beth. From now on her healing must come from within.

"My favorite's the triple scoop of double-chocolate-chip-mocha ice cream exercise." Her voice quavered but grew stronger with each word.

Hugh swallowed his own emotion and said, "I might even start seeing a shrink if that's what she recommends."

"Oh, Hugh." She managed to laugh. "I miss you. I know I don't tell you that often, but I do. I wish you were here to back me up with Jamie's mother. As soon as she walks in the door I'll be so nervous I'll agree to anything she asks, I can't seem to help myself." There was real fear underlying the lightness of her words.

Hugh felt his hand ball into a fist again and deliberately made himself relax. "You mean Lorraine and Harold are coming to Houston?"

He could almost see Beth's earnest nod, her silvery hair swinging against her pale cheek. "They'll be here day after tomorrow."

Hugh made up his mind in a flash, shouldering aside his own doubts about the wisdom of what he was planning. "But you won't be."

"What do you mean?"

"Get your suitcase packed. I'll call from here and get you on the first available flight into Cincinnati."

"But Hugh, it's too late tonight." She sounded hopeful despite her objection.

He raked his hand through his hair. "Okay, first plane out in the morning. You're coming to Ohio to stay with me."

"But what about—"

"Harold and Lorraine Sheldon can go to hell."

He wondered what Faith would say when she learned that Beth would be coming to Painted Lady Farm. What reaction would she have to the sight of his sister? And if his gut instinct was right, and Caitlin was Beth's lost child, would the woman he was coming to care about more than he would admit, ever willingly speak to him again?

CHAPTER FIVE

BETH PROPPED her good leg on the dashboard of the Blazer and surveyed the view through the windshield. She was feeling less anxious now that they'd left the interstate behind and were traveling east along a county highway that Hugh informed her would take them within a mile of their destination. She knew it wasn't logical to feel this way but it had spooked her more than she wanted to admit to find some of the road signs giving the mileage to the town in Indiana where the accident had occurred.

Of course, she hadn't a single memory of the accident or the town, but that didn't seem to matter. Now she calculated they were at least a hundred miles east of that terrible place, and she tried not to think about it anymore. She was getting good at not thinking about things that troubled her. At least some of the time.

"You're sure it's all right with this woman if I share the cabin with you?" The question was out of her mouth before she could stop it.

"It's fine. I told her you were coming this morning before I left for the airport."

"I've asked you that already, haven't I?" Her

mind still played tricks on her like that. She would blank out on a word, or an object, stuttering and stammering as she tried to bring the errant image to mind, or she would forget whether or not she had asked a question, or received a reply, until she heard herself repeating it. Kind of like having Alzheimer's at twenty, she often thought with a shudder.

"Yes, but only once since we left the interstate."

"There's a sign for Painted Lady Butterfly Farm. Two miles straight ahead." She pointed out the window, pleased that with all the stress of the past forty-eight hours that her mind hadn't decided to play tricks on her eyes, too. She knew she was blessedly lucky that other than the amnesia, she had very little residual brain damage.

She shifted position on the hard seat. Her hip was throbbing and she could feel a cramp coming on in her calf. She was glad they'd be arriving soon. She needed a good stretch. "Pain is good," she mumbled, massaging the incipient cramp. She'd probably never be comfortable wearing shorts or a bathing suit in public with all the scars from the surgeries. But, at least she was wasn't walking on an artificial leg.

And she wasn't dead and buried like Jamie. *And their baby? Was she dead and buried, too?* As usual those kind of thoughts threatened to drown her in guilt and sadness. She fought to beat them back.

"Leg bothering you?"

She took a deep breath and sat up a little straighter. Hugh was with her; this time the darkness wouldn't win. "Just a little."

"We're almost in sight of the place. I'll help you walk it off. Then I'll take you into Bartonsville for the meat loaf special at the Golden Sheaf."

"I don't eat red meat."

"I know. I'll eat yours. You can have the salad and mashed potatoes. I don't suppose you've sworn off banana cream pie, too?" His grin was devilish. Hugh was a really good-looking man, even if she was prejudiced in his favor. He looked a lot like pictures of his father, who had been a Green Beret. He'd died when Hugh was eight, six years before she was even born. She used to pretend he was her father, too, instead of Trace. Trace wasn't father material at all.

"Don't even think about it. Especially if it has whipped cream on top instead of meringue."

"It does."

"I'll fight you to the death for it." The exchange brought them to the cabins. Beth opened the door of the truck and was engulfed by the steamy heat of an early June afternoon. "Whew, it's hot."

"Yeah, but not as hot or humid as Houston."

"Nowhere is as humid as Houston. So this is our new abode?" Beth looked at the cabin and liked what she saw—steep-pitched roof, green window boxes overflowing with spicy-scented geraniums, funky red lawn chairs and a real wooden screen door. She got stiffly down from the high seat of the Blazer. "This place is stuck in the fifties."

"Faith will be thrilled to hear you say that. I think she worked hard to get that ambiance. Wait until you see the refrigerator. It's vintage *Happy Days*. And it doesn't keep ice cream. You'll have to get your double-chocolate-chip-mocha fix at the Dairy Barn in town.'' Hugh pulled her bag from the back as she limped past the cabin to stare down at the farmhouse. There were big trees in the yard and an even bigger red barn, a pond with a swinging rope and green fields stretching for miles in all directions. A woman was out in the yard picking up branches, probably from the hailstorm Hugh had told her about.

She was being followed by a dog that looked like Lassie, only way smaller, and a little girl. A toddler, dragging a stick almost as long as she was. She appeared to be two or two and a half. The same age as her daughter would be. Comparing children of similar age to her lost baby was a habit she needed desperately to break. She turned hurriedly and saw Hugh coming back out of the cabin. The screen door slapped shut with a bang.

''That sounds like the one on *The Waltons*,'' she said too brightly. She watched a lot of classic TV shows when she couldn't sleep.

Hugh's eyes moved past her, and spotted the three figures in the yard. ''That's Faith Carson and her daughter,'' he said. ''Do you want to meet them?''

''Sure.'' Hugh had told her the owner of Painted Lady Farm was a young widow with a little girl. Faith was her name, and the little girl was Caitlin. She shouldn't have trouble remembering those names.

''You're sure the butterflies aren't going to be a problem?''

She wasn't going to let them be a problem. It was a weird coincidence that the place where Hugh was staying was a butterfly farm. And her nightmares had come to be filled with images of blood and butterflies, but she could handle it. She used to love the damn things. She had even wanted to be an entomologist once, a lifetime ago. That was the kind of useless thing she remembered with no problem at all.

Hugh was looking down at the woman and child, his expression guarded. "You've asked me that before," she said, giving him a little punch on the arm. His muscles were rock hard and she winced. "You've been working out, again."

"I've been working. Period."

"To tell you the truth I'm looking forward to being a lady of leisure." She was amazed to find she meant it. The time since the accident had been like running a nonstop marathon—on crutches, rehabilitating her body and mind, getting her strength back and staying one step ahead of her nightmares. Now she just wanted to do some reading, walk the trail along the creek Hugh had told her about, swim in the pond, even if the fish did nibble her toes. Maybe she'd even go in the butterfly house. If facing your demons was something you had to do, she could think of worse ways to go about it.

"Ready?" Hugh tucked her arm through his. "Just take it slow until you get the kinks worked out." She was surprised to see a flicker of nervousness in Hugh's dark eyes. Hugh never looked nervous. Almost against her will her gaze skated past him to focus on the woman and her little girl still picking up sticks in the yard. She shivered and didn't know why. A premonition?

The scene before her looked like something out of a Norman Rockwell painting. Nothing threatening except a glass house of butterflies, which she could stay out of if she wanted to. She was just tired, that's all. Time to suck it up and move on. "I'm ready," she said. "Introduce me to Faith Carson and her little girl."

IT WASN'T ONLY CHANCE that made Faith look up from her task of collecting downed twigs and branches to see Hugh and a slight, blond woman walking arm and arm toward her. She had spent entirely too much time watching for them...no, for him, over the course of the last hour, and entirely too much time thinking about what might have happened if he'd taken her in his arms the other evening. She'd dreamed about it, as well, and her dreams had gone much further than a kiss.

He had come to the greenhouse early that morning, while the mist was still on the meadow and the sun barely over the horizon. Caitlin was asleep in the house. Faith was relying on the intercom that connected her daughter's bedroom to the greenhouse to give her warning when Caitlin woke up.

Hugh had accepted a cup of coffee, black, no sugar, but declined a cranberry muffin. He'd explained his sister was coming in on a flight from Houston in the afternoon. There had been a sense of urgency about him, a grimness in the hard line of his jaw, or so Faith had fancied. She had attributed it to worry for his sister, and approved of his concern. Family was important to Faith. She was glad to know it was important to him, too.

Faith's heart almost stopped beating as the young woman stepped out of the glare of the sun and could be seen clearly. She was the last person on earth Faith expected to see.

She was Caitlin's mother.

The girl Faith had thought dead two and a half years before.

"Hi," the apparition said in a light, sweet voice that Faith recognized even without the overlay of pain and fear it had once had. "I'm Hugh's sister, Beth Harden. Are you okay? You look as if you've seen a ghost."

"I... No," she said, and forced a smile onto her face. "I...I straightened up too quickly, that's all. I'm fine. It's...it's nice to meet you, Beth. Welcome to Painted Lady Farm." Inside she was shaking so hard she thought her knees might buckle, but her voice sounded almost normal.

"It's nice to be here, Mrs. Carson."

"Faith. My name is Faith." She heard the echo of her words that stormy November day and wondered if Beth recalled them.

"Thanks, Faith. My brother said you had quite a storm go through here yesterday." Beth looked around the yard, noting the broken twigs and branches, the mud-splatted pansies in the bed at their feet. "Hugh also said Painted Lady Farm was a lovely place. He was right."

"Thank you. I've worked very hard on it the past three years." Faith could scarcely form sentences. Why the polite small talk? Why didn't Beth and her brother get it over with, state their claim to Caitlin and end Faith's life?

"I can tell."

The young woman's smile was pleasant, but distant, a stranger's smile. Sudden unreasoning hope hit with the force of a blow. Was it possible Beth didn't recognize Faith as the woman who had delivered her baby? How could that be?

Behind her, Faith could hear Caitlin crowing with laughter as she played tug-of-war with Addy. The moment she had dreaded for two and a half years had arrived and passed. The sun hadn't fallen from the sky, the world hadn't stopped turning. The slender ghost from her past hadn't pulled Caitlin into her arms claiming her as her own.

Still, the urge to grab Caitlin and run away, as far and as fast as she could go, was strong. But Faith knew if she made any move toward Caitlin at all, Hugh Damon would notice. Her first impression of him had been the right one. He *knew,* and nothing she said or did would convince him otherwise. Her world was in danger from this man. She should have heeded her intuition and sent him packing the moment he had first set foot in the greenhouse.

But she hadn't, and now she had no other choice. She would have to play the game. "Let me show you around." She forced the muscles of her mouth into a smile and lifted her hand toward the greenhouse. Everything around her had taken on an aura of unreality, except for the steady regard of Hugh's eyes and the gurgling laughter of Caitlin playing with her dog. "There are no other visitors at the moment. Would you like a tour of the butterfly house?"

Now Beth looked as if *she* had seen a ghost. "I...I'm a little tired from the flight," she said, glancing up at her brother. She was as slender and petite as Faith remembered, but her hair was no longer the color of moonlight. It had darkened to gold, the same color as the highlights in Hugh's dark hair.

"Perhaps tomorrow morning, then? The butterflies are early risers and it will be cool enough to sit for a while and enjoy them."

"Thanks. I...I'll think about it."

Addy had tired of playing tug-of-war with Caitlin and had come prancing over to sniff at Beth's pant leg. Caitlin followed close on the sheltie's heels. She wrapped her grimy little arms around Faith's leg and peeked up at Beth. "Hi. I Caitlin."

Faith didn't dare look down at her daughter. Her reluctance was mixed of equal parts wariness and fear. Wariness that Hugh was watching and cataloging her every reaction. And fear that Caitlin would feel some connection to Beth, and with the complete honesty of small children voice that emotion and bring down Faith's carefully constructed web of lies.

Beth leaned forward but didn't stoop to Caitlin's

level. "Hi. I'm Beth." Her smile was warm, genuine, but still one of a stranger.

Any lingering doubt Faith had as to Beth's utter obliviousness of her relationship to the two of them vanished. She could not be such a good actress that she could suppress all emotion at the first sight of the child she had lost.

Faith glanced at Hugh and saw doubt and shock flicker across his face before he mastered the emotions. Had he thought the same as Faith? That Beth couldn't possibly fail to recognize her own child? Now that she hadn't had he been thrown off balance?

"My dog," Caitlin said, pointing to Addy. "Watch out. She'll smell your bottom."

"Caitlin." Faith's admonition was automatic.

Beth's laughter was as unguarded as Caitlin's comment. "I'll remember that. She's a nice dog." Beth leaned a little farther forward, holding out her fingers for Addy to sniff. A spasm of pain crossed her face and she stumbled slightly. Hugh was beside her in a moment, steadying her with a hand under her elbow.

"Are you okay?"

She jerked upright, color rushing into her pale cheeks, a look of annoyance on her face. "I'm fine. My knee just gave out on me. It still does that sometimes. I should have worn my brace, but I didn't want to get stopped going through security at the airport."

"Would…would you like to sit down for a few minutes?" Faith gestured to the Adirondack chairs under a nearby oak. The last thing she wanted was to spend more time in their company but she had to play her part. She had to carry on as if nothing was out of the ordinary. Instead of ordering the two of them off her property and out of her life, she would have to be the gracious hostess without a care in the world beyond their comfort.

"No, thanks. I think I'd like to go back to the cabin."

"I'll go get the Blazer." Hugh's expression was unreadable. Once more she had the impression that this meeting had not gone as he had expected. How had he tracked her down? Something had brought him to her doorstep. Some scrap of knowledge, some tidbit of detail gleaned from Beth, perhaps? She would never know because she would never dare to ask.

And she would never dare to be alone with him. She wasn't fool enough to think that he intended to let matters stand as they were. He would confront her with his knowledge at the first opportunity. And, God help her, she was as loath to lie to him now as she had ever been.

"YOU'RE UP EARLY." Hugh came out of the cubicle-size bedroom of the cabin the next morning, pulling a shirt on over his jeans. It was barely daylight, the sun just peeking over the rolling farmland to the east. Beth was sitting at the small Formica-topped table with a bowl of cereal in front of her and orange juice in a vintage jelly glass in her hand.

"I'm always up early these days," she said not

quite evasively. There were faint shadows under her eyes, but she didn't look as if she'd spent a sleepless night tossing and turning, the way he had.

He didn't question her any further. He wasn't quite sure what to do next. He'd acted on impulse the past couple of days and that was sure as hell the last thing he should have done. He'd brought them both to the edge of disaster yesterday, and today the risk was just as great. *Engineers* and *impulse* were not words that belonged in the same sentence.

"I made coffee." Beth gestured over her shoulder with her spoon. "This place is seriously retro, but it's got a modern-day coffeemaker. Although I was kind of hoping I could take a crack at making it in one of those old aluminum pots with the little glass domes on top. You know, like the ones in the old Maxwell House commercials."

"I need a cup. I don't care how you made it." The floor was linoleum and cool to his bare feet, but the day promised heat and humidity.

"I bet you do." Beth let the spoon drop into her empty bowl and stood up. "You tossed and turned all night. Bad dreams?"

"No. Just a hard mattress," he lied. The wide-awake memories of introducing Beth to Faith and Caitlin the afternoon before were nightmare enough. Deep down inside he simply hadn't believed the doctors. Couldn't believe that Beth wouldn't have some remembrance of what had happened to her once she confronted the woman who was raising her child.

Whatever other doubts he had he still believed that Caitlin was Beth's child.

Beth moved over to the sink to rinse her bowl and glass. She was wearing long-legged flannel pajamas even though it was too warm for them in the barely air-conditioned cabin. She was still sensitive of the scars on her leg. Four surgeries, eleven pins. She was lucky to be walking at all. Not lucky, Hugh reminded himself proudly. She'd worked damn hard to come this far.

"What do you want to do today?" he asked.

She paused with the bowl suspended under a stream of water. "I...I don't think I'm quite ready for the butterfly tour yet."

"Did you have the dream again last night?" he asked too sharply. She turned her head and gave him a considering look. His guilty conscience was working overtime and she'd picked up on the vibes in his voice.

"No. I don't remember dreaming at all."

What did that mean? Hugh wondered, but he was relieved that Beth didn't seem to have suffered any psychological damage from his aborted attempt to jump-start her memory. Still, he didn't want her around Faith Carson until he could find the words to tell his sister why he'd brought her here. And how he was going to do that, he had no idea. Except he couldn't do it at Painted Lady Farm. "We could do some sightseeing today if you want. There are a couple of antique places nearby. And a farmer's market. The strawberries are coming out around here."

"You hate antiquing." On the other hand she loved poking through the nooks and crannies of antique shops.

"For you I'll brave the dust and mildew of every junk shop we can find in a fifty-mile radius."

"Great. I'll jump in the shower and be ready in fifteen minutes."

He'd brave more than a couple of musty antique shops to see her smile that way. They'd spend the day together. He'd find some way to ease into the subject of her lost baby. And then, later, he'd strap on body armor and track down Faith Carson to have it out with her.

He wasn't joking about the body armor. He had no illusions whatsoever that the woman was now his enemy. He had seen it in the fierce protectiveness in her eyes yesterday, in the way her hands had tightened into fists on the branch she'd held. She would fight him to the death to keep what she claimed was hers.

His pager went off. He grabbed it off the counter. "Damn. It's Higgins at the site. I'll have to call in."

He punched in the number on his cell phone and thirty seconds later he was listening to the half-hysterical voice of the site boss. The EPA inspectors were on their way and his secretary hadn't passed on the message the evening before. Hugh had to get his butt to Cincy before the Feds arrived or there would be hell to pay.

There was no getting out of it. Hugh was going to

have to spend the day on site. He'd have to take Beth with him.

But when she came out of the shower ten minutes later, dressed in a sunny-yellow top and thin white cotton slacks, she surprised him by shaking her head and turning down his offer of a day in the city. "I've had enough sitting around in airplanes and trucks. I think I'll rent a bicycle and take off on my own."

"Rent a bicycle?"

"Yeah, from Faith. How long have you been here? Haven't you read that note on the end of the cupboard?" She wrapped the towel she'd been using into a turban and marched over to tap a pink-tinted fingernail on the sheet of paper tacked to the cupboard. "Faith rents bicycles. It says here there's a bike trail that starts at a little roadside park—" she tilted her head and then pointed west "—just down the road. I'll check with her and see if any of those antique shops are close enough to go to on my own."

He opened his mouth to protest and she cut him off.

"Don't thank me, big brother. I know how much you hate poking around in dusty shops while I try on vintage hats and paw through stacks of old table linens."

"You just got here. I haven't seen you for weeks." He felt like a jerk for trying to manipulate her this way, but the last place on earth he wanted her to be today was in close proximity to Faith.

"You can take me out to dinner tonight to make up for it. They're featuring fresh strawberry pie at the Golden Sheaf. I saw it on the menu last night. Besides, I want to get to know Faith better.''

"What?'' He searched her face for any clue that she had recalled something, but he saw only a hint of laughter and mischief in her eyes that brightened them to the color of the sky on a midsummer afternoon.

"I want to check her out. See if she's good enough for you.''

"What the devil are you talking about?''

"I think you're just the teeniest bit interested in our landlady,'' she said.

"What gave you that idea?''

"Woman's intuition, I guess. Something about the way you look at her. The way you talk about her.''

"I was making conversation. Filling you in on what it's like around here, that's all.''

"If that's all you were doing then why are the veins standing out on your neck? And your face is turning red.''

He made a grab for her. She'd always been ticklish, and when she was little he'd used it to his advantage when she was teasing him.

"I'm too old for this,'' she giggled, wriggling like a fish, as he reached out and reeled her in for a bear hug.

"You're not even twenty-one.''

"I will be next month.''

"Practically an old woman,'' he growled, noting how light she felt in his arms.

She went quiet very suddenly. "Some days I feel like an old woman."

He set her gently on her feet. "Beth, honey—" Once more words failed him when he needed them most.

"No poor-Beth talk. I shouldn't have said that. I'll be fine, really." She clasped her small hands around his wrists and squeezed hard. "Go do your job."

He had to tread very carefully. He'd foolishly brought his sister to this place, and introduced her to the woman who might hold the key to her past without learning the truth from Faith first. But today he had nothing to fear. Unlocking that mystery was the last thing Faith Carson wanted. He was convinced of that. She had become his unwilling ally, whether she liked it or not.

CHAPTER SIX

THIS TIME she was ready for the appearance of Hugh's sister. Faith was watering the last of the flats of red, white and what passed for blue petunias that were always popular for bedding plants in and around Bartonsville, not only because people liked to wave the flag, but because the Bartonsville high school sports teams were known as the Patriots. Beth's limp was less noticeable this morning, a slight hesitation in her gait, the only indication of the accident that had almost taken her life.

"Good morning," Beth said, shoving her hands into the pockets of her white slacks. The high for the afternoon was predicted to be ninety. Even though she had paired the slacks with a sleeveless yellow T-shirt she was going to be uncomfortable in the outfit before long.

"Good morning. I hope you slept well. Have you had breakfast?" Faith was proud of the nothing-out-of-the-ordinary tone of her voice, but she hoped her smile didn't look as forced as it felt on her lips.

"Yes and yes." Beth's answering smile was genuine and free of guile.

Faith relaxed a fraction. She had lain awake most

of the night reliving the moments of their first encounter, searching her memory for any inkling of recognition she might have missed and had found none, but still she worried. And with good reason. Hugh Damon didn't suffer from amnesia as she'd begun to believe Beth did.

"And your brother?"

"I'm afraid he has to spend the day on site in Cincinnati. Something about the EPA and drainage variances." She lifted slender shoulders in a shrug. "He left almost an hour ago." Faith knew exactly when he'd left. She had watched the Blazer drive away as she'd gone to feed the barn cats.

"Then you've come to see the butterflies. It's a good time. I'm just getting the feeding trays ready."

Beth was standing before a table of garden herbs. She had picked up a small clay pot of rosemary to sniff, but now she set it down with a thump. "I...I don't think so. Thanks, anyway. Actually, I came to see about renting a bicycle for the day. The flier in the cabin mentioned a biking trail."

"Yes, it starts at the park about a mile from here and follows an old railroad right-of-way. About two miles farther on it crosses the river on a trestle bridge. It's a very pretty ride at this time of year."

"Sounds exactly right...if the grades aren't too steep."

"Nothing steeper than the lane from here to the road."

"I think I can mange that." She went back to examining the herb pots, as though she needed something to do with her hands. Beth appeared restless and on edge, although she tried not to show it. Faith wondered how much of that edginess might be caused by the first faint stirring of returning memory?

"I'm afraid I don't have much of a selection of bikes. Only a couple of old three-speeds, but you really don't need anything fancier around here." Faith turned off the wand sprinkler and motioned for Beth to follow her toward the barn, where the bicycles were kept.

"Mommy," Caitlin yelled, hopping down the back steps, pulling thirteen-year-old Dana, Steve's niece, and Peg along with her. Her daughter tugged free of Dana's grasp and flung out her arms as she ran, apparently as thrilled to see Faith as if they'd been parted for twenty days instead of twenty minutes. Peg and Dana followed more sedately and nodded pleasantly to Beth.

"I got Barbie shoes on. See." She held up one little foot shod in a pink Barbie sandal. "I'm be-oo-ti-ful."

"You are beautiful." Faith picked her up. "Are you all ready to go bye-bye with Dana and Auntie Peg?"

"I go potty like a big girl. I brushed my teeth." Caitlin gave Faith a Cheshire cat grin that showed two rows of shiny white teeth.

"Good girl."

Caitlin wrapped her arms around Faith's neck and gave Beth the once-over. "Hi," she said, growing suddenly shy. Again Faith felt a sharp lance of anxiety pierce her. Was it possible for Caitlin to feel some connection, however tenuous, with the woman who had given her life?

Beth's smiled wavered for a moment but the darkness passed quickly and the smile returned. "Hi, Caitlin. Do you remember me? I'm Beth."

Caitlin nodded, looking over Beth's shoulder, then up the lane to the cabins. "Where's Hugh? I like Hugh. Get him."

Beth's laughter was high and tinkling. "Uh-oh. Sounds like my brother's made another conquest."

Faith didn't want to talk about Hugh. "Beth Harden, this is my sister, Peg Baden and her husband's niece, Dana."

"Hello, Beth," Peg said. "Welcome to Ohio."

"Hello," Beth said politely. "It's nice to meet you."

Dana added a shy hello, which Beth returned.

"Baby school." Caitlin started to fidget. "I go baby school."

Beth's expression was puzzled. "Baby school?"

Caitlin nodded vigorously and then went limp, hanging over Faith's clasped arms, her silvery-blond hair floating around her face as she reached for the ground. With a little grunt Faith set her on her feet. "Go," the toddler demanded, tugging on the hem of Peg's denim skirt.

"Caitlin, that's not polite. Remember we must use our manners. The grown-ups are talking. Please be good and wait until we finish, or you'll have to stay home," Faith said as sternly as she could manage.

"Caitlin is going to be Dana's study subject for her baby-sitting certification course at the junior high school," Peg explained. "Evidently potty-trained, two-a-half-year-olds are very desirable specimens."

Dana nodded. "Brittany Weisman can't use her little sister because she's still wearing diapers. Her mom says she's not going to bother to potty train her until summer's over."

"You'll graduate with honors if you last two days with Caitlin," Faith added.

"It sounds like fun," Beth said.

"Go now, Dana. C'mon, Peg-peg." Caitlin was dancing up and down again. Beth was watching Caitlin's antics with interest, but nothing more, no hint of recognition or connection showed on her face.

"All right already." Dana scooped Caitlin up and swung her onto her back.

"Yay! Piggyback." Caitlin giggled.

"I put her new Barbie and her favorite sippy cup in her bag and the phone number's in the side pocket."

"I've got everything in the van already," Dana assured Faith.

Peg rolled her eyes. "I don't think it's Caitlin that's having separation anxiety here."

Faith felt her color rise. She tried hard not to be overprotective, but today she couldn't help it. She wanted to shut Caitlin safe in her bedroom and throw away the key.

"We'd better be on our way. Steve is watching

the boys, but he has work to do so I need to get back. Nice meeting you, Beth,'' Peg said.

Faith excused herself to Beth and followed Peg to the van. "Are you okay?" Peg asked as Faith buckled Caitlin into the safety seat.

Faith snapped the harness into its lock and didn't look up. "I'm fine." But, of course, she wasn't, and Peg had noticed. Her sister, although only five years older, had been more of a mother to her than the frail, pretty woman who had borne them. Faith had made up her mind not to tell her sister who Beth was. She couldn't add that extra burden of secrecy to Peg's marriage. She was going to have to face this alone.

Peg climbed into the driver's seat and stared at Faith as she brushed Caitlin's hair behind her ears. She spoke quietly while Dana strapped herself in beside Caitlin. "You're all jumpy. You've got big circles under your eyes. You look as if you haven't slept in days. Are you coming down with something?"

"No. I'm fine, really. But you're right. I haven't been sleeping too well."

"Take a nap this afternoon. I'll keep Caitlin until after supper."

"You don't have—"

"I know I don't have to." Peg gave her a saucy grin. "I promise we won't keep her too late. And I won't let the boys feed her too much ice cream." A trip to the Dairy Barn at the edge of town would be the highlight of Caitlin's day. There was no way Faith could say no.

"Okay." She leaned over and gave Caitlin a peck on the cheek. "Bye-bye."

"Bye." Caitlin gave her a happy wave.

She watched her sister drive away, then turned to find Beth wheeling a bicycle out of the barn. "Do you want me to leave the deposit with you?" Beth asked. She pulled a couple of bills out of her pocket and held them toward Faith.

"No need. You're welcome to the bicycle."

"You can't make money that way."

"I don't need the money. Let's just call it a perk for long-term guests. But I do have to ask you to sign a waiver. My insurance company demands it."

"No problem." Beth leaned the bike against a post and followed Faith to the greenhouse.

"You're welcome to tour the butterfly house whenever you like," Faith said as she showed Beth where to sign the simple liability form. "In fact, if you're interested now would be a good time. It's sunny. The butterflies are always more active when it's sunny."

Beth spoke quickly, shaking her head. "Maybe tomorrow. I'd really like to ride this morning."

"All right."

The note of uneasiness had returned to Beth's voice. It was faint but evident. She didn't want to be around the butterflies. Faith wondered why. She was finding it too easy to talk to Beth, and she mustn't allow herself to drop her guard that way. The girl's next words confirmed the wisdom of that internal warning.

"Your little girl's adorable. I wish I had hair that color."

"You do have hair that color," Faith said, swallowing against the sudden constriction in her throat.

"I used to have hair that color. Now it comes out of a bottle. So do my eyelashes and eyebrows. Your little girl has lovely eyelashes and eyebrows, darker than her hair."

"She...she takes after her father." Jamie had been blond, with dark eyelashes and eyebrows, Faith recalled. But if Beth couldn't remember Caitlin's birth, or Faith, had she also lost her memories of her baby's father?

"She's lucky, believe me. After my accident my hair got dark, but my eyebrows and eyelashes didn't. I looked weird. Of course, for six months I didn't know how I looked. And I couldn't have complained about it if I had. Every word that came out of my mouth made no sense." Beth had been running her fingertip along the edge of a hummingbird figurine on the shelf just inside the door. She broke off suddenly. "I'm sorry. You probably don't want to hear all this, do you?"

"No. Please. I—I'm a nurse. I know a little about brain injuries. You don't have to go into detail if it makes you uncomfortable, but please feel free to do so if you want to."

"Thanks. I—I don't usually care about that anymore. It's—" Beth shrugged and set the little figurine back on the shelf very carefully. "This will sound silly but this is as close as I've been to where the accident happened. Seeing the road signs on the interstate gave me the willies." She rubbed her hands up and down her arms.

"Where did your accident happen?"

"A little town in Indiana. About a hundred miles or so from here. You've probably never heard of it."

"Probably," Faith agreed. "I only moved here three years ago after my husband died. Were...were you alone?"

"I was with my boyfriend. He was driving. There was a terrible ice storm."

Faith caught her breath and knew she must speak. "Caitlin was born during an ice storm. I was here by myself."

Beth's face was suddenly very white. "When?"

There was no way Faith could avoid answering. "She'll be three in November."

"I thought she m-m-must be about that old. T-t-two and a half." Beth seemed to force each word from her lips, her stutter was very pronounced.

"Yes, she is."

"That's when my accident happened."

"It was a very bad storm. It covered most of three states, all the way from Chicago to Cleveland. Caitlin and I were trapped here for days." Faith waited for Beth to ask Caitlin's exact birth date, her heart beating hard and fast in her chest, but the question didn't come. Instead, Beth reached out for another figurine. Her hand was shaking badly enough that Faith could see the tremors from several feet away. She busied herself straightening a stack of invoices before putting them in the drawer below the cash register. She needed to change the topic. But first she must learn all she could without Hugh's hard, seeking gaze pinned on her. She could never show such interest in Beth's past in front of him.

"Were you and your brother living in Indiana at the time?" She was taking a great risk. Anything she said could lead to the younger woman remembering everything.

"No. I was living with Father and my stepmother in Boston. Hugh was out of the country. My boyfriend was killed. A semi truck jackknifed and started a chain reaction. W-we were running away from our parents. His parents mostly." The words were defiant, but the slighter stutter betrayed Beth's agitation. She gave a harsh, quavering little laugh that betrayed her still more. "I still am. I came here to get away from them. They keep badgering me...about things I can't remember."

"I'm sorry." Faith bent down to the little refrigerator so that Beth couldn't see her face. She wasn't especially knowledgeable about brain injuries, but one thing she did know was that there were no absolutes. Faith's whole world was in danger from any of a thousand small associations that could bring about the return of Beth's memory.

She brought out a plate of watermelon and orange slices and set them on the counter with a thud. Her hands were shaking as hard as Beth's had been. She rubbed them together and reached for the paring knife and plastic container of wooden skewers she kept beside the refrigerator.

"What are you doing?" Beth asked. If she wanted to change the subject, Faith would go along with her. She had had enough of this dangerous game.

"I'm getting ready to feed the butterflies. They love fruit. Especially watermelon."

"Maybe because it's the closest to nectar?"

It was an astute observation. "I sometimes think that myself, although there's plenty of nectar flowers blooming in the habitat. And I set out nectar feeders, too." While Beth watched, Faith threaded pieces of fruit onto the skewers and placed them in a grid pattern to hold them up off the plate, giving the butterflies more surface to feed from.

"Butterflies taste with their feet and hear with their antennae."

"That's right. The school groups always get a laugh out of me telling them if they were butterflies, they'd have to stick their bare toes in their hot fudge sundaes to taste it."

"I remember all the oddest things," Beth said softly. "I wanted to be an entomologist...until the accident. Bits and pieces of things I used to know pop into my mind all the time. But I can't—" She stopped abruptly. Faith held her breath wondering what she would say next.

I can't remember what happened to my baby?

"But huge chunks of the most important months of my life are gone." Her voice trailed off. "I really am sorry I've dumped all this on you. It's strange. I don't usually talk about the accident. And I never ramble on this way. Especially—''

''With a stranger?'' Faith was slightly ashamed of herself for putting the words in the girl's mouth.

''I was going to say with someone I just met. *Stranger*'s such a hard word.''

''It is, isn't it?'' Faith said softly, speaking from her heart. Beth looked so lost and confused. Only a monster wouldn't feel compassion for her. And Faith wasn't a monster, just a mother terrified of losing her child to another woman. ''I don't think we're strangers anymore, either. Would you like to help me feed the butterflies?''

''No.'' Once more the denial was swift and immediate. ''No. I think I'd better get on with my ride. It's getting hotter by the minute. Where did you say that little park was?''

''It's at the bottom of the next hill. Go out to the road, turn right past the cabins. First you'll see the cemetery and at the bottom of the hill a road off to the right. The park's at the end of it.'' Faith gestured with a skewer. ''It's only a half mile or so across the fields. You can't see it from here because of the woods that run along the creek. But you can't miss it. There's a sign. The county renamed it Sylvan Lake, but everyone around here still calls it Carson's Pond.''

''Turn right. Cemetery. Bottom of the hill. Sylvan Lake.'' Beth's eyes were huge pools of blue misery.

Faith began to be alarmed. Perhaps she shouldn't let her go off by herself this way.

"Beth, what's wrong?" She couldn't stop herself from asking. It was hard for her to see this girl in such distress, even though self-preservation prevented her from offering too much comfort.

"I—I'm afraid of butterflies. Isn't that a hoot? I dream about them. I'm cold and scared and hurting. There are thousands of butterflies. And they drop into the snow and turn to drops of blood—" Once more she stopped, as though torn between wanting to tell Faith what was on her mind, and in fear of doing so. "I told you it was weird." She squared her narrow shoulders and started backing toward the door. "I recommend never getting your brain scrambled in a car accident."

"Beth."

"Don't worry about me. I stammer a lot and get words all mixed up. But I'm not crazy, even if I do rattle on. And look, if I said anything earlier to make you believe my brother's some kind of lady-killer, he's not."

"What?" Faith was taken off guard by her words. "Your brother?"

"When Caitlin asked for him. I—I made some comment about him being a lady-killer. It's the truth. But it's not because he encourages them. I don't think he's even had a date since I got hurt. I don't want you to get the wrong idea about him."

"Your brother...has been the perfect gentlemen since he arrived."

''He's a great guy.''

''I'm sure he is.'' It was Faith's turn to be evasive. She shooed away an inquisitive fly from the fruit plate with a wave of her hand.

''I'll go now so you can feed the butterflies.''

''Beth.''

She had already reached the doorway of the greenhouse by the time Faith spoke. She turned back, her defiance melting away, as though she expected to be told to take a pill and forget all the things that tormented her.

''Have a good ride.''

Beth held her gaze for a long moment. So long Faith was tempted to look away, lest Beth read the secret she kept so carefully. ''Thanks,'' she said, a tiny curve of a smile touching the corners of her mouth. ''I'll do that.''

IT WASN'T EVEN ten o'clock and it was already as hot as a Houston summer morning would be. But the humidity wasn't as bad, at least not yet. Beth leaned the bike against the wrought-iron fence of the small cemetery and looked back at Painted Lady Farm.

''God, what a fool you made of yourself this morning.'' She talked to herself when she was alone. It wasn't something that she'd started doing since the accident, though. She'd been talking to herself since she was a little kid. Hugh always used to tease her about it, peering behind the curtains and lifting up the cushions on the couch to find whoever it was she was talking to.

"Oh, Hugh. I still think I'm losing my mind, no matter how hard you try to convince me I'm not."

She looked down. Her hands were shaking and dark spots danced before her eyes. Her therapist would be mad at her for getting this upset. If she didn't settle down before Hugh got home he'd insist she take a sedative, and if she did that the dreams would be back in earnest.

She couldn't go on like this. She needed exercise. Exertion would lead to oblivion. She had to find the bike trail and go as fast and as far as her unreliable leg would take her. She coasted down the slope of the cemetery hill and found the gravel lane leading to the park just where Faith said it would be.

The lane angled up another gentle hill, winding through a grove of big oaks and maples and finally opening into a small parking lot. The trail head was clearly marked, a wide asphalt-paved path that would make for easy riding. It was shaded by a row of small trees and big sumac bushes at this time of day, and inviting. There was only one car in the lot, a beat-up looking Buick that had to be at least as old as she was.

A set of steps led up a steep bank to where the ground leveled out again. Beth decided to take a look at the park, maybe find a fountain or a spigot and get a drink of water. She'd taken off in such a state that she hadn't stopped at the cabin to get her pack. It would be a hot ride without water, but she wasn't about to use that as an excuse to turn back and spend the rest of the day pacing in the cabin's cramped main room.

She topped the rise, puffing just a little from pushing the bike up the banked slope, and looked down on a meadowlike setting. The lake was very small, more like a large pond really, narrow at one end and rounded at the other. A little hump-backed bridge crossed a marshy stream at the narrow end and a path led to a stone and wood picnic shelter. There was a play area for children on the shore of the lake, a big wooden jungle gym, swings and a slide. Primitive outhouses stood against the tree line.

There was an old-fashioned pump with a long handle in front of the shelter like the one she'd seen in Faith's backyard. She would get a drink before she began her ride. She started down the slope, pushing her bike, when a sudden wave of vertigo washed over her, leaving her shaken and sweating. Bright spots danced before her eyes, the sun whirled in the sky, and somewhere far away she heard a baby crying. Not now. Not the dream. This had never happened to her before. The dreams always came in the darkest, loneliest hours of the night. She shivered and felt the first sharp claws of a panic attack steal her breath.

"I've had too much sun," she said out loud. "Or I'm getting sick." But neither of those explanations accurately described the way she felt. Something was drawing her toward the picnic house, a sense of mingled familiarity and fear. "I know this place."

But she didn't. Couldn't. She had never set foot

in Ohio, or anywhere within a hundred miles until yesterday. The police, Jamie's parents, Hugh. They all had retraced their flight from Boston using several different routes, hoping to find the spot where she'd given birth, where she'd left her baby behind. But Bartonsville, Ohio, had never been mentioned.

Whatever it was about this place couldn't be related to her past. She took heart from the thought and opened her eyes, brushing away the tears that had fallen on to her cheeks.

"Hey! Wait."

Beth looked around to see a male figure on a black dirt bike come racing down the slope toward her. He skidded to a stop, blocking her path. If he was some kind of a pervert, or country-style purse snatcher, she'd never be able to outrun him. Better to stand her ground and not show any fear.

"You don't want to go down there," he said, leaning his weight on the handlebars, breathing heavily. He was wearing a navy-blue ball cap and cutoffs that were so thin and well washed they might have been made of tissue paper. A faded red Bartonsville Patriots T-shirt stretched across his chest and flat stomach. His hair was red, not auburn, or chestnut, or ginger. Just red. He had freckles everywhere she could see, and warm brown eyes. She relaxed a little. He didn't look like a rapist. He looked as innocent as Beaver Cleaver. And he wasn't so intimidating after all, not with that grin. He was maybe five-seven or five-eight. Although, he did have broad shoulders for his height, and well-muscled thighs below the cutoffs. She jerked her gaze upward. She didn't notice things like that about boys anymore.

"I want a drink of water." She tried to sound as old, and as annoyed as she could manage. "Please get out of my way so I can get to the pump."

"That's what I'm trying to tell you. If you go that way you'll be up to your knees in mud. The town fathers saw fit to build that cute little bridge over the stream, but they didn't appropriate any money for draining the path. It's like a swamp down there this time of year. If you were from around here you'd know that."

"You're right. I'm not from around here." She sounded churlish and felt slightly ashamed. He wasn't a rapist. He probably played halfback on the Bartonsville high school team, or maybe he wrestled. And now that she looked at where he was pointing, she did see that he'd saved her from getting stuck in the mud. He might not be quite the boy she'd first thought him to be, either. Something about the way he held his body, the directness of his gaze bespoke a measure of maturity. "You're a man," she blurted in one of those horrifying lapses of control that still plagued her in stressful situations.

He laughed, a rich full-throated, masculine laugh that made her add another two or three years to her estimate of his age. "Last time I checked."

"I—I'm sorry. I m-m-meant to say I thought you were just a kid when you came barreling down that hill." The effort to keep her brain and tongue from tying themselves in knots was causing her to break out in a cold sweat. And the continued unsettling pull of the picnic shelter added to her distress.

"I know I look like a kid," he said without offense, pulling the ball cap off his head and wiping his forehead with the back of his forearm. "Makes my job hell some days. Look, it's too damn hot to stand out here. Come on, I'll show you the dry way to the pump. And don't worry. Faith Carson will vouch for me. I'm Kevin Sager. I teach science at Bartonsville Junior High. I just had my kids out there to see the butterfly house a week or so ago."

"How did you know I was staying at Faith's place?" Almost against her will, Beth turned her bike and followed him along the bank until they came to a narrow path leading down to the picnic shelter. She kept her eyes averted from the building. No matter how ordinary—even inviting—it looked, she would rather die than go inside.

"The Painted Lady decal on the back fender of your bike. I run across renters of hers biking here every once in a while."

"Oh." She hadn't noticed the butterfly decal before he pointed it out.

He dropped his bike in the grass beside the pump and started working the handle. Beth just stood where she was, staring at the sparkling flow of water. "Cup your hands," he said, after a few moments. "My good manners only last so long. I'm dying of thirst and I forgot my water bottle this morning."

"I—I—?" For a terrible moment her mind came up entirely blank, unable to grasp the concept of making a cup with her hands. She looked at him helplessly, blinking back tears. She hadn't had this kind of block for months and months.

"You must be a city girl," he said, laughing again, as though nothing were terribly wrong.

"I am." What had she expected him to say?

"Thought so. Do this." He placed his hands side by side, scooped up a palm full of water and brought it to his lips, slurping noisily. "Ahhh, the only thing that could beat that right now is an ice-cold beer. Come on, your turn." He went back to pumping.

Beth dropped the kickstand on the bike and balanced it carefully on the grass. Trembling she laid one hand over the other and stared down at her stiff fingers. Something wasn't right? But what? She felt panic nipping at the edges of her thoughts again and battled it back. She took a deep breath and closed her eyes, recalling the movements he'd made. He had nice hands, she thought, big and square with a dusting of hair on the knuckles. And his name was Kevin. She liked that name. Suddenly, the concept clicked into placed. She curled her fingers upward and stuck her hands under the falling water.

"It's cold," she said, bringing her hands to her mouth.

"Spring fed. So's the pond. Want to go skinny dipping?"

"I—I— No." He was flirting with her. He was treating her like a normal girl...woman...not an invalid, not a mental case. Not a mother who might have done something so terrible to her baby her mind refused to remember a single thing about her birth. She didn't know how to respond. She took a too hasty step back and he grabbed her wrist to keep her from tripping over her bike. He let go of her as soon as she was steady on her feet, but the warmth of his wet hand lingered on her skin.

The devilish grin he'd been wearing disappeared, sharpening the angle of his jaw, dispelling any notion that this was a boy and not a man. "I'm sorry. I was just teasing. Not good form when you don't even know the name of the person you're teasing. What is your name, by the way?"

"Beth Harden."

"From?"

"Houston. Houston, Texas."

"I know where Houston is."

She felt herself blushing.

"And I'm Kevin Sager, fourth generation citizen of good old Bartonsville, Ohio. There we are, properly introduced. The formalities are over, right?"

"Right."

"Okay, no more teasing. Now can I make a serious request? Beth Harden from Houston, Texas, do you want to go skinny-dipping with me?"

CHAPTER SEVEN

HUGH HADN'T REALIZED how worried he'd been about leaving Beth alone until he pulled the Blazer to a halt beside the cabin just before sundown and saw her peering at him through the old-fashioned screen door. She was wearing shorts and a halter top, something she never did in public.

"You look like you could use a cold beer," she said, holding open the door. "Too bad we don't have any here."

"We do now." He pulled two plastic bags of groceries and a twelve pack of beer out of the back of the Blazer. "I stopped to get a few essentials."

"Like taco chips and salsa?" Beth asked with a smile, taking one of the bags and peering inside. "And cheese spread in a squirt bottle?"

"Hey, I like the stuff."

"It's pure fat. It will clog your arteries while you sleep."

"I like living dangerously."

"You always have."

He changed the subject. "No neighbors for the night, I see."

"Nope. But a couple did stop to look at the place

for a week later in the fall. I wasn't eavesdropping. The guy must have been deaf. He talked so loudly I imagine Faith's ears were ringing for an hour after they left." Hugh watched her closely. She seemed relaxed and untroubled. Her speech was clear, her movements smooth and coordinated. If she'd had a bad day, he would be able to tell. And she wouldn't be wearing shorts. On bad days she layered on the clothes no matter what the weather was like, cocooning herself against the world like the butterflies that haunted her dreams.

He relaxed a fraction. It seemed whatever interaction she'd had with Faith Carson hadn't upset her. But what did that mean? Had Beth made no connection with the woman or child in her damaged brain whatsoever? Or was he was one-hundred percent wrong in his speculation that Caitlin Carson was Beth's lost child? He'd have to tread carefully in his attempt to find out which it was.

He'd taken the time to remedy one of the other glaring omissions he'd made. He pulled a cell phone out of his pocket. "Here, I thought you might need this to keep in touch with the world."

"I don't know about keeping in touch with the world. But I'm glad I can keep in touch with you. And the pizza place out by the highway delivers within a fifteen-mile radius. I hear they make a great veggie sub."

"How do you know that?"

"I met a guy. He told me."

"You met a guy? Where? Who? We're out in the

middle of nowhere and you don't have a car.'' It was the last thing he'd expected her to say. She hadn't shown any interest in dating since the accident. At first Hugh had figured it was because she'd focused all her energies on her recovery. But over the past few months he'd begun to worry that it was because she felt herself too damaged to enter any kind of a relationship. He'd been searching for a way to bring up the subject, but now it seemed events had overtaken him.

"I had a bike. Maybe I shouldn't tell you his name. You sound as if you're going to track him down and beat him up." The sparkle he saw too seldom in her blue eyes faded away.

"Sorry. Big brother protocols kicking in." He turned to put the beer in the small fridge, squatting on his heels to place each can in the door shelf while he talked.

"Tell me about him. Is he from town?"

A smile curved her lips. "Yes. His name's Kevin Sager. He teaches junior high science. This is just his second year, so you can't complain he's too old for me," she said, anticipating his next question. He popped the top on a can of beer and motioned for her to keep talking.

"I met him at the park down the hill that Faith told me about when she loaned me the bike. I was going to take a ride along the bike trail, but it was too hot by the time I got there, so I thought I'd stop for a drink of water. I was kind of…wound up…and the place gave me the creeps for some reason." She faltered for a moment. "I haven't the slightest idea why. It's just a nice little country park." The statement caught Hugh's attention but he didn't let his interest show. He'd learned early on in her recovery not to show worry for her, or she would clam up, unwilling to confide in him further if she thought he was upset by her anxiety or pain.

"Okay, so far so good. We've got an age-compatible, gainfully employed, single male here. He is single, isn't he?"

"He's single. At least he told me he was and I believe him. He told me to check with Faith if I wanted a character reference. He's had his class out here to study the butterflies. He...Kevin..." She threw up her hands and laughed. "He rode up like a knight in shining armor on his bike and stopped me from walking into a swampy place, and probably wrenching my knee. And then he asked me to go skinny-dipping with him."

"He what?" So much for the nonchalant approach. Hugh crumpled the empty beer can in his fist. He was hot and dirty and he needed a shower and another beer, but first he wanted to get the low-down on this character who was hitting on his sister.

Beth laughed again, and the sound went straight to his heart and settled there with a warm glow. "Don't get yourself worked up. I admit it was a terrible pickup line, but he was just kidding." She colored slightly, and Hugh guessed the guy probably damn well had wanted to go skinny-dipping with his sister. He wouldn't be human if he didn't. "He's a nice guy, really. We rode back here together. He's coming back tomorrow and we're going to ride the trail to the river. He says it's great at sunrise. What time is sunrise anyway?''

''About six this time of year.''

She wrinkled her nose. ''Oh, well, I guess I can struggle out of bed that early if I have to. Do you want me to fix you a salad or something?''

''No. I grabbed a burger and fries on the way out of the city.'' Hugh decided he would play it cool and not ask any more questions about the school teacher his sister had taken a fancy to. But that didn't mean he wasn't going to get some answers somewhere else. He hadn't been around to keep her from tragedy with Jamie Sheldon, but he wasn't going to stand idly by and let her get her heart broken a second time.

''Want to come sit outside with me and watch the sunset? The TV reception is lousy today.''

The remark hit another sore spot in his conscience. ''Beth, are you sure you're going to be okay out here? We can look for a place closer to the project. I'll rent you a car on the days I'm working. You can do some shopping....''

''I don't want to move into the city. But maybe I will take you up on the rental car. I think it will be easier to get comfortable driving again here in the country, instead of in freeway traffic, don't you?''

Her breezy tone didn't fool him. She wanted to stay here, and he should be glad. He wanted answers to all the questions that had eaten at him like acid since the moment the doctors had told him Beth had given birth, probably just hours before the accident.

He wanted to know what Faith Carson knew.

But there was something more than concern for his sister and her lost child driving him, something deep inside him that would not be denied.

God help him, he also wanted to learn all there was to know about Faith Carson for himself.

HE CAME TO HER in the moonlight, as she stood at the edge of the meadow. There was a slight breeze blowing from the west, ruffling the surface of the pond, keeping the mosquitoes at bay. The movement of the air cooled the nape of her neck, but it wasn't strong enough to ground the fireflies, or lightning bugs, as they were known in these parts. They danced and sparkled above the meadow flowers as thickly as stars in the sky.

"Hello, Faith," Hugh said, and the low, rough timbre of his voice caressed her skin like the wind.

"Good evening."

"Are you out stargazing?" he asked, resting one foot on the bottom rung of the rail fence that divided the lawn from the butterfly meadow. He was wearing cutoffs and a white T-shirt that stretched across his chest. She pulled her gaze upward, to his face. His expression was lost in the shadows, but she felt him watching her.

"Just enjoying the evening."

"It's just about perfect. Enough breeze to keep away the bugs and no clouds to block the view." He was looking up at the thin crescent moon. She leaned her elbows against the top rail of the fence and tipped her head back. The Big Dipper was directly overhead, and she concentrated on tracing its outline. She simply couldn't allow herself to be drawn in by the warmth of his low, rough voice. He was her enemy, not a man that she might find pleasure in conversing with on a moonlit night.

"Is Caitlin asleep?"

She jerked her head around. An ordinary question, but fraught with hidden meaning. Nothing about this meeting was ordinary, and they both knew it. Faith answered carefully. "She had a long and exciting day. She almost fell asleep in her SpaghettiOs." She slipped her hand into the oversize pocket of her sundress and touched the remote unit for the nursery monitor.

"My sister told me about it. Baby-sitting school, I believe she said."

"Yes, Caitlin loved it. She was the star pupil today. She can't wait for tomorrow. She'll be up with the sun."

"She's a sweet kid."

"She's my life," Faith said, unable to stop herself in time.

He didn't seem to notice, or ignored the opening she had given him to pounce. And pounce was the right word. He seemed as dangerous and predatory as a hunting cat.

She waited, tense and alert, but he changed the subject, throwing her off balance once more. "My sister had an exciting day, too,'' he said, resting his palms on the top rail. His arms were as well muscled as the rest of him. And once more she felt a flash of longing for those arms to be wrapped around her. ''She met a man.''

''A man? But where? I mean, she went to the park down the road, but she was back in an hour. I know because she brought the bicycle back to the barn.''

''She met him there. He was bicycling, too. He says he knows you. That you'd give a reference to his good character.''

''Me?'' The number of men in her life were few. There was Steve, and Reverend Kanine at church, Dr. Elliot at the hospital. ''What did he say his name was?''

''Kevin Sager. Is he the pillar of the community he says he is?''

''Kevin Sager? Yes, I know him slightly. He's the new science teacher at the junior high. His father's a county commissioner. Good family, as they say around here.''

''Thank you, I appreciate that. Beth hasn't had a lot to do with boys since her accident.''

''Kevin's not a boy. He's a man, although a young one. And your sister is a grown woman who probably won't appreciate you vetting her choice of friends.''

''But she's fragile as hell.'' He was protective of Beth. A man of honor and loyalty, as Mark had been. Faith knew that instinctively. But he was still her enemy. She could not forget that for a moment.

He had the power to destroy her.

And he would soon tire of this polite game and begin to question her in earnest, demanding answers she dare not give him. For a brief, wrenching second she wished she could lay the whole burden of her secret life on him, so they could work through it together, the way she and Mark had worked through their problems.

But that could never be. And she shouldn't succumb to such weak moments even in her fantasies.

"I really should be going inside. Even with the monitor on, I don't like to leave Caitlin alone in the house."

"Why is my sister afraid of the park?" Hugh asked. He moved to block her path to the house so quickly she gasped. His broad shoulders blocked out the moonlight and left her standing in darkness, alone and scared.

"I—I don't know what you're talking about."

"I think you do. Something about that little way-side park at the bottom of the hill upsets her. Why should that be? There's nothing out of the ordinary there. I've seen the place. Just a shelter, a pond, some swings for the kids."

"Yes. That's all it is. I walk Addy there often. There's a path from the backside of the meadow through the woods." Another incriminating bit of knowledge he might not have discovered for himself. His eyes gleamed in the moonlight, like the hunting cat she'd compared him to earlier, and she suppressed a shiver.

He let the silence drag on a few moments longer.

"I think you know why I'm asking, don't you, Faith?"

"On the contrary, I don't have any idea at all."

"Beth told you about her accident this morning."

"Yes. A little." She would stick to the truth as much as possible. She curled her hands around the top rail until the splintery wood bit painfully into her palms.

"Did she tell you about the child?"

"No." She had answered too quickly. She dared not let herself break eye contact, hopeful that the moonlight hid her expression at least as well as it did his. "She...she didn't mention a child. Not a word. What...what happened to it?" How much curiosity was normal? How much was too much, not enough?

He was silent, long enough for her to take two deep breaths to try to slow her racing heart. "She didn't have to tell you about what happened to the child, did she? You already know."

The accusation that had lain unspoken between them was finally in the open. She surged away from the fence, but he moved too quickly for her. He braced one long muscled arm on either side of her, keeping her captive where she stood.

"You know why being at the park upset her. She's been there before, hasn't she?"

"I don't have the slightest idea what you're talking about. Let me go." She didn't attempt to hide the panic in her voice. His actions, what he was saying were surely enough to panic any woman, not just one with secrets she didn't want him to learn.

"Is Caitlin truly your daughter, Faith?" There was no threat in his voice, only the implacable will to discover what she wanted no living soul to know.

His wording gave her an opening. "Yes, she's my daughter. Do you want to see her birth certificate?" She let her fear turn into rage. She would not be intimidated by him. "Although, I don't know why in hell I should show it to you. Now let me pass."

"No, I can't let you go. Not yet. Not until I've had my say."

"I can't help you." Dear Lord, that was the truth, and the conviction in her tone shook him momentarily, but only momentarily.

"I think you can. I'm not trying to frighten you, Faith."

"You *are* frightening me. You're not making any sense. And I don't like being threatened like this." That also was the truth. Did he mean to claim Caitlin here and now? Did he want to make her confess to Beth what had happened and hand over her child? But Beth wasn't blameless. She had abandoned the infant. The authorities wouldn't automatically take her from Faith and give her to his sister. Didn't he realize that Caitlin would be the biggest loser if he pressed the issue?

Hugh took a step back, but didn't let her go. "I've spent the last two and a half years trying to find my sister's child," he said. His voice was hard and intense. "A child she doesn't remember giving birth to."

"Amnesia." The word sifted past her stiff lips. It

was the only explanation. True amnesia was rare, but it did occur.

He nodded once. "She was badly injured in the accident. She lost a huge amount of blood. There was some brain damage. The doctors say she may never remember any more than she does now. But she has nightmares of blood on the snow and a baby crying."

"I'm sorry she has nightmares." Again, she could speak the truth.

He continued to watch her closely. "There are butterflies in her dreams."

Faith closed her eyes. She could not hold his searching gaze one second longer.

"So that's why you came here. Because of the butterflies?" She recalled as clearly as if the moment had just happened, Beth's pain-filled gaze fixed unblinkingly on her butterfly-covered sweatshirt. The image had somehow been retained by her damaged brain and translated into a recurring nightmare. Such a small detail to be of such importance to them all.

"Yes. That's the one clue that's been missing for all the other searchers. And there are other searchers out there, Faith. Did you know that?"

"Why should I?" Her throat closed and she swallowed hard. Did he realize that fact terrified her more than anything else he could have said? She had thought her days of looking over her shoulder, of being suspicious of every car that came up the lane, were over.

"The Indiana police searched for the baby for weeks, but found nothing. They checked birth records in Ohio and Kentucky, too. All babies born within seventy-two hours of the time the doctors estimated Beth's baby was born. That was the criteria they used.''

''No one ever questioned me. No one.''

''Probably because they didn't look at records this far east. And maybe because you didn't register Caitlin's birth until almost a week later. I checked.''

''I wasn't able to get to the courthouse before that time.'' Short sentences. Just bare facts. ''I was alone. All alone.'' She didn't have to fake the tremor in her voice, it was all too real. Then she betrayed herself. ''You said you weren't the only one looking for...for Beth's baby.''

''Her boyfriend's parents are looking, too. They have been all along. They have money. They hired private detectives, but by then the trail had grown cold. But they were concentrating on a much smaller area near the accident site. Jamie and Beth paid cash for everything they bought from the time they left Boston, so there was no paper trail. They were traveling east when the accident happened. Jamie's parents think it was because they'd given up on getting to me through my old firm in Texas, and were coming back to Boston. I think it was because they were coming back for their baby. Coming back to you. It was the butterflies that gave you away even though you didn't start operating the farm until the next year. What happened, Faith? Did you stumble across them in the park? Was Beth in labor? Did you deliver the baby?''

Too close. He was too close to the truth. Faith pushed at his arm but she might as well have been trying to push over one of the fence posts. "I don't have to stand here and listen to any more of your wild accusations."

"They're not wild accusations, Faith. They're facts. You have a child born on the same day as my sister's. You were alone when you gave birth. No witnesses. You raise butterflies."

"But you just said it yourself, I didn't start raising butterflies until after Caitlin was born."

"But you were interested in them. So was your husband. He died trying to get to the place in Mexico where monarchs winter over close to a year before you broke ground for the butterfly house."

"Who told you that?"

"It's common knowledge in town."

He was right. She had no reason to lie about Mark's death, or that she had been only slightly injured in the crash. The only lie she told about that day, was one of omission. That their baby had not died, too.

"Beth has nightmares of butterflies and snow and a baby crying. Why does she dream of them, Faith? Because you talked with her about butterflies as you delivered her baby?"

"I don't know why she dreams of butterflies," she said desperately. "I can guess why she dreams of a baby crying. I would have that dream, too, if I had lost my child." He didn't move. "Let me go. I need to be with Caitlin." This time she pushed against the wall of his chest with as much force as she could muster. The air rushed out of his lungs with a whoosh and he took an involuntary step backward. She surged past him, but he reached out and stopped her with a hand on her arm.

"Beth needs to learn her child's fate," Hugh said quietly. His grip on her wrist was loose. She could pull away from him easily. It was the force of his will, his conviction, that held her there. "I have to know the truth for her sake."

"I can't tell you anything. Nothing."

"Faith, you don't need to be frightened of me," he said quietly.

She pulled her hand loose and whirled on him. She laughed, a sound harsh with nerves and incipient panic. "Not be frightened of you? Of course I'm frightened of you. You came here under false pretenses. You have me investigated behind my back. You question my friends about me. You accuse me of—" She stopped herself before she said the betraying words aloud. "You believe my daughter is another woman's child. I'm crazy for not sending you packing yet tonight."

"You can't send me packing. If you do, it's the same as admitting I'm telling the truth."

"It is not! It's the only sane thing to do."

He covered the distance between them in an instant. Faith knew she had made a mistake by not running as fast and as hard as she could into the house and locking the door when she had the chance.

He gripped her arms with both hands and his touch was not gentle. His face was only inches from hers.

"I'm not here to threaten you, or to take your child away. I'm here to try to salvage my sister's happiness. Don't send us away, Faith. Beth needs to be here. I can see the difference in her in only two days. Regardless of what you think of me, don't turn her away. Please."

"What can I do for her?" He was so close she was seared by the heat of his body radiating toward her. She could see the glint of gold flecks in his eyes, feel the tension in the muscles of his arms. He could kiss her, or strangle her, before she could cry out for help. But she had lied when she said he frightened her. She wasn't afraid of what he could do to her physically. She held herself as stiffly as he did. God help her, it was the only way she could keep herself from closing the small distance between them.

"You can be her friend."

"She isn't going to remember anything about this place, or me." The words were a prayer as much as anything else.

"I'll accept that if I have to." His mouth hardened into a straight line.

What choice did she have? She couldn't go to the sheriff and accuse Hugh of anything.

He had said there were others searching for Caitlin, too. She dared not take the risk of stirring the calm surface of her life in Bartonsville for fear that all the secrets that were buried beneath would rise to the surface. She had to agree to what he asked, at least for now.

"You can stay. Now let me go."

He dropped his hands and stepped back. "Thank you, Faith." He didn't say anything more, didn't give her false assurances that she would not regret her decision. She already regretted it. She didn't for a moment think that Hugh Damon would give up his quest. She must be on her guard every moment of the day and night.

And she could never, never be this close to him again.

CHAPTER EIGHT

"WHAT ARE YOU planning for the rest of the day?" Beth asked, her good leg drawn up against her body as she painted her toenails on the hard, stiff-cushioned sofa in the main room of the cabin. It had been one of her goals in therapy to regain the dexterity to paint her toenails whatever damn color she pleased.

"Work," Hugh admitted.

Beth had been busy over the past week. Small vases of blue cornflowers, yellow mustard weed and Queen Anne's lace graced the table and windowsills. Kevin had taken her antiquing three days in a row and she'd brought home vintage crocheted throws, "afghans" she'd called them, to drape over the back of the sofa and arm chair. She'd even gotten Faith's permission to hang a picture or two. Paint-by-numbers renditions of country mills and barns that Beth assured him were the next rage in collectibles. Slowly but surely she was turning their temporary quarters into a home.

"You've been on site every day since I got here. It's Sunday. You need a day off."

"Things are finally getting on track. I need to stay ahead of the game."

Beth looked up, the nail polish brush poised above her shocking-pink toenail. "Kevin and I have something special planned for today."

"I figured as much. What is it? Antiquing? Driving into Cincy?"

She jumped in with her defense. "I need the practice. Most sixteen-year-olds have more driving time under their belts than I do."

"Especially nighttime driving hours." Hugh grinned back at her from the table where he was perusing schematics on his laptop.

She rose from the couch and padded across to him. She put her arms around his neck and rested her chin on the top of his head. Hugh went very still. She was rarely demonstrative. "We haven't been out that late. Only a little after midnight a couple of times. Poor old Hugh. You've been lonely."

He grunted in a noncommittal tone and shut down the laptop.

"I have been spending a lot of time with Kevin, haven't I?"

"Ten evenings in a row, but who's counting?"

"I never thought the time here would go so quickly."

Neither had he, but not for the same reasons as his sister. He had finally accepted what the doctors had said all along. Beth's memory would not return. She still had no recollection whatsoever of Faith Carson.

And Caitlin was just a cute little kid as far as she was concerned.

Hugh would have begun to doubt his own certainty of Caitlin's parentage, except for two things. Beth would not set foot in the butterfly house or go back to the little park. He'd even, God forgive him, driven her there himself, on the pretext of checking out the bike trail. She'd stayed in the Blazer, her face pale, her lower lip caught between her teeth in the nervous gesture she'd had since she was a child. He could feel her watching him as he explored the stone-and-wood shelter. Back inside the truck her uneasiness was palpable. That evening she'd turned down Kevin's suggestion of a swim in Faith's pond and went to her room, lying on the bed in the darkness, listening to her portable CD player.

Hugh felt like a jerk for days afterward and swore that he wouldn't try to force her memory anymore.

"Well, you're not going to work today," she said decisively. "We're having a cookout with hot dogs and hamburgers and potato salad and baked beans and s'mores. The whole nine yards."

He pushed the laptop to the middle of the table. "Where's this all-American cookout going to happen?"

"At Faith's. Kevin and I were discussing the idea this morning when I was helping out in the greenhouse. The plans were getting complicated, trying to decide whether to go to Wal-Mart and buy one of those little bitty charcoal grills, or borrow your Blazer to haul Kevin's dad's gas grill out here, and then haul it back to town. And, well, to make a long story short Faith said we could use her grill. And then I finally remembered my manners and insisted that she and Caitlin join us. You don't mind, do you?'' She swept right on past any objection he might have made. ''But Kevin started grousing about it being as much work to haul her grill up here to the cottage as it was his dad's. And—''

''And?''

She spread her arms. ''Kevin looked so put upon that now it's going to be a family affair out by the pond. Steve and Peg and the boys are coming, too.'' Beth leaned around him so that she could see more than his profile. ''You don't sound very enthusiastic about the cookout. Don't you want to spend some time with Kevin? I thought you liked him.'' She looked worried, and he could see her beginning to form all kinds of wild conjectures, like giving up the boy she was infatuated with to please her ogre of a big brother.

''I like Kevin.'' It was Faith he was reluctant to spend time with. He had promised her that he would stay out of her way and he'd done his best to keep his word. But living here meant he did run into her. And the more he and Beth did things with Faith and Caitlin the more he began to dream of what it would be like to be part of a family again. To have a woman…to have Faith to love and cherish and bear his children. He'd even caught himself fantasizing that there might be a way out of this tangled and dangerous mess he'd created. One that would bring a happy ending for all of them.

"Then it's settled. I know you like Faith so that's not a problem. But—" Beth laughed self-consciously "—I was afraid you thought I shouldn't be seeing Kevin."

He uncrossed her arms from around his neck and turned in his chair. "Why the hell would you think that?"

"I—I don't know. I guess because of all that's happened. My—my problems."

"Nothing that's happened to you should keep you from spending time with a great guy like Kevin." He lifted her chin so that she had to look him straight in the eye. "Do you hear me, Beth? Nothing."

"Do you think he's really that great?" she asked wistfully. "Do you think he won't look at me like I'm some kind of monster when I say, 'Oh, by the way. I not only got my boyfriend killed in a car accident. I had a baby that same day and I misplaced her? I haven't the slightest idea where she is or what happened to her?'" Tears glistened in her blue eyes and she blinked furiously to hold them back.

"No more of that talk, Beth," he said forcefully. "Listen to me. I don't think he'll look at you like you're a monster, because I think he's a bright, intelligent guy who cares for the woman you are now, not the scared, confused kid you were three years ago." He hoped to hell he was reading Sager's character right. If he wasn't and he hurt Beth, he would have to answer to Hugh, and the outcome wouldn't be pretty.

She sniffed and gave him a tentative smile. "Okay, big brother. I'll do it your way. I'll wait for just the right moment and then dump my sordid past in his lap. If he's got the right stuff I'll know it then, won't I?"

"Don't let him push you past the point you want to go, Beth." He'd begun to worry about the physical aspects of the relationship in the past few days.

She didn't pretend to misunderstand. "Don't worry about that. He's been a perfect gentleman. He hasn't even tried to get my bra off, even when we were parking in the moonlight." She sounded a little miffed.

"Good for him."

She gripped his hands with her much smaller ones. "Hugh, don't worry. I'm not going to make the same mistake I made with Jamie. I won't let him make love to me until everything's right between us—no matter how much I might want him to before then."

He knew Beth wouldn't make love just for the physical release. She was too emotionally scarred to be promiscuous. If she made love with Kevin Sager it would be because she had given him her heart. "Are you that serious about him?"

"I could be," she said softly, and smiled.

THERE WAS A DULL throbbing ache behind Faith's eyes but it wasn't caused by the fact that she'd forgotten her sunglasses, at least not entirely. The sun was well down on the horizon, almost ready to disappear. It was warm and muggy, and now and then a mosquito sang past her ear. Spring had turned into full summer, even though the official start to the season was still a couple of weeks away. The source of her discomfort was the usual one these days, the continued presence of Beth and Hugh.

Every hour that went by increased her guilt and remorse. Beth spent time each morning in the greenhouse, taking over bit by bit the chores Faith had saved for Steve's niece, Dana, who was busy with the American Legion traveling softball league on which she was the star first baseman.

Beth had waved off her objections that guests weren't supposed to act as unpaid laborers, and kept right on showing up to dust figurines in the gift shop, deadhead the butterfly bushes and the coneflowers and pinch back the pots of kitchen herbs.

And while they worked they talked, about all manner of things, from fashion to hair color, to books and music, to politics and world events. Beth was eager to learn, to catch up on the parts of her life she'd lost out on during her recovery and rehabilitation. But she also fell silent for long periods of time, and Faith stayed silent too because she still didn't know when a simple word or phrase, or glimmer of an idea might spark Beth's memory of the day Caitlin was born. Yet despite these sometimes awkward moments, Faith was certain Beth considered her a friend and that was another burden she had to bear because there was no way that Faith could feel the same.

And then there was Hugh. Always watchful, always in her thoughts, always a threat. But also a man of quiet strength and dignity, who appealed to her on so many levels, not all of them having to do with the workings of her mind.

She watched him now involved in the volleyball game with Steve and Kevin and Dana, who was spending the night with Peg and Steve. Beth was acting as linesman and referee and her laughter carried out over the still water of the pond and echoed along the tree line. Jack, Guy and Caitlin, Addy at their heels, were darting in and out between the player's legs. Every once in a while Hugh or Kevin or Steve went sprawling in the grass avoiding a little one. The game was spirited, but good-natured and not for the first time Faith found herself watching Hugh as he moved with the kind of effortless grace of a man completely at home in his body.

Perhaps she had let her gaze linger on him too long, because now Hugh glanced her way as he set up for an overhand serve. Their eyes caught and held for a fraction of a second before Faith looked away, as a now familiar shiver of awareness danced up and down her spine.

She poured herself a glass of iced tea from the thermos sitting on the tailgate of Steve's truck, and walked out onto the wooden decking that served as dock and diving platform. She sat down on one of the built-in benches and turned her back to the sunset, looking instead out over the rolling farmland.

She waited as Peg left her lawn chair on the sidelines of the game and came toward her. Faith scooted over so that there was room for her sister to sit beside her. "Can I beg a swallow of your tea?" she asked. "I left my glass by my chair and I'm too lazy to go back and get it."

Faith handed over her glass. "Are you sure you're okay? You barely touched your food." It wasn't the first meal Faith had noticed her sister not eating in the past week or so.

"Hey, that's my line, remember?" Peg countered. "You still look as if you're not getting enough sleep."

"We're not talking about me. I'm fine," Faith insisted.

"So am I. Or I will be in eight months or so." The sun had set but there was still plenty of light in the sky, so she easily saw Peg's lips curve into a smile.

"You're pregnant!"

Her sister's smile grew wider and she nodded. "Yes. But just barely. Only a few weeks. We haven't told the boys. It's a long time for them to wait for a new baby."

"Oh, Peg, I'm so happy for you." And so thankful that she'd resisted each and every temptation to break her promise to herself and tell Peg about Beth. Peg's boys had been strong, healthy babies, but her pregnancies had been difficult. There was no way that

Faith would add stress to this one if she could avoid it. She leaned over to wrap her sister in a hug just as the volleyball sailed over their heads and landed with a splash in the pond.

"Heads up, ladies." Running feet came pounding onto the deck. Faith and Peg broke apart with a gasp as Kevin made a shallow, running dive to retrieve the ball that sent a shower of cool spray over both of them.

"Man overboard!" Guy hollered, executing a perfect cannonball that sent water cascading onto the deck, soaking his mother and aunt. His brother was only two seconds behind, and his splash was even bigger. The boys were wearing swim trunks and inflatable arm rings and had been in and out of the pond a half dozen times during the course of the afternoon.

"You monsters," Peg sputtered. "And to think I was just congratulating myself on replicating the little beasts."

Steve ambled onto the deck and Faith reached out to squeeze his big work-roughened hand between her own. "Congratulations. Peg just told me the news."

"Thanks," he said, resting his other hand on Peg's shoulder. "You're the first to know. We haven't even told Mom and Dad yet."

"I promise not to tell a soul. What do you want?" she asked, low-voiced. "Boy or girl?"

"A girl," Steve said without a moment's hesitation. "Just like Caitlin." Faith's throat tightened at his simple declaration.

"But we'll take another boy." Peg gave her husband a peck on the cheek. "I probably won't have a choice. The Badens tend to breed a lot of boys."

Beth and Dana followed Steve onto the deck, with Hugh a couple of steps behind. The girls held Caitlin's hands as she hopped along between them. Faith was no longer nervous when Beth spent time with Caitlin. The little girl liked Beth, and Beth seemed to enjoy being with her daughter, but Faith detected no deeper attachment growing between them, and in the most private places in her heart she rejoiced at the knowledge. Caitlin clambered up onto the bench beside Faith and sat on her lap.

"I could use some help out here." Kevin came up sputtering, as the boys ganged up to try to shove him under.

Steve lifted his leg. "Sorry. Bad knee. Old basketball injury."

"I never swim before the middle of August. The water's too cold," Peg demurred with a shiver.

"And I have Caitlin to look after." Faith was glad the light was beginning to go. She was wearing a sundress with thin little straps and no bra. The bodice was lined, but she could feel her nipples contract as the wet fabric was cooled by the evening breeze.

"Hugh?"

"You're on your own, buddy." Hugh laughed and Faith warmed to the sound. What would it be like to be able to relax in his presence and enjoy his company with no reservations? She would never know and that realization hurt.

"Beth, you aren't going to let them drown me, are you?" Kevin was treading water, effortlessly, fending off the boys with one hand. He looked to be in no danger at all from his small attackers and Beth said so. She was wearing shorts and a football jersey with the Bartonsville Patriot mascot on the front and Sager emblazoned across the back above the number. The jersey was faded and frayed at the hem and sleeves. It was obvious it had been a gift from Kevin.

Jack and Guy hooted and hollered and dared Beth to come in so they could dunk her, too.

"You're bad boys," Caitlin said, and promptly snuggled closer to Faith.

Kevin swam over to the deck, shrieking little boys still clinging to his back, reached up and closed his hand around Beth's ankle. He tugged lightly, being careful not to pull her completely off balance. "Help me, Beth. The two of us can take these guys."

Beth had her hands braced on the deck railing. She was shaking her head, but was laughing at the same time. "I don't have a suit on."

"Neither do I," Kevin said. He'd jumped in wearing cutoffs and a T-shirt. "C'mon. You won't melt." He tugged once more and Beth threw up her hands. "Oh, why not."

She jumped lightly off the deck and disappeared in the dark water, surfacing with a squeal. "It's freezing," she shrieked.

"I told you it would be cold," Peg said. "No one listens to me."

"Get Beth," Jack yelled and both little boys attempted to swim away from Kevin in favor of their new victim.

"Oh, no, you don't." Kevin grabbed first one boy then the other and tossed them toward the shallow end of the pond. "Go let the bluegills nibble on your toes for a while."

"No!" Both were shrieking with laughter.

"They're not bluegills. They're piranhas," Jack said, menacingly.

"Your toes won't last too long," Kevin said with a diabolical laugh. "No one can save you now."

"Aghhh, they've got me," Guy screamed, arms and legs flailing as he splashed around in mock terror.

Kevin put his arms around Beth's waist and began towing her out into deeper water. "Now that I've provided a diversion for the man-eating bluegills we can have our moonlight swim without getting nibbled on ourselves."

"You think you're very clever, don't you," Beth said, but let him pull her toward the shadow of the willow tree that overhung the far bank.

"Jack. Guy," Steve called, leaning out over the deck railing. "It's almost dark. Time to get out of the water."

The boys began loud protests that ceased immediately when Dana announced that if they wanted to stay in the pond, she'd eat all the S'mores herself. She swung Caitlin onto her hip and marched off, initiating a mad dash for sneakers and towels.

"C'mon, Steve. You're the best marshmallow

toaster in the county.'' Peg and Steve went off arm in arm, leaving Faith and Hugh alone on the dock.

Faith looked up at the stars, remembering the last time they'd been alone like this. Hugh put his foot on the bench and leaned his forearm on his knee. ''The moon is brighter than it was the last time we were alone together.''

''It will be full in a few more days.''

He fell silent, watching Beth and Kevin as they floated beneath the willow's overhanging boughs. ''He's good for her,'' he said at last. ''He's brought her out of herself when I couldn't. Do you know this is the first time I've seen her wear shorts in public since her accident?''

''They do seem to be a good match.''

''Beth is almost ready to confide in him.'' Hugh's words stole the warmth from her blood.

''About…about the accident.'' She couldn't say *about the baby*.

''About everything.''

She had been dreading the day that Beth's feelings for Kevin overcame her fear of rejection. One more person who might put two and two together and come up with four. A man who hadn't suffered traumatic brain damage and who might think it was more than a coincidence that Caitlin and Beth's lost baby had the same birthday.

''Faith, I want her to be happy. I want the empty places in her mind and her heart to be filled. I want her to have what she has right now.''

Kevin had wrapped his hand around the trailing

willow branches to hold them in place, his other arm was around Beth's waist. They must think they were lost in the shadows of the big tree but a last glimmer of twilight outlined them and the kiss they were sharing.

Faith clasped her hands in front of her. She wanted those things, too, including a man who would make love to her under the trailing branches of a weeping willow tree.

"I want Beth to know the truth." Hugh's voice was pitched low so it wouldn't carry over the water to Beth and Kevin. "You have the key to that truth, Faith."

Faith rose and put her hand on his arm so that he turned to face her. "You're asking me to confess to a crime, a very serious crime," she said. "Do you realize that?" Another of her fears. One she'd thought banished to the darkest corner of her subconscious. She should hate him for being the catalyst to revive all her nightmares, but she could not. She had chosen this road, knowing it was one way only with no exits to happy-ever-after.

A frown furrowed his forehead. "What you tell me would never go further than the three of us. I mean you no harm, Faith."

She laughed in disbelief. "You're threatening everything I hold dear in this world. My very life, if anything should happen to Caitlin. And if you're right and Caitlin is not my daughter but Beth's, your sister might not be held blameless, you know. If your theory is right, she abandoned her baby in the middle of a terrible storm. More than likely the authorities would take Caitlin away from all of us. Is that what you want?''

He dropped his head to stare down at the dark water below the deck. The breeze had begun to ripple the surface of the pond. It stirred the thick layers of his hair and brushed against her cheek. ''Of course not. I want to—''

''You want to mend what can't be mended.'' She attempted to tug her hand free of his without success. She gave up the struggle. She wanted his touch, even though, at the same time, she longed to be somewhere safe and alone.

''You can trust me, Faith,'' Hugh said quietly so that the words wouldn't carry out over the water. Kevin and Beth had broken their embrace and were swimming lazily toward the deck.

''No,'' she said unable to filter out the regret she felt at the words. She did want to trust him. She had been fighting against that weakness for days and days. She looked down at their joined hands, willing him to set her free. He did, moving a step away.

She shivered. She couldn't confide her secret to any man, certainly not this one. Pain, greater than she should have felt, shot through her when she admitted the truth. She had never thought to love again, but if she did, Hugh Damon would be the kind of man to whom she could give her heart. If he had been anyone other than who he was. ''You're wrong. You're the last person on earth I can trust.''

Headlights sliced across the surface of the pond as a car turned into the lane.

"I wonder who that is?" Beth asked, climbing onto the dock. She was shivering and her teeth were chattering. Kevin came up behind her and grabbed a towel from the bench, wrapping it around her shoulders.

"It's probably the couple who've rented the cabin on your left," Faith said. She was still trembling from her conversation with Hugh, but she managed to keep the tremors from reaching her lips. "Excuse me, I need to go greet them."

She began walking toward the luxury sedan as it pulled to a halt before the greenhouse. The security light gave Faith a good view of the couple. He was of medium height, thin, with a full head of silver-gray hair, dressed in a casual open-necked shirt and khakis. The woman beside him was also thin, and almost as tall as her husband. She was wearing a sleeveless T-shirt and cream-colored pants with a matching jacket thrown over her shoulders. Her hair was shoulder length, and curved smoothly against her cheek. The color was hard to gauge in the security light's glare, but it seemed to be golden brown.

"Who is that?" Beth asked. Faith was already several yards along the path. She turned back, surprised to see Beth's face was chalk white.

"Their name is Templeton. They've booked a cabin for the rest of the week."

Beth's eyes were wide and fearful. She shook her

head. "No," she said. "Tell them they can't stay. Tell them to go away."

"I—I can't do that." She lifted her hand in a gesture of supplication. Beth's panic was infectious. Faith felt her heart rate speed up. "Hugh?"

He had his arms around Beth's shoulders and his face was expressionless, hard and cold. "Their name isn't Templeton. It's Sheldon. Harold and Lorraine Sheldon. They're Jamie's parents. And it looks as if they've finally tracked us down."

CHAPTER NINE

BETH PUT THE CAP on the toothpaste and set it back on the shelf of the white enamel medicine cabinet. She shut the door and stared at herself for a moment in the slightly wavy mirror. She didn't look too bad for six o'clock in the morning. She was getting used to being an early riser.

Especially these past few days, when it seemed the only time that she wouldn't encounter Jamie's mother or father. Beth hadn't believed for one moment that they'd only tracked her and Hugh down because they were worried about her, afraid that Lorraine's insistence on her seeing a hypnotherapist had caused her to run.

Avoiding the hypnotherapist had been why she'd left Houston, of course, but she wouldn't give Lorraine Sheldon satisfaction by admitting the fact. She may have run away from Texas, but she was glad Hugh's work had brought them to Painted Lady Farm. She liked Faith and Caitlin. And Kevin.

She might even be halfway to falling in love with Kevin.

She certainly hadn't planned to feel this way about him. But she didn't regret it.

Even more importantly, she was starting to know and like herself again. She hadn't had the butterfly dream since she'd arrived. Not once. She still didn't want to be around the insects, but they no longer frightened her.

And she was learning to be at peace with the things she couldn't change. She no longer tortured herself with endless hours of trying to remember something, anything, about her baby's birth and disappearance. That didn't mean she didn't want to know. She did, sometimes so much her heart ached with the wanting. But she had begun to accept that she might never be granted that knowledge. That she would have to go on with her life.

And she would start by telling Kevin what had happened to her three years ago. She wanted him to know, and not just because she had caught him talking to Harold and Lorraine more than once, and she was afraid they might give away her secret first. The desire to tell him everything had been growing steadily, almost from the first day they'd met.

She closed her eyes because for a moment the face reflected in the mirror had been her face a month before. Scared and uncertain.

No more. She was in control now.

She hurriedly rinsed her mouth and ran a comb through her hair. She needed to vacate the bathroom for her brother.

Something was bothering Hugh. Every night she heard him tossing and turning. Sometimes she would awake and see the glow of his laptop screen coming from the main room.

She was coming to the conclusion Faith Carson had a lot to do with her brother's condition. Sadly, he didn't seem to be making much headway with her. Beth didn't know what she could do about that, either, but she'd keep working at it. Heaven knew, she'd sung his praises to Faith until she was breathless. Unfortunately, Faith seemed as reluctant as Hugh to take their relationship any further.

It wasn't because the attraction wasn't there. They just weren't acting on it.

Maybe they needed a push in the right direction. Would Hugh ask Faith out if she offered to baby-sit for Caitlin—

Baby-sit for Caitlin. The thought brought Beth out of her matchmaking reverie. Was she ready to take on the responsibility for a child even for a few hours? For almost three years she'd barely been able to take care of herself.

She closed her eyes and looked inward, searching for that kernel of confusion and fear that always lurked inside her. She took a deep breath and exhaled slowly. If it was still there it was buried deeply. She felt good about herself. She felt good about the future—

She glanced at the clock. Not quite six-thirty. Hugh should have been up pounding on the bathroom door by now. She padded across the linoleum and knocked lightly on his door. ''Rise and shine, brother dear,'' she sang out.

His only reply was a muffled groan. "Go away."

"Hugh. It's six-thirty."

"Damn, my alarm didn't go off."

A few moments later he appeared in front of her in a T-shirt and cutoffs.

He ran his hand over the stubble of beard on his face and wiped the shadows away. "I'll shave and jump in the shower and we can head into town for breakfast."

"Faith's expecting me at the greenhouse. Why don't you come down there? I'll treat you to a blueberry muffin."

The furrow between his dark brows returned, as it always seemed to do when she mentioned Faith. "You're not punching a time clock, are you? Let's give the blueberry muffin a pass. I've got a hankerin' for sausage biscuits and gravy."

The Sheldons usually didn't get up very early, but she didn't want to meet them at the greenhouse if they did. She'd do whatever it took to avoid them until she told Kevin the truth. Maybe that was cowardly, but she didn't care. She had too much at stake to take any chances with Jamie's parents. "Okay," she said. "I guess Faith can hold down the fort without me for an hour or so. The Golden Sheaf for breakfast it is. But no sausage gravy and biscuits. That's just a heart attack on a plate. Oatmeal and fruit, okay?" She brightened a little inside. "Maybe we'll even run into Kevin if we get a move on."

"Mrs. Sheldon. Good morning." Faith was fixing the feeding trays in the greenhouse. She'd wakened at sunrise and had been unable to go back to sleep. Caitlin had heard her in the shower and was wide-awake and bouncing on her bed when Faith came out of the bathroom. Now she was sitting at her little table behind the counter with a bowl of Froot Loops, out of Lorraine Sheldon's view. She was surprised to see Jamie's mother up and around. It was by far the earliest either of the Sheldons had risen since they arrived.

"Good morning, Faith. I decided to come and see the butterflies before it gets any hotter. Is that convenient?"

"I'll be changing the feeding trays in a few minutes. I'll be happy to have you join me," she said as politely as she could manage.

"Thank you." Lorraine rubbed her hand up and down her arm, looking around at the figurines and potted plants that still remained for sale. Summer travel was in full swing and Faith had been kept busy with visitors to the butterfly house, so her contact with the Sheldons had been blessedly brief.

"Would you care for a cup of coffee? Or tea?" Faith took a step to her left, obscuring Caitlin from the other woman's view.

"Tea would be nice." Lorraine was wearing linen slacks and a silky sleeveless shell in shades of pistachio and cream. A finely woven straw hat protected her makeup from the strong morning sun. Her jewelry was gold and heavy, her manicure flawless. She looked as if she were ready for a day's shopping on

Fifth Avenue or Rodeo Drive. Faith wondered how she'd made it down the lane in her Italian leather sandals without twisting an ankle.

Faith wasn't certain where to place Lorraine's age. She supposed she must be in her midforties or older. After all, she would have had a son in his early twenties if Jamie had lived. One thing was certain. She was years younger than her husband. Harold Sheldon was pushing sixty. Had she been a trophy wife? Indulged by an older, wealthy husband, her only child the center of her existence? That would go a long way in explaining why she had tracked Beth and Hugh down at Painted Lady Farm.

"I'm afraid all I have are tea bags. But I do have English Breakfast."

"Oh." Lorraine made a little moue of disappointment. "In that case I'll just have juice."

"Orange or cranberry?"

"Cranberry." Faith stooped to get the bottle from the small refrigerator. "Thank you," Lorraine said when Faith handed her a glass. "I thought perhaps Beth would be here this morning."

"She does usually show up about this time."

Lorraine took a delicate sip, then fixed Faith with a practiced smile. "I've had so little time to talk to her. She's miffed with me, I'm afraid." She made a little face. "I hope you aren't, as well."

"I don't understand."

"I mean, because I booked our reservations under my maiden name—"

"It wasn't necessary to employ a ruse," Faith said

coolly. She would never have rented a cabin to the couple if she'd had any inkling they were Jamie's parents, of course, but she kept that damning detail to herself.

"I should have explained the whole situation to you the moment we arrived...." Lorraine's voice trailed off and she shrugged her thin shoulders. "It's all so very complicated."

"I know some of Beth's story," Faith said carefully. She felt as if she had walked to the edge of a crumbling cliff and was looking down into an abyss.

"She seems to be doing very well here."

"Painted Lady Farm is a wonderful place to heal, as I found when I moved here after my husband was killed."

"I'm sorry for your loss," Lorraine said. "I know how hard it is to deal with losing a loved one." There was genuine sorrow in her voice, and Faith thought back to the tall, good-looking boy she had met. Would he have grown up quickly enough to become a strong and loving man and face his responsibilities if he'd lived? Faith hoped that would have proved to be the case.

"Beth is making a future for herself. I think she'll do fine."

"I pray you're right. My husband and I are very fond of Beth. We were very, very worried about her when she disappeared from Houston that way without a word. I couldn't be at ease until we had tracked her down and seen for ourselves that she was all right."

"Why wouldn't she be?" Faith couldn't stop herself from asking, although she knew she should change the subject. "She's with Hugh and he seems to be very solicitous of her."

"I didn't mean to imply otherwise. But he's a man, and they have different priorities. I just don't think he realizes how—" She stopped talking and took another sip of her juice. "Beth seems to have made a friend since she's been here. Kevin Sager. My husband and I have met him at the cabins. He seems like a nice young man."

"He is. He grew up here and he teaches junior high science. I like him very much."

"I'm glad. I wouldn't want Beth to be taken advantage of."

As Jamie had taken advantage of her? Faith caught herself before speaking the words aloud. No wonder Beth was a nervous wreck when Lorraine was around. The woman was relentless in probing every aspect of her life. "If you're finished with your juice I'll take you into the habitat," she said to forestall any more questions.

"I'm ready." Lorraine placed her glass on the counter, peering over at Caitlin. She was still in her pajamas, her flyaway hair in pigtails. Addy stood protectively at her side, keeping watch for wolves and rustlers and the occasional dropped Froot Loops. "Your little girl is adorable.

"Thank you."

"I haven't seen her much since we came."

"She's been spending several hours a day with my

brother-in-law's niece and two of her friends. They have started a temporary play school for two- and three-year-olds for their 4-H projects.'' Faith felt her throat tightening. She didn't want Lorraine showing interest in Caitlin.

''I'm two,'' Caitlin said holding up two sticky fingers as she shoveled cereal into her mouth with the other hand. ''This is my dog. Her name's Addy.'' She gave Faith a sly look. ''Watch out. She sniffs your bottom.''

''I…I'll remember that.'' Lorraine didn't smile at Caitlin's favorite joke. Instead, a small frown appeared between her carefully arched brows. ''She's left-handed.''

''Yes. She's very definitely left-handed.'' Caitlin had had a decided preference for her left hand since she was very little.

Lorraine kept on staring at Caitlin. Then she moved around the counter and asked the question Faith had been dreading. ''You're two, are you? Do you know when your birthday is?''

The toddler shook her head. ''When it gets cold again.'' Caitlin changed the subject with lightning swiftness. ''I'm going swimming today.''

''You are? That's nice.''

''Would you care to see the butterflies now, Mrs. Sheldon?'' Faith interrupted. She didn't want the older woman to put the clues together. She picked up a plate of fruit and stepped toward the entry to the habitat. ''The less time the door is open the better,'' Faith prompted.

"What? Oh, yes. The butterflies."

"I come, too." Caitlin pushed back her chair.

"Why don't you stay here and finish your cereal, Kitty Cat?" She didn't usually leave Caitlin alone in the greenhouse—once or twice Faith had caught her leaving the building on her own to play on her swing set or look for a strayed Barbie—but it would only be for a minute or two. She would change the feeding plates and then leave Lorraine alone to wander among the butterflies.

"I come." Caitlin could be stubborn when she set her mind to it.

"All right, but you must be a good girl and leave the butterflies alone."

"I be good. Addy, stay here," Caitlin commanded. The sheltie whimpered and looked up at Faith.

"Stay, Addy." Addy dropped to her belly with the guilt-inducing look in her brown eyes that all shelties had perfected.

As consolation, Caitlin dribbled a spoonful of soggy cereal on the ground for Addy to eat. "Good dog," she pronounced and skipped over to the door. Pretty butterflies. One. Two. Three. Four. A. B. C. D," she began to sing the familiar ditty in a high, clear voice, hoping from foot to foot.

"She's very vocal for thirty months," Lorraine said. Her tone was conversational but her eyes were sharp and questioning.

"She is very quick. And so eager to learn. She'll be going to preschool three mornings a week in the fall.'' Faith left the feeding dishes sitting on the counter and picked Caitlin up.

"She said her birthday is when it gets cold again. So she'll be three before the end of the year?'' Before Faith could object Lorraine reached out and brushed her fingertips over Caitlin's pigtails.

"Yes.'' Faith opened the habitat door and gestured Lorraine inside. She launched into her standard tour patter to avoid any more questions from the older woman. "On the left is the chrysalis room. I have about seventeen species of butterflies here. I have them shipped in from a breeder in New Jersey, although someday I hope to obtain the licenses I need to breed the tropical species here. But right now the habitat isn't winterized so that's not possible.''

"Interesting.'' Lorraine smoothed her hair with both hands, barely glancing at the pupae hanging from their colored pins.

"All of the butterflies in the habitat are tropicals. But you can usually observe a number of local species along the meadow walk. And, of course, you probably noticed the monarchs in the walk-in cage in the greenhouse. We tag all the monarchs we find here in the meadow, although only the last generation to hatch each season actually migrates south to Mexico.''

"How can you tag a butterfly?'' Lorraine looked puzzled.

"You net them and then very carefully affix a tiny color-coded sticky dot to their wing. It doesn't hurt them if you do it correctly. You're welcome to come along and watch next time.''

''Perhaps I will if it's not too hot.''

Caitlin had gone to the waterfall the moment she was inside the habitat. She was sitting on the edge, dabbling her fingers in the small pool at the base. She looked up and smiled at Faith, pointing to a huge iridescent blue butterfly with a wingspan the size of a saucer. ''Blue morpho,'' she said in a stage whisper.

''Is that what it's called?'' Lorraine's attention was focused on Caitlin, not the butterfly.

''Yes. From Costa Rica. One of the most beautiful butterflies in the world.''

''How many more does she know?''

''Not many, really. Monarchs and painted ladies because of our logo. She recognizes the large moths and the zebras.''

''And she isn't even three. Such a pretty child. I had a son. He died in a car accident. Perhaps Beth told you of it?''

''I knew that Beth's boyfriend was killed in the accident that injured her. I didn't know he was your son until you arrived,'' Faith reminded her.

Lorraine ignored the reference to her duplicity. ''There's more to the story. I don't suppose Beth or her brother told you that part?''

''I don't think—'' Faith began but Lorraine went right on talking.

''Beth was pregnant when she persuaded Jamie to run away with her. I'm not blaming her,'' she said, but the tightening around her mouth told Faith she did hold Beth responsible for Jamie's death. "I—I made a mistake. I—I thought it would be better if Beth didn't have the baby. When I realized that was the wrong thing to ask of her, I made a second mistake. I tried to persuade her father and stepmother into pressuring her to give the baby up for adoption. Now Beth hates all of us."

"I don't think Beth is capable of hating anyone."

Lorraine didn't acknowledge Faith's reply. "I have a grandchild. A little girl," she said quietly. "Somewhere. When is Caitlin's birthday?"

"November," Faith responded, feeling panic slithering along the edges of her nerves. She fought it down. She could do this. She had lied to Hugh, to Beth, to the world. Lorraine Sheldon was no different than the others.

"When in November?" Lorraine wrapped her arms around herself as though she were standing in the middle of the ice storm that had greeted Caitlin's birth, instead of a tropical butterfly house.

"The eleventh."

Lorraine sucked in her breath. "My granddaughter was born on the eleventh. At least we believe she was. And Caitlin is left-handed, just like Jamie. He got his left-handedness from me. It's much less common in girls. You're not left-handed, are you?" She glanced sharply at Faith who met her gaze without hesitation.

"No, I'm not. But my husband was left-handed."

Dear Mark, another small detail of heredity that might save her.

"She has Beth's hair coloring and slight build—" Her voice dropped to a whisper. "And Jamie's eyes."

"No," Faith said firmly. "She has my eyes."

Lorraine made no indication that she had heard Faith's words. She looked blindly around her and sat down abruptly on one of the wooden benches lining the path through the habitat. "Oh, dear God. Why did Hugh Damon come here?" she asked abruptly.

"I—" Faith knew she had to get hold of herself. She was only giving Lorraine more reason to doubt every word she said each time she hesitated in her response. But panic had engulfed her. Her legs became too wobbly to hold her upright. She stiffened her spine. "He found Painted Lady Farm on the Bartonsville Chamber of Commerce Web site, exactly as you told me you did."

"His work is forty-five miles from here. We passed it on our drive in. That's hardly convenient."

"He feels it is."

"No. There's another reason he's here."

"If there is, I have no idea what it might be. I suggest you ask him for yourself," Faith said.

Lorraine's gaze was fixed on Caitlin with total concentration. "I know why he came here. He found some clue that our detectives missed. It's Caitlin, isn't it? That's why he's stayed here these past weeks. She's my Jamie's baby."

"You're wrong," Faith said evenly, no trace of

doubt or fear tinging her voice. "She's mine. No one else's. It's all just coincidence, nothing more."

It was all suddenly very clear. This woman was the embodiment of her nightmares. The faceless being who sat in judgment of her and came down from the shadows to take her baby away. Lorraine Sheldon was her enemy, not Hugh Damon.

Lorraine was convinced that Caitlin was her son's child. Faith wanted to sweep her daughter into her arms, and run until they were both so far away Lorraine Sheldon could never find them again, but she resisted the frantic urge.

Still, she was filled with fear because she was a mother, too. And she knew without doubt that Lorraine Sheldon would not change her mind. She would do whatever she must to prove Caitlin was Jamie's daughter.

CHAPTER TEN

HUGH SAW the Closed notice swinging beneath the Painted Lady Farm sign and Kevin Sager's beat-up old Buick parked in front of his cabin at the same time. The closed sign was unusual enough for a weekday afternoon, but the sight of Kevin sitting with his back against the front door was even odder.

"Hugh, I'm glad you're home." Kevin jumped up as Hugh got out of the Blazer. "Beth's been locked inside all day. She won't come out or let me in."

"What the hell happened?" Hugh glanced at the cottage where Harold and Lorraine had been staying. Their Lexus was gone. There had been a car with Indiana plates parked at the third unit when he left that morning, but it was gone, too.

"I don't know what happened, but it must have been bad. Faith was almost as upset as Beth."

"Is the door locked?"

Kevin nodded. "From the inside."

Hugh knocked on the dark green door. "Beth, it's Hugh. Let me in."

For a long moment there was only silence from the other side. Hugh considered kicking the door in.

It opened, and Beth stood before them, tearstained

and pale. The room was stifling. Beth hadn't bothered to turn on the never more than adequate air-conditioning unit. "Are you alone?" she asked, as she stepped back to let him in.

"I'm still here." Kevin entered before she could shut the door on him. Hugh followed him inside.

Beth dropped onto the couch and pulled her knees up to her chin, wrapping her arms around her legs. "Have you been sitting out there all this time?"

Kevin leaned over the back of the couch so that his face was close to hers. "I told you I was staying put until you let me in. I meant it. I always mean what I say, Beth."

She lifted her hand and touched the tip of his nose. "You're sunburned."

"It's damn hot out there."

"Beth, what happened?" When he saw that she was not physically ill, Hugh had gone to turn on the air conditioner and cool down the overheated room.

He needn't have bothered, the anguished look she gave him froze his heart. "Oh, Hugh. Why didn't you tell me what you believed about Caitlin? Why did you let Lorraine tell me?"

"Caitlin? What are you talking about, Beth?" Kevin sat down beside her and pulled her against him. She turned her face into his chest and started to weep.

"I wanted to tell you. I was going to tell you, but this— I—I j-j-just can't take it in. I c-c-can't remember."

The heartache in her voice cut through the shock

that had held Hugh motionless. He had waited too long to tell her what he believed to be the truth, and now he was going to pay the price of losing his sister's confidence once more. He'd known it was only a matter of time before Harold and Lorraine Sheldon figured things out, yet he hadn't done anything to prepare Beth.

And what of Faith—and Caitlin?

"Tell us what happened," Hugh prompted. For a moment he thought she would ignore his question, but finally she began to speak.

"After you dropped me off I w-w-went down to the greenhouse to help Faith like I always do. Faith came out of the greenhouse with Caitlin in her arms. She looked—I don't know—frightened, angry, both those things at once. Caitlin was crying and Addy was jumping up and down, barking like crazy. Lorraine was right behind them. She was crying, too. The way she always does when she's upset about Jamie. And—" she gave a harsh little laugh "—I should have known then." She looked at him once more, heartbreak in her eyes. "Oh, Hugh...you should have told me."

"What happened next?" He couldn't begin to make things right until he knew the extent of the damage Lorraine had caused.

"W-w-we all stood there staring at each other. Then Lorraine turned on me and said, 'My God, Beth, how could you not—'" She stopped abruptly and dropped her head in her hands. "I—I... can't—"

"Yes, you can. You can tell me, Beth," Kevin said, rocking her against him as though she were a child. Hugh stood where he was, silent and grieved, and for the moment completely shut out. It was Kevin Beth had turned to in her need, not him. He had failed her once more.

"You'll hate me," Beth whispered. "I hate myself."

Kevin lifted her chin and looked at her. "I won't hate you, Beth. I... Never mind that for now. Why does Jamie's mother upset you so?"

"I told you that Jamie died in the accident."

"I remember. But there was more you didn't tell me, wasn't there?"

"I w-w-was going to tell you. Soon. Today. Really I was." She started to cry again.

"I believe you. Go on."

Hugh snagged a box of tissues from the counter and handed them to Kevin. That was all he could do for her right now, all she would let him do. Beth sat up, took a tissue and blew her nose. As upset as she was, she was trying to pull herself together. Hugh's chest tightened with pride.

"Something happened before the accident, didn't it?" Kevin urged once more.

"I was pregnant. I had a baby. A little girl. I know that much from my diary. But when the accident happened she wasn't with us. She was gone." Her voice was low, a tremulous whisper tinged with an old horror brought to the surface. "There was no trace of her. The police searched. Hugh searched. Lorraine and Harold are still looking. But nothing for all this time. Every day I wake up wondering if she is alive...or dead. And then somehow...today... Lorraine got it into her head that Faith's little girl isn't Faith's child at all. She's mine.''

She started to cry once more. She seemed to remember Hugh for the first time in several minutes. ''Hugh, you don't think that, too. Do you?'' She turned to him but her hands were clasped firmly in Kevin's. ''It's impossible, isn't it? It's just a horrible coincidence that Caitlin was born on the same day as my baby, and that Faith delivered her here at Painted Lady Farm with no one to help her. We're miles and miles from where the accident happened. The police said they had no proof we'd ever even been in Ohio. It's just a coincidence we came here. The butterflies are a coincidence. The park—''

She stood up, pulling her hands free of Kevin's grasp. ''The p-p-park.''

''Is just a park, Beth,'' Hugh said. He had to pull her back from the nightmare that had nearly claimed her sanity after the accident. If he had to lie to her now to spare her more misery, he would. And he would go on lying. ''I admit it was the butterflies that first brought Faith to my attention. But she didn't open the butterfly farm until after Caitlin's birth. That Caitlin was born on the same day as your baby? Chance. Coincidence. Nothing more.'' He was lying to protect her—and Faith and Caitlin—from Lorraine Sheldon. She was the greatest threat now.

Beth stood and came toward him, walking a little uncertainly. Hugh took a long stride around the table and she came into his arms. "I'm sorry I jumped on you the way I did. It's j-j-just that I thought you weren't telling me the truth. You promised to always be straight with me, remember?"

"I remember." Her happiness and well-being meant everything to him. He folded her into his arms because he couldn't chance her reading the guilt he knew clouded his expression.

Beth sniffed and wiped her nose again. "I knew it. If Caitlin was my flesh and blood I'd feel something, wouldn't I? I don't. At least I didn't at first. Now she's like a little cousin to me. Or a friend's child. But not mine. Wouldn't I feel it if she were mine?"

The last of the fading hope Hugh had cherished of Beth recovering her memory died at those words. He had felt a connection, tenuous though it might have been, the moment he'd laid eyes on Caitlin. Lorraine Sheldon had felt it, too, and it was strong enough for her to have acted on it. But Beth felt nothing.

She was trembling harder than before, and he knew she was close to breaking down again. He tried to get her to think of something else. "Where are Lorraine and Harold?" Hugh asked, releasing her so that she could return to Kevin.

"They're gone. Faith insisted they leave." She almost smiled. "You should have seen her, Hugh. She stood there with steel in her eyes. Lorraine started crying again, but Faith wouldn't change her mind.

Harold tried to get me to open the door for a long time after I ran back here, but I wouldn't talk to him. I thought maybe they'd grab me and haul me off to the hypnotherapist. Or the cops. Finally they left when Faith threatened to call the sheriff. I heard it all from in here.'' Her voice cracked, then she gave a watery little laugh that twisted Hugh's heart. ''But I wouldn't let Faith inside, either. Or Kevin. I was a little crazy there for a while, I think.''

''Where are Faith and Caitlin now?''

''She's at her sister's,'' Kevin interrupted. ''She insisted on staying here in case Beth needed help, but Caitlin was getting hot and fussy. I suggested she close the butterfly house for the rest of the afternoon. She headed off about two hours ago.''

''She probably won't even let me near Caitlin again after that awful scene with Lorraine.'' Tears blurred Beth's eyes once more and she wiped them away with the back of her hand.

''Faith will understand,'' Hugh said, but he wasn't so sure it was true.

''I hope so. We'll work it all out later, right?'' Beth recited the words as though she had practiced them over and over again in her sessions with the therapist. She rubbed her temples. ''I...I have a terrible headache.''

''I don't doubt it. It's after seven,'' Kevin said. His voice was steady, his tone bracing. ''Have you eaten anything since breakfast?'' She looked puzzled for a moment, then shook her head. Kevin stood up. ''That's one thing we can put right. I'll take you to a little place I know that's got great food. It's far enough away that not too many people from Bartonsville go there. Do you want to wash your face and comb your hair first?''

Beth reached up and ran her fingers through her tangled hair. ''Yes, I must look like a madwoman.''

''You look like you're roasting in those clothes. And you look like you've been crying all day, but nothing worse than that. Don't dress up. It's an old-fashioned drive-in with carhops and trays that hook onto the car window. Burgers as big as plates. You'll love it.''

''I don't eat red meat. How many times do I have to tell you that?''

''A chicken sandwich, then.''

''How's the root beer?''

''The best I've ever tasted. Let's go, I'm starving.''

Beth took a shaky breath and managed a smile. She lifted her hand and touched Kevin on the cheek. ''You sat out there all day in the sun with nothing to eat?''

''Damn straight. And you know how I hate to miss a meal.''

''You did that for me?''

''I told you—''

''You'll always be there for me,'' she whispered.

''Yes. But I'd rather be there on a full stomach.''

She smiled and this time it was real. Hugh felt the tension inside him unknot slightly. Kevin would look after her. ''I'll be ready in ten minutes.'' She turned toward the bathroom then pivoted back to face Hugh. "Will you be—"

"Don't worry about me. I'm fine. You go with Kevin. Everything will look better when you've had something to eat."

She shook her head. "It won't look better, but maybe it won't look like the end of the world."

Kevin rested both hands on the back of the couch, but remained silent until the sound of running water from the bathroom covered his words. "I suspected there was more to Beth's story than just running away from home because she didn't get along with her dad and stepmom. But this?" He dropped his head and stared down at his hands. "It's a hell of a thing to have to live with."

"She wanted to tell you about the baby."

He nodded and looked up again. "I know that. But you took a hell of a risk bringing Beth here if you thought Faith Carson's little girl is really hers. You must have known there was a chance something like this would happen."

Hugh turned his back on Kevin, struggling to get his feelings under control. Anger flared and died within him. Kevin was right. It was his fault, his alone. He should have come clean the moment the Sheldons arrived. Now he'd have to face the consequences of his own inaction. He just hoped he didn't end up losing his sister's love along with her respect.

"Tell me exactly what's going on here," Kevin said. "I need to know for Beth's sake."

"Beth is my responsibility."

"For the time being." Kevin met Hugh's gaze with steady regard. "I intend to make her my responsibility if she'll have me."

"Beth isn't in any shape for a love affair."

"It isn't going to be an affair. And I know she's not ready for anything too serious right now. I'm just telling you it *is* serious on my part. I won't be shut out of her life because her big brother is trying to fix the major screwup he's gotten us all into."

Once more Kevin had cut straight to the heart of the matter. Hugh balled his hands into fists, but he was far madder at himself than at Kevin. Keeping her boyfriend in the dark wouldn't help Beth face the mess he'd made of everything. Kevin Sager had to be trusted with what he knew, and what he suspected.

"Beth started having nightmares about six months ago. She kept dreaming of a baby crying, butterflies changing to drops of blood on the snow. She'd wake up night after night, crying and terrified. I'd damn near given up trying to locate any new leads on the baby. But when the dreams started I gave it one more shot, added butterflies to the mix, widened the search area and came up with Faith Carson. Widow, nurse, mother of a daughter born the same day as the doctors said Beth's baby was born."

"And owner of a butterfly farm. Not your everyday occupation." Kevin nodded. "Okay, so far I see where you're coming from."

"It was just one too many matches to be coincidence. I signed on to the Cincy job when the structural engineer they'd hired died of a sudden heart attack. It was the perfect cover, but I would have come here anyway. I'd have found some excuse."

"You could be right," Kevin said, leaning forward. "Faith's made a lot of friends in town the past couple of years, but I'd be lying if I told you there wasn't talk when she first showed up on Main Street with a baby. I remember my mom and her friends discussing it. Not that anyone saw much of her those first few months after she moved here. But she didn't look pregnant, you know, and people remembered. And then to have the baby all alone in the middle of the biggest ice storm in twenty years. Well, it was sure something to talk about for a while."

"And it will be again if the Sheldons start asking questions about Faith and Caitlin."

"You don't think they're gone for good?"

"Lorraine will move mountains to find the truth now that she's convinced Caitlin is Beth and Jamie's child."

"I think you're right to be worried about Lorraine Sheldon. She looks like the kind of woman who gets what she wants regardless of the consequences. Bartonsville's a good place to live, but people are only human. There are plenty who love a good scandal, and this would be a doozy."

"I thought Beth might remember if I brought her here," Hugh admitted, feeling the discouragement seep into his very bones. "She didn't, but I kept hoping, for her sake, that she would. Maybe that's why I let it go on so long."

And because he wanted to be near Faith for his own reasons, an equally bad decision.

"So far it's your word against Faith Carson's."

"I have no proof but my own suspicions."

"Stalemate."

"Exactly, until Lorraine Sheldon arrived. I want Beth to have peace and happiness. But I don't want Faith Carson branded as a baby stealer. I've been feeling my way since the day Beth got here. I waited too long to tell her what I suspected. Instead of a miracle, I got the Sheldons breathing down our necks. Then it was too late to leave. Lorraine would have thought that was suspicious, too. And it would have put Faith into an untenable position." Which, of course, had happened anyway. He heard the water shut off in the bathroom. Beth would be back with them in a minute or two.

"What are you going to do now?" Kevin asked. "This could get really ugly if Mrs. Sheldon decides to keep poking and prodding. And I have a nasty suspicion she'll do just that. Faith could end up in jail. And Child Services would certainly take Caitlin."

"Don't you think I know that?" Hugh growled. "All I wanted was for Beth to be happy and whole."

"At the expense of Faith and her daughter?"

"No, damn it. Of course not."

The bathroom door opened. Beth came out, still red-eyed but composed. She'd traded the heavy sweatshirt for a tank top but she still wore her jeans.

Kevin glanced across the room, a smile on his lips for Beth, but the words he spoke, low enough that only Hugh could hear, were blunt. "Then I suggest you figure out a way to do something about it."

CHAPTER ELEVEN

"NO MORE SQUIRTING your brother in the face, Jack," Peg informed her older son in her I-mean-it-or-else voice that Faith remembered from her own childhood. "Dana will have to be in charge of the hose if you do it again." She settled back in the wooden swing that hung on the deck of her twenty-year-old brick rambler. She and Steve had bought the house when they'd become engaged a year ago from friends of his parents who were retiring to Arizona. Peg's decorating expertise had brought her quite a bit of business when prospective customers saw what she'd done with the interior.

Caitlin was sitting on top of the slide on the boy's swing set with Dana hovering protectively nearby, as she watched her cousins chase each other with the hose. The last of the afternoon's warmth was fading into a cool, June twilight.

"Dana's going to deserve a baby-sitting medal before the summer is out." Faith propped her elbow on the back of the swing and rested her cheek on the back of her hand.

A drumbeat of tension still beat behind her eyes, but it had faded to a dull ache and she ignored it. "I have to be getting back to the farm,'' she said. ''I can't have it look as if I let the Sheldons run me off my own property. And I'm worried about Beth. I shouldn't have left her alone for so long.''

''We've been over this. You said Kevin Sager was there.''

''Sitting outside the cabin.''

''He'll look after her. I'm more worried about you. Do you want Steve to follow you home, just to make sure those people are gone?'' Her sister was stroking Addy's silky ears, and the little sheltie, worn out from following Peg's big yellow Labrador retriever around all afternoon, snuggled closer to Peg's thigh and began to snore gently.

''Of course not. I'm fine. But sneaking around behind Steve's back to lay my troubles on you is one more thing I have on my conscience.''

Peg didn't pretend ignorance. She covered Faith's hand with her own. ''I have a confession to make. I told him about Caitlin right after we were married. And I called him to tell him about what happened this morning when you were putting Caitlin down for her nap.''

''He's known all this time?'' Faith thought back over the time since the wedding. Not once had her rock-solid brother-in-law given her any inkling that he knew she was not Caitlin's birth mother.

''I know I promised I would keep your secret.'' They were in shadow on this side of the house but Faith had no trouble detecting the sheen of tears in her sister's eyes.

Faith leaned forward, took Peg's hands between her own. "I should never have asked that of you."

"At the time it seemed the most natural thing in the world. I never intended to become involved with another man. Ever. Thank goodness I can be easily swayed." Peg laughed, and the sound held such happiness that Faith felt a quick jab of longing for what Peg and Steve shared, and that she would never know again.

Peg rested her hand on her slightly rounded belly. "I didn't think second-time-around miracles like Steve happened to women like me."

"He's worthy of your love and your trust," Faith whispered.

"And your trust," Peg responded.

Faith closed her eyes against a sudden sting of tears. "I know." She remembered what Steve had said at the picnic by the pond the night the Sheldons arrived. "I hope we have a little girl like Caitlin." He had known then that Caitlin was not her flesh and blood and he had said it anyway.

"He thinks you should get a lawyer—"

"No." Faith wasn't ready for that step. "No. Not yet."

"Honey, we have to be prepared. Maybe not for what Hugh and Beth might do, but for what the Sheldons certainly will."

"Beth and Jamie drove away. They abandoned Caitlin to a stranger in the middle of a storm."

"I know, honey. Those kids weren't blameless. At least Jamie wasn't. But Beth must share some of the responsibility. Hugh probably realizes that and doesn't want to see his sister branded an unfit mother.''

"I agree with you. That's partly why I let him stay. I...I knew he couldn't make a claim on Caitlin without hurting Beth.'' Hugh. Loyal, devoted, his sister's champion. Could he be her champion, too? Somewhere deep inside her she kept hoping that they could forge some kind of alliance for Caitlin's sake. *For her sake.*

"But the Sheldons. They're something different, aren't they?'' Reality washed away her momentary fantasy.

"Lorraine Sheldon wants her grandchild. She doesn't care who she hurts achieving that goal.''

Peg had been pushing the swing with her foot. She stopped, and planted both feet on the deck, her hands braced on her knees. "I hope you're exaggerating. Surely she can be made to see it's Caitlin who would be hurt most if she's taken away from you.''

"Don't ever say that out loud again,'' Faith begged. "Don't you know how often I've awakened in the middle of the night imagining that very thing?''

"I'm sorry,'' Peg said, leaning across Addy to give Faith a reassuring hug. "We're both on edge.'' She sighed. "I should have known. I should have recognized Beth—''

"How could you? Why should you have even thought twice about her? She and Caitlin don't resemble each other that closely. Until this morning she had no idea that Caitlin might be her missing child. I'm convinced of that.'' Poor Beth. She had been stricken dumb by the scene she'd walked into.

"No. But I should have picked up on things. There was her name. The accident she was in. How upset you've been since she came. And here I thought it was because you had the hots for her brother—'' Peg stopped talking abruptly. She whipped her head around, her eyes raking Faith's face. "You look as if you've been hit by a two-by-four. You do have feelings for Hugh Damon. I knew it. I told Steve so after the picnic.''

"I do not. How could I? He's done this to me.''

Her sister wasn't impressed by her protest. "He's also your best ally against the Sheldons.''

Hugh had said they were allies that night in the moonlight.

"He's only interested in his sister's welfare.''

"And I'm interested in yours and Caitlin's. Steve and I will always be here for you. We'll help you any way we can, you know that.''

"I've never doubted it for a moment. And I can't fault Hugh for wanting to know what happened to Beth's baby. If the situations were reversed you would have done the same thing for me.''

"Yeah, he's a knight in shining armor, all right.'' Peg leaned over once more to enfold Faith in a hug. "I'm just sorry my little sister is the one who gets stuck fighting off the dragons. Why don't you leave Caitlin here for the night just in case the Sheldons decide to stage a repeat performance? She and the boys can have an indoor camp-out. Dana's staying, anyway, since Steve and I both have to be up and gone at the crack of dawn tomorrow.''

Faith looked out at her laughing, bright-eyed daughter. She hadn't seemed unduly alarmed by the morning's events, but Faith dreaded the possibility of Caitlin encountering the Sheldons again. ''Thanks, Peg.''

''We love having her.''

Steve walked out of the barn, and the sisters watched in silence as he crossed the yard and came to stand beside them, resting his arms on the top rail of the deck. ''From the look on your faces, I guess Peg 'fessed up to what she's told me.''

''Yes, she has.''

''Good. I don't like keeping secrets from family. I want you to know Peg and I will stand by you,'' he said. ''I think you made the right decision for Caitlin. She would have gone into the system if you'd turned her over to the authorities. There's no guarantee she would have been given back to Beth when they were finished investigating. The law might not agree with me, but as far as I'm concerned, she's yours. She's one of the brightest and happiest little girls I know. I meant it when I said I hope we have a daughter just like her.''

Faith swallowed the lump of tears his words had brought into her throat. Peg squeezed her hand, hard, and Faith squeezed back.

''Thank you, Steve.''

''I'd better be getting the boys dried off and settled

down, or we'll be up until midnight.'' His voice had roughened around the edges, telling Faith her brother-in-law was more emotional than he wanted to admit. He turned away and jogged off to join the melee around the swing set.

"Where do you think the Sheldons are tonight?" Peg asked after a moment.

"Not far away, I imagine."

"There's nothing fancy enough for the likes of her within fifty miles of here."

"I think she'd set up housekeeping in a barn if she thought it would get her what she wants."

Her sister's next words sent an icy tremor down Faith's spine. "And what she wants is Caitlin."

THE SUNSET WAS incredible, red and orange below, streams of mauve and purple above. The twilight was long, lingering well into the evening, now that the first day of summer was near. This was beautiful country, Hugh had come to realize. The kind of place where people watched the cloud patterns in the sky, and the leaves change color on the trees. A man could settle down here, grow old and die in peace and prosperity. For a man who had spent close to a dozen years building dams and bridges on every continent on earth, it suddenly didn't seem like such a bad way to go.

The sound of a car engine approaching ended his reverie. Hugh watched Faith drive slowly past the cemetery as he rubbed a last bit of polish onto the hood of his long-neglected Blazer. He'd had a lot of nervous energy to burn off after Kevin and Beth left. He'd needed something to do with his hands, something that would let him think as he worked. He'd settled on washing and waxing the Blazer, but always one small part of his brain had been listening for Faith, watching for her to come home.

She slowed, but didn't stop at the ornate wrought-iron gate that marked the entrance to the cemetery. In life Mark Carson had loved her and cherished her; in death he had given Caitlin a name. But a dead man's memory couldn't help her now. She must face the future alone.

Unless she faced it with him.

He didn't know when the idea had come to him, that standing together they would be better able to protect Beth and Caitlin from the Sheldons' interference. It would be a partnership, legal and binding. A marriage of convenience, it used to be called. Would she agree to it?

He wondered if he could bring it off. Have her be his, but not his. The thought of being married to Faith Carson heated his blood and filled his head with images that would send her running if she could read his mind.

Except for Addy, ears pricked as she sat in the seat beside Faith, she was alone in the minivan, Hugh noticed. She must have left Caitlin with her sister for the night. She stopped the car, slipping out to take the Closed sign from the hooks where it was hanging. Regardless of what had happened that morning, it was obvious, tomorrow Faith intended to return her life to normal. But she was more upset than she let on, he surmised, or she would have her daughter at her side.

Addy sniffed around the base of the sign then looked in his direction, barking a greeting, but waiting at Faith's side. She saw him watching her and came toward the Blazer. Her arms were folded beneath her breasts, emphasizing their soft roundness. He kept his gaze on his work, but the sheen on the hood of the Blazer reflected her image like a dusky mirror.

"Is Beth okay?" she asked, as soon as she moved into earshot.

He wadded the old T-shirt he'd been using as a polishing rag into a ball and threw it into the bucket that had been hanging beneath the outside spigot on the side of the cabin.

"She's doing all right. Kevin took her to get something to eat a couple of hours ago."

"I knew she was in good hands with him. That's the only reason I left her."

"How are you?" he asked, moving around the front of the Blazer to stand beside her.

A hawk cried out overhead and in the distance a dog barked, causing Addy to give a quick yip in reply and warning.

"I'm fine."

"I don't believe you," he said quietly. There were dark circles under her eyes and faint stress lines bracketed her mouth.

"I'm still shaking inside," she said bluntly. "For

the second time in two weeks someone has accused me of taking another woman's child as my own.'' She met his eyes with proud defiance, but he saw the terror beneath. ''Did Beth believe Lorraine?''

He shoved his hands in the pockets of his jeans and leaned back against the fender to keep himself from taking her in his arms.

''No.''

''Did you tell her *you* believe that Caitlin is her child?'' She emphasized the pronoun very slightly.

''No.''

''Why not? It's the truth, isn't it? You're just as certain Caitlin is Beth's daughter as Lorraine is.''

''Faith, we don't have to be on opposite sides here.''

She gave a startled little laugh of disbelief, then her eyes narrowed. ''You denied it, didn't you? You didn't tell Beth why you brought her here.'' She backed away. ''Why?''

''Because I have no proof. I thought—'' He dropped his head back, staring at the darkening sky, searching for words that wouldn't come. He had thought they could work it out, he and Faith, come to some understanding, some arrangement that would give all of them what they wanted. Beth, her peace of mind, Faith, her child. And him? What did he want? A wife, a lover, a mother for his children?

''She trusts you,'' Faith said. ''How long can you lie to her about what you believe before she begins to suspect?''

She had touched a nerve rubbed raw by his own restless thoughts. "As long as it takes."

"As long as it takes for what? For me to confess what you want to hear? That won't happen until the sun falls from the sky." She whirled away as though to leave.

Hugh's hands came out of his pockets and fastened around her shoulders. "Don't go. We have to talk this through." He wanted to pull her closer. He wanted her tight against him, but he loosened his grip, holding his breath that she wouldn't turn and walk away.

"We have nothing to discuss," she said wearily, wrapping her arms around her waist, as though to ward off a chill. "Caitlin is my daughter."

"And she needs our protection. So does my sister. Don't you see what I'm asking, Faith?"

"No, I don't."

"We need to form an alliance, a partnership." He raked his hands through his hair. "Hell, maybe even a marriage."

Her eyes grew round, and darkened to the same color as the pond water beneath the willow. "What are you talking about?"

"Together we can keep Harold and Lorraine from ever learning the truth about Caitlin."

"No." She shook her head, rejecting his idea, rejecting him. "They would see it as a threat. A—a declaration of war. They'd suspect there was an ulterior motive and they would be more determined than ever to find out what happened the day Beth's baby was born.''

He drove home his point, trying to overcome her objection. ''Together we double our strength, our resources. Our ability to protect your daughter and my sister from the Sheldons.''

''No.'' Her voice had risen slightly. She closed her eyes refusing to look at him again. ''There has to be some other way. I—I can't marry you. I—I don't love you.''

He reached out then and gathered her into his arms without thinking. He cradled the back of her head with one hand, holding her gently, but firmly so that she couldn't run away. ''Does love have to be part of the equation?'' he asked, searching her face for some sign that she would soften. He found none, but he refused to accept that. Hugh lowered his head and kissed her. He felt her stiffen and her hands came up to push against his chest. He gentled his mouth on hers, willing her to open for him.

And then with a small sigh of surrender she did. Her mouth opened beneath his. She tasted of honey and mint and she smelled of sunflowers and summer grass. She wrapped her arms around his neck and let his lips skim over her eyelids. her cheeks, the curve of her ear.

When his lips returned to hers she leaned her full weight against him. She was soft and round in all the right places, and holding her in his arms was just as glorious as he had imagined it would be. He wanted to sink down onto the soft green grass and take her then and there, but he held back. When the kiss ended he didn't attempt another. He let her rest her cheek against his shoulder as she caught her breath, then let her step backward until only the tips of his fingers connected her to him.

"Together we could take on the world," he said.

"Not as husband and wife, no matter how important the cause. There has to be some other way. I can't marry without love. And you're not in love with me." Tears glistened on her lashes.

He lifted her chin with the tip of his finger. "Maybe not." He let the words hang in the air for a long time. "But I don't think that would be such an impossible thing to do."

She turned and fled, her dog at her heels.

HUGH FOLDED HIS HANDS across his bare chest and leaned one shoulder against the door frame. He looked out over the starlit fields, watching the mist swirl in the hollows. It was after three. The moon had set hours ago. Beth and Kevin had not returned and he couldn't sleep.

He couldn't sleep not only because he was worried about his sister, but because he couldn't get the memory of holding Faith out of his mind.

God, he'd screwed up big time tonight. He'd meant to present his proposal of an alliance in a no-nonsense, businesslike way. Instead he'd taken her into his arms and all but admitted he was more than halfway to falling in love with her.

She'd run from him as though he were a madman.

And to her way of thinking he probably was. She saw him as less of a threat than the Sheldons only because she trusted him not to do anything to hurt Beth. But now she would believe she couldn't trust him even the little amount she once had, because he'd shown her his attraction.

He wanted to protect them all, Beth and Caitlin and Faith. But he had blown his best chance of doing that. From now on Faith would do everything to keep him at arm's length—and set herself to face the challenge of Lorraine and Harold Sheldon alone.

CHAPTER TWELVE

HE SNORED. Not loudly, but she supposed she could get used to it. And his beard was a much darker red than his hair. She reached out and touched his chin, very lightly. Kevin frowned in his sleep and brushed at her hand as though she were a fly.

Beth stretched gingerly. Sleeping in the back seat of a twenty-year-old Buick was not like spending a night in a suite at a fancy hotel. She was stiff all over, and she had at least a half dozen mosquito bites in places she wasn't sure she could reach to scratch. Still, she wouldn't have traded the past twelve hours for anything in the world.

They hadn't made love. She had wanted to, but Kevin had held back. "Not tonight, Beth," he had told her. "When we make love the first time, it's not going to be because you want to forget all the pain you've got bottled up inside. And it's not going to be in the back seat of this damn car."

He had held her and comforted her, kissed her and stroked her hair, but he had gone no further. And he hadn't said he loved her. But he did. She knew because she was falling in love with him, too. But she wouldn't say it aloud, either. Not until she had come to terms with what happened yesterday.

She needed time, and Kevin knew that, too. He would wait for her to make sense of the jumble of emotions inside her. Was Lorraine right? Was Caitlin her child? Her lost and longed for baby? If she was, then all the feelings she thought she would have if they were ever reunited, were not the ones she was feeling right now.

She liked Caitlin. She was a sweet little girl, pretty and smart. But she didn't feel like Beth's child. Like the baby she'd dreamed of holding in her arms every night and day for almost three years.

She was Faith's child.

And Beth couldn't imagine what she could do to change that perception in Caitlin's mind—and in her heart. And did she even want to?

Kevin woke up with a little grunt and his arms tightened around her. "Good morning."

"Good morning," she said back. She kissed him lightly on the tip of his nose, then buried her face in his shoulder. They had spent the night together, but that was a long way from being comfortable waking up beside a man, when you had morning breath and tousled hair and no makeup.

"How did you sleep?" Kevin asked, sitting up with a groan and pulling her up beside him.

Beth thought back over the night just past. "I…I slept all right. No bad dreams."

"Good. I'd better get you home. Your brother's

probably waiting by the door with a baseball bat right now.''

''I'll protect you. But we should get home. I don't want Hugh to go off to work worrying about where we are.''

''Or what we've been doing.'' Kevin wriggled his eyebrows and she laughed.

''Or what we've been doing.''

But she did need to know what Hugh really believed. Was it all just coincidence as he had assured her yesterday? Or *was* he convinced that Caitlin was her baby?

If he did believe that, then he'd been lying to her for weeks. And Hugh had never lied to her before.

Kevin opened the car door and climbed out. The sun was up and the birds were singing, although it was still very early. They had spent the night on the riverbank at the end of a rutted and overgrown lane that Kevin had had no trouble finding, although it was almost invisible to Beth. She had a good idea why he knew it so well. It was a perfect make-out spot, but she didn't ask how many other girls he'd brought here in the past. ''C'mon. I'll take you home, unless you want to pee in the bushes.''

''No, I don't.'' Beth laughed. That was one of the things she liked about Kevin. He didn't treat her as if she were made of glass. Even after yesterday. ''And I do have to pee so step on it.''

''I will after we get back on the road. Otherwise I'll bounce us around so much it will be too late by the time we get back to the cabins.''

"Do you have to work today?" she asked, as he maneuvered the car in the narrow space and headed back up the lane.

"No. I'm yours. You can decide what you want to do while I go home to shower and shave." Kevin worked several part-time jobs in the summer. He lived with his parents and was saving for a house of his own. She liked that about him, too. He wasn't ashamed to say he lived with his parents. Family was important to him.

"Good. I..." She took a deep breath and slowed down a little. She wasn't going to stutter, or forget the words, or lose track of what she was going to say. Her mind was clear as a bell. "I need to talk to Faith sometime today."

"What are you going to say to her?"

She turned her head toward him. "I don't know," she said simply and truthfully. "But I do know one thing. I think it's time for me to see what the butterfly house is like inside."

FAITH OVERSLEPT the next morning. Caitlin was reluctant to leave the boys and Dana, so it had taken an extra twenty minutes to finish her toast and cereal and round up the toys she'd taken with her to Peg's. They barely made it back to the farm before a bus tour of thirty senior citizens arrived. It was the middle of the morning before Faith could take the time to clean the Sheldons' vacated cabin, and to leave fresh linen for Beth and Hugh.

She assumed Beth was all right because she had

seen Kevin Sager's car parked in front of the cabin beside Hugh's Blazer as she went to fetch Caitlin. When she returned, the vehicles were gone. Hugh had gone to work, as usual. She was doing her best to pretend everything was the same as it had been yesterday, too, but she couldn't maintain the illusion when she thought of what had passed between them last night.

A partnership. A loveless marriage to a man whose loyalty was divided between two women? Was she willing to go so far to protect her secret?

Faith pulled herself up short. Once again her longing to turn to Hugh had nearly betrayed her. She could not count him as an ally, as a partner, certainly as a husband, because she could not confide in him. She was as alone as she had been on the day of Caitlin's birth. She must never forget that, not for a moment. She would never have a man like Hugh to stand beside her.

"Look, Mommy. I made a house." Caitlin was busy playing in a turtle-shaped sandbox that Hugh had brought home in the back of his Blazer one day and set up in a corner of the greenhouse. Beth had found it "for a steal" at a Bartonsville yard sale and Caitlin had been so delighted with the gift that Faith would have seemed churlish refusing it. She had thanked Hugh and Beth, and felt another small weight added to the guilt in her heart. "I make a big house." Caitlin upended another bucket of damp sand and began patting it into a more interesting shape.

"It's time to go clean the cabins, Kitty Cat. Do you want to help me?" Faith asked and knew immediately she'd made a mistake. You never, ever, gave a two-year-old a choice. They would pick the one you didn't want them to every time.

"Stay here," Caitlin said, not looking up.

"We'll take the wagon," Faith tempted. "I'll pull you up and we'll coast back down the hill if you're a good girl."

Caitlin's face lit up. "Okay." Sand, toys and pigtails flying, she scrambled out of the sandbox. "Let's go."

"Just as soon as I load the linens and cleaning supplies into the wagon. And you go potty and wash your hands."

"Don't have to potty," Caitlin announced. "But I'll wash my hands. I'm a good girl, aren't I, Mommy?" *Mommy.* She loved this child so much. How could she face life without her? She would do whatever she must to keep her as innocent and happy as she was this very moment. Even give herself to a man who loved his sister, but didn't love her?

Unwilling to explore those thoughts any further, Faith swept Caitlin up in her arms and whirled her around until she squealed with joy. "You're the bestest little girl in the whole, wide world."

It was hot inside the cabin where Harold and Lorraine had been staying. Faith opened the windows and both doors. A nice breeze was blowing, keeping the day from being too hot. The cabin wouldn't take long to clean. It was the smallest of the three, one bedroom, a minuscule bathroom and a main room with a small kitchenette.

There was no sign of the Sheldons except for the dirty towels in the bathroom and the unmade bed. She stripped the linens and cleaned the bathroom while Caitlin played on the small patio at the back of the cabin with two of her Barbies and a stuffed kitten that she'd insisted on bringing along for the promised coast back down the hill.

Faith had just taken the clean linen into the bedroom when she heard a car drive up and a door open and close. Faith brushed her hair behind her ears and walked to the screen door, aware that it might be the Sheldons returning. Instead she came face-to-face with Beth. Kevin lifted his hand from the steering wheel in a wave, then drove off, leaving the two women alone.

Beth's expression was strained, but she tried to smile. She was wearing shorts and a Baylor T-shirt, and she'd pulled her hair into a little ponytail on top of her head. She looked about sixteen and scared. ''Hi, Faith. I'm glad you're back. I sent Kevin away. I...I—'' Faith waited as she took a deep breath and gained control of herself. ''May I come in? I think we need to talk.''

Faith opened the screen door. Beth stepped inside, blinking to adjust to the change in light. She scanned the cleaning supplies Faith had laid out on the kitchen table, and the clean linen piled beside it. ''I guess I needed to see for myself that they're really gone.''

"I doubt they've gone very far."

Beth looked around the little cabin, as though reassuring herself her eyes weren't playing tricks on her. "No, they won't have gone far. And they'll be back. Lorraine wants to know what happened to my baby more than anything. Now that she thinks she's found her, she won't give up. I'm sorry." She lifted her hand and let it fall back to her side. "I'm sorry about yesterday. I didn't know what to do, or to say to make it better."

"It was as difficult for you as it was for me." Faith chose her words carefully as she always did with Beth. The problem was that she liked Hugh's sister. She wanted her to be happy and successful. She just wanted her to do it without ever knowing that Caitlin was her daughter.

"Where is Caitlin? Did you send her away?"

"She's out on the patio." Faith motioned toward the open back door of the cabin.

"Is she all right?" Beth walked around the bistro table that sat in the middle of the room and looked out at Caitlin playing on the paving stones. "I mean, is she all traumatized, or anything? Did Lorraine's crying and calling her Jamie's darling and wanting to hold her frighten her?"

"A little," Faith admitted.

Beth turned her back on the door. "It frightened me, too. She's like that. Really excitable. I can't remember if she was like that before, but she probably was, or why would we have been so hell-bent to get away from her?" She shrugged. "Or maybe it has something to do with her age? You know, hormones and menopause and all that. She's almost fifty, you know.'' Faith hid a smile. Beth was so young, really. Being fifty was as impossible to imagine as being two hundred was. ''She ties me up in knots. I feel like I'm back in the hospital and can't even remember how to say my own name. It's as though she can't really believe I don't remember what happened that day. If she just asks me often enough, or finds someone else to ask me often enough, I'll be able to tell her where I left my baby. Doesn't she know I'd give my life to be able to remember what happened to her? Doesn't she think I would feel something, some extra special connection to Caitlin, if she really was my child?''

Faith felt her heart hammer against her chest. Beth did not feel a connection to Caitlin. She had said it clearly and emphatically. She was *right* to keep her silence. ''She loved Jamie very much. She's a mother, too. She's desperate to find the part of him that remains.''

''Yeah, that's something I can understand about her. The wanting. Jamie was an only child. He wasn't spoiled, though. At least not too much. He was cool and rich but he never treated me like I wasn't as good as he was. At least that's what I wrote in my diary. I don't remember him at all. Maybe he got the good genes from his dad? Harold isn't such a bad guy. I can talk to him when Lorraine's not around. But he thought I should give my baby up for adoption, too. He thought we were way too young to raise a child.''

"You probably were," Faith said quietly.

Beth smoothed a wrinkle from the pillowcase on top of the pile of linen. "I wanted someone to love, who loved me, too."

"I think that's a common emotion for teenage mothers."

"I know it is. I've had enough therapy, and read enough to figure that out. And I've also figured out I'm in charge of the rest of my life, so you don't have to give me the standard riff."

Faith chuckled, she couldn't help herself. "Oh, dear, was I so obvious?"

Beth smiled, too, the same mischievous grin that Caitlin had. It was the first Faith had noticed it. She wished she hadn't because now she knew Harold and Lorraine could also see the similarities between the two.

"No. I don't think there are too many other ways you can say it. Poor Hugh, he wants to make everything right again, and there's no way he can. We both know it, but he keeps on trying. He's that kind of guy. Never give up. Never say die. Maybe if Hugh told me he thought Caitlin was my baby I'd start to believe, too. But he says it's all a coincidence. And if I can't believe Hugh, than I can't believe anything or anyone else." She gave the pillowcase another pat, then picked up the stack of linen. "I'll help you make the bed."

"Thank you." Faith could barely get the words past the constriction in her throat. Dear God, what had Hugh done in trying to protect Beth with his well-intentioned lie?

Faith unfolded the bottom sheet and flipped it over the mattress. Beth continued talking as they worked. "Hugh explained to me last night why he came here in the first place. It was the dreams. My...my dream about the butterflies." Her voice was slightly muffled. She had a pillow tucked under her chin to anchor it while she placed it in the pillowcase.

It was the first she had stuttered in some time. Faith watched her closely. Her hands were trembling slightly, but she seemed to be in control. She had been right when she'd told Lorraine Sheldon the day before that Beth had come a long way in her healing. "He told me that, too."

"But he doesn't believe Caitlin is my baby. I want you to know that."

Faith tucked the pillows beneath the chenille bedspread, grateful for something to do with her hands as they talked. "Caitlin is my daughter, Beth."

"Please don't blame Hugh for the Sheldons coming here. It's all coincidence—the date of her birth and the butterflies and...and everything—" She seemed to want to say more, but stopped. "Just coincidence."

"You can accept that?"

"Yes." She lifted her shoulders in a sad little shrug. "I have to, don't I? Faith, would you tell me something?"

"If I can."

"You're a mother. You'd never not recognize your child, no matter what had happened—"

"Mommy! Mommy!" Caitlin's shrill cry was a full-blown scream by the time she'd come to the last drawn-out syllable. Addy began to bark in sympathy, adding to the din.

The color drained from Beth's face and her eyes grew huge, terror filled. "Caitlin, my God. What happened to her?"

Faith dropped the pillow she was holding and skirted the bed but Beth was already at the back door. She dropped stiffly to her knees and pulled Caitlin close against her. "What's wrong, Kitty Cat? Are you hurt?"

It didn't take more than a glance at the handful of blossoms scattered at Caitlin's feet, and the red swelling on the back of her hand she had cradled against her chest, to conclude she'd been stung by a bee while picking flowers from the beds bordering the patio.

"Kitty Cat, tell me what's wrong," Beth begged.

"Owie! Owie! Mommy!" Caitlin held out her arms and reached for Faith, crying all the harder. "Nasty old flower bit me."

Faith ignored the pain of seeing her daughter held and comforted in her birth mother's arms. She sat down on one of the red metal chairs, warm from the sun and took Caitlin onto her lap. "Let me see your owie." Beth rose stiffly, using the other chair to help her stand.

"Is she okay? What happened?"

"It's a bee sting." Faith held the dirty little hand cupped in her own and pointed to the "owie," raising her voice just enough to be heard over the wails. "See. There's the stinger. Mommy will make it better." Faith smoothed her thumb over the stinger, which showed up as a dark center to the welt. Caitlin sobbed harder, her eyes screwed shut, anticipating more pain. "There," Faith said. "All gone."

Caitlin opened her eyes and looked down at her hand. "Nasty gone?"

"All gone," Faith assured her.

"It still hurts. Need med'cine."

"Beth, could you do me a favor?"

"Yes. What do you need?" Her blue eyes were still wide and dark with anxiety but color had come back into her cheeks and she no longer looked on the verge of panic.

"There's a box of baking soda in the door of the fridge. Mix a spoonful with a little water in a glass to make a paste. It's the best *med'cine* there is for a bee sting."

"Baking soda?" Beth looked momentarily blank. "Baking soda. I don't—"

"Yes, you do. It's a white powder in an orange box," Faith said patiently.

"Orange box?" Her anxious expression cleared a little. "I remember. Baking soda. Brush your teeth. Make cookies."

"Now you've got it." Faith used the same soothing tone for Beth as she had for Caitlin.

"Make a paste. In a glass or a dish?"

"Either will do." Faith smiled. "And a cold compress. There are clean cloths with the cleaning supplies on the table."

"Cold compress. That, I remember."

Five minutes later Caitlin's cries had dwindled away to a few hiccuping sobs. Her hand was smeared with baking soda paste and wrapped with a cool, wet cloth. She was leaning against Faith's shoulder as she rocked in the red chair, Addy on guard at her feet. Beth sat beside them, looking out over the meadow toward the house.

"I think she's falling asleep," she whispered.

Faith nodded. "She's had a very busy week. She's behind on her sleep."

"I thought she must have fallen and broken both her arms and legs the way she was crying," Beth confessed.

"She has very good lungs." Faith kept a straight face with difficulty.

"You acted as if it were all just so ordinary."

This time Faith did let her smile break through. "She's two and a half, Beth. Bee stings and bumps and owies are all in a day's work for mommies."

Beth relaxed against the back of the chair. "You're right. I don't remember being around little kids very much. I haven't had any contact with them since my accident. I haven't trusted myself to be alone with anyone else's child since my baby disappeared."

Faith felt tears sting the back of her throat. So much guilt for Beth to carry, but Faith could do nothing to alleviate the pain without betraying herself. "You did very well with Caitlin today."

"Once I got my brain working again, maybe. But not at first. At first I panicked."

"Only for a moment."

"We both know that's long enough for something terrible to happen," Beth said quietly. Faith was aware she wasn't thinking only of Caitlin's bee sting. She didn't respond. There was nothing she could say.

Caitlin sat up. "Go home. My owie still hurts."

"Let's go watch a video and have something cool to drink," Faith said. She knew better than to suggest a nap. "We'll come back to finish the cabin when it's cooler."

"Let me clean it for you," Beth said quickly, forestalling Faith's automatic protest. "I need something to keep me busy. Kevin won't be back for a while. We're going through the butterfly house later. It's time to get over this butterfly phobia of mine. I'll probably never know where it came from, but I'm going to try to figure it out by bearding the little monsters in their lair." She laughed, trying to make a joke of what was obviously going to be an ordeal.

"If you like, I'll go with you and Kevin, and give you the grand tour."

"Lend some moral support?" Beth stood up smiling and entered the cabin.

Faith felt small and low. "Yes, exactly. And perhaps it won't seem so much of an ordeal with others about."

Beth held open the screen door for Faith to carry Caitlin inside. "I like that idea. It's a deal."

The sound of cars turning into the lane caught their attention at the same time. The Sheldons' green Lexus rolled past the cabins.

"Oh, no." The smile disappeared from Beth's lips. "They're back."

A second car followed, a county sheriff's cruiser. Faith's throat closed, and she fought a sudden wave of nausea as the blood rushed from her head to pool in her stomach.

"What is the sheriff doing here?" Beth stepped back into the main room of the cabin so that she couldn't be seen by the cars' occupants.

"I don't know." Faith saw her own fear mirrored in the younger woman's eyes. For a moment she felt exactly as Beth must feel when words or concepts refused to come to mind when she required them. It was like treading water in a vast sea in the middle of a starless night. "I'd better go see."

"No, don't go," Beth pleaded.

"I have to. I have nothing to hide from Lorraine Sheldon or the sheriff," Faith lied.

Tears welled up in Beth's blue eyes and spilled onto her cheek. She shook her head, looking miserable and torn. "If I go with you they'll start asking me questions about the baby again."

"Stay here. You don't have to talk to them if you don't want to."

Beth was shaking like a leaf, but Faith had no other comfort to give her. She needed it all for herself. It was no coincidence that a sheriff's deputy had accompanied the Sheldons to her home. Lorraine had taken her suspicions to the authorities, and they were here to learn if there was any truth to her accusations.

If Faith couldn't convince them otherwise, her worst nightmare would come true. Her secret would be revealed to the world, and Caitlin would be taken from her.

HUGH WAS ALREADY three-quarters of the way back to Painted Lady Farm when he got Beth's call. Her voice was shaking, and her stutter had returned, but he had no trouble understanding what she was trying to say. The Sheldons were back, and damn them, they'd brought the law. How many strings had Harold and Lorraine pulled to get the sheriff to listen to their story?

Maybe not as many as he'd thought they'd need. The case of Beth's missing baby was still an open one. The authorities would be interested in any new lead that came to their attention.

He could hear the struggle in her voice as she battled to hold back tears. "When can you come back?"

"I should be there in twenty minutes." Or less, he told himself.

"Thank God, but how did you know I needed you here?"

"I didn't know. We had to shut down early today. A city utility crew broke through a water main and flooded the entrance to the access road. Just hang in there. I'll be as quick as I can."

He heard her take a deep breath. "I ran back here when Faith went to meet the Sheldons, but I can't let Faith face them alone. Maybe I should go down to the farm. I—I can tell the deputy he's got the wrong little girl. Caitlin isn't my baby. You were right. It's all just a bunch of weird coincidences. I'd know if she was mine. I'd feel it in my heart even if my brain's forgotten, you know that as well as I do. My baby is still lost."

"Beth. Beth, wait." She'd broken the connection. He pulled the cell phone away from his ear and glared at it as if sheer force of will could get her back on the line. "Damn." Two miles to his exit, then another ten to Faith's farm. Fifteen minutes. Long enough for Lorraine Sheldon to wreak havoc. He tossed the phone onto the passenger seat and stomped his foot down on the gas pedal.

He had set this whole mess in motion and now he had damn well better be able to do something to put it right. Something that wasn't going to break Beth's heart.

And Faith's.

CHAPTER THIRTEEN

FAITH WISHED she and Caitlin didn't look quite so bedraggled. She walked across the parking lot, pulling her daughter in her red wagon and feeling hot and sweaty. Caitlin was still tear-streaked, pouting because she couldn't coast down the hill. Addy had decided to play watchdog and was growling at both the Sheldons and the sober-faced sheriff's deputy standing beside his patrol car.

"Addy, quiet," Faith ordered sharply. The sheltie quit growling but stayed beside the wagon. She bent to brush Caitlin's hair from her eyes, knowing the others had noticed both the makeshift bandage on her hand, and the mulish look on her little face. "Go play on your swing, Kitty Cat. Momma has to talk to these people and then I'll come swing you."

"No," she said folding her arms in front of her and sticking out her lower lip. "Stay here." She glared up at the sun. "I hot."

Faith pulled the wagon farther under the huge maple that shaded most of the backyard. "Does this feel better? It's cooler here." Caitlin rested her elbows on her knees and continued to scowl at all and sundry.

"She's hurt," Lorraine said, pointing to the bandage. She took a step toward Caitlin, but her husband put his hand on her arm and she remained where she was.

"A bee sting, that's all," Faith said. She turned to face the deputy. She held out her hand. "I'm Faith Carson. I'm sorry to keep you waiting. How may I help you?"

"Chief Deputy Gibson, ma'am," he said, touching the brim of his hat with the tip of his finger before shaking her hand. "Mr. and Mrs. Sheldon have come to us with some serious accusations."

Faith was shaking so hard inside she wanted to wrap her arms around herself to hold in the tremors, but she kept her hands at her sides. "And those accusations would be?"

"That you are not the mother of this child." He glanced at Caitlin. "Would you prefer we do this without the child present?"

"I am a widow, Deputy Gibson. My daughter is only two, too young to be left alone in her room. She is tired and hot, and probably frightened by the three of you. What do you suggest I do with her?" She had no intention of inviting the Sheldons, or the deputy, into her home.

The deputy reddened slightly. "I see your point."

"Where's Beth?" Lorraine interrupted once more. "She should be questioned as well."

"I don't know where Beth is at the moment," Faith said, selecting her words carefully. "I was cleaning one of my rental units when I saw your cars turn into the lane. I came as soon as I could.''

''Beth is off somewhere with that boy she's been seeing, isn't she? It doesn't matter. She will only claim she can't remember anything.''

''Lorraine, you're not being fair. You've seen the doctors' reports. Beth isn't faking her amnesia.'' Faith was somewhat surprised that Harold Sheldon had contradicted his wife so publicly. In the short time Faith had known them he'd mostly remained silent.

''It was you who was hysterical yesterday, Mrs. Sheldon,'' Faith couldn't stop herself from saying, ''not Beth.''

Deputy Gibson cut in. ''Beth is Beth Harden, the missing baby's mother?''

''Miss Harden has been staying in one of the cabins with her brother for several weeks. He's an engineer working on a project north of the city. Mrs. Sheldon and her husband arrived several days ago. She told me she found Painted Lady Farm on the Bartonsville Chamber of Commerce Web site, just as Mr. Damon did. I had no idea there was a connection between them until that time. Mrs. Sheldon believes that Beth Harden is my daughter's real mother. When she made her belief known to me I was very upset, as you can understand. I asked her and Mr. Sheldon to vacate their cabin and leave my property.''

''Can't say as I blame you,'' the deputy said under his breath. He was a sandy-haired, whipcord-thin man about her own age. ''But enough of what Mrs.

Sheldon claims checks out that my boss asked me to come out here and talk to you.''

''Am I under arrest?'' Faith asked.

He hooked his thumbs in his gun belt and looked down at Faith from under the brim of his hat. ''Did I say that?'' he asked.

''No. I'm sorry, Deputy. This is all very upsetting, surely you must see that.''

''I admit it's one hell of a story.'' He leaned his hip against the fender of his car and turned to Lorraine and Harold. ''Why don't you start at the beginning so I can get this all straight. What makes you think that the little girl is your grandchild?''

''So many things,'' Lorraine said.

Harold spoke up. He and Lorraine were standing in a pool of hot, yellow sunlight while Faith and the deputy were in the shade. He squinted against the sun. He wasn't wearing a hat and perspiration began to bead on his forehead. ''Caitlin was born the same day as our son died. We have searched the country over for the past two and a half years. We had no idea Beth's brother was still searching for the child, too.''

''Something led him to this place and this woman and child,'' Lorraine broke in. She, too, was looking flushed. She held out her hand as though to implore the deputy to see her reasoning. ''It's not just coincidence that Hugh Damon brought Beth to a place where a woman with no husband gave birth to a baby without a single witness on the same day our grandchild was born. He knows something more, I'm convinced of that.''

While Lorraine had been talking the sound of a car engine approaching underscored her passionate words. Faith felt the knot of nerves in her stomach tighten still further. She didn't want to deal with a carload of tourists wanting to tour the butterfly house. She didn't want friends or neighbors to see her being interrogated by the police.

Or, perhaps it was Peg. Dear, loyal Peg, who would stand by her side and compromise herself still more to keep Faith's world intact.

But it was neither tourists nor her sister who pulled into the parking lot. It was Hugh's black Blazer. And he wasn't alone, Beth was with him. Faith hadn't expected him to return for several hours. Even if Beth had called him as soon as she got back to their cabin, there was no way he could have made it back to Painted Lady Farm so soon. He'd obviously returned for some other reason and found Beth, who'd told him everything. Hugh parked beside the deputy's cruiser and walked around the truck to help Beth out of the vehicle.

Faith searched his face for some clue to his thoughts as he held out his hand to the deputy and introduced himself and Beth. His expression gave nothing away. Faith had no idea what he would say. Since she had dismissed his offer would he add his accusations to the Sheldons' and strengthen their claim?

"We have a pretty good idea of why you're here," Hugh said to the deputy without preamble.

Deputy Gibson was equally blunt. "Your sister is the mother of the missing baby?"

"I am." Beth looked pale but composed. She kept her gaze averted from Harold and Lorraine and stood close to Hugh.

"This is a very unusual case. You all understand why the sheriff wanted me to check it out."

"We understand," Hugh said. "We all want to believe we'll find Beth's baby someday. But Mrs. Carson's daughter is not my sister's child." Faith fought to keep her relief from flooding her face and giving her away. He was only trying to protect Beth, she warned herself. He had not had a change of heart.

"Can you prove that?" the deputy asked. He spoke to Hugh but he looked at Beth. She stayed silent. It was Lorraine who spoke.

"If she's not Beth and Jamie's baby, why did you come here in the first place? Why did you bring Beth?" she demanded, crossing the sun-dappled space between them.

"I came because of my work." Hugh stepped forward, blocking Lorraine's path to his sister.

"You came because something drew you. What was it, Hugh? I don't know what clue led you here but I intend to find out."

Hugh's voice was as steady as his tone was unyielding. "There's no clue, Lorraine. I admit there are coincidences. Caitlin's birth date is the most obvious."

"Mrs. Carson, your daughter was born at home and not in the hospital, am I correct?" Deputy Gibson asked. He had taken a black spiral notebook from his shirt pocket and flipped it open.

"Yes." She was on familiar ground here, she didn't falter. "My husband had died six months earlier. I was alone. I went into labor early, in the middle of that terrible ice storm we had three years ago in November. The phone was out. I couldn't drive myself to the hospital because the roads were so bad."

"You also didn't seek any prenatal care from any doctor in the area, is that correct?"

The question caught her off guard. No one had asked it before. She supposed it was because most people assumed she had been seeing a doctor. They were always more interested in the story of the delivery. "That is correct. I—I wasn't thinking very clearly after my husband died, but my pregnancy was uneventful and thankfully Caitlin was born healthy." She never embellished her lies.

But as she spoke a frightening new possibility had entered her mind. Was it possible the authorities, or the Sheldons—or Hugh—would now try to track down the doctor in the remote Mexican village they'd taken her to after the accident, and prove she had never carried her baby to term?

"You registered your daughter's birth at the county records office six days after she was born."

"Yes, that was the first day I felt safe enough, and strong enough to leave the house."

"I still can't believe this state doesn't demand more concrete proof of maternity than just turning up with a baby in your arms," Lorraine said scathingly.

"You'll have to take that up with the state legislature, ma'am," the deputy said dryly.

"She's not my baby, Deputy." Beth blinked back tears and her voice rose a little even as she struggled visibly to control it. "No one will believe me. I don't remember anything about this place. I don't remember ever seeing Faith until my brother brought me here."

"If you'd only allow the hypno—"

"No! I won't. I'm not going to remember what happened that day, no matter how many therapists you try to bully me into talking to, don't you understand that?"

"I only understand my son is dead because of you and the one thing that would give me comfort, my grandchild, might be dead because of you, too." For the second time Faith saw Lorraine Sheldon shaken out of her polished calm, her face was contorted with grief and frustration.

"Shh, Lorraine. Don't say anymore. You'll regret it later, you know you always do." Harold put his arm around her shoulders and drew her against his chest. Every day of his sixty-some years was visible on his face. The sorrow in his expression was of a man who knew he might never see his only grandchild before he died.

Hugh had his hands on Beth's shoulders, steadying her, comforting her. Only Faith stood alone. She knew it was the way it had to be, but she longed for someone to stand beside her.

The longing surged into her veins. Longing not for Mark, the man who had once held that place in her heart, but for Hugh, the one man she could never have.

She felt a tug on the hem of her shorts. "Mommy. I'm hot. I want a drink."

She looked down. Caitlin had climbed out of her wagon and stood looking up at her, tear streaks dried on her face. "Don't like them," Caitlin said, pointing her finger at Lorraine and Harold. "Go away," she said loudly. "You're bad."

The pronouncement had the effect of drying Lorraine's tears. "Don't be angry, Kitty Cat," she whispered cajolingly. Faith wanted to scream at her not to call Caitlin by the name Faith had given her when she was only hours old and had made little mewling sounds as she tried valiantly to suckle from the makeshift nipple. "I like you very much."

"Don't like you. Go away," Caitlin repeated.

"Yes, please. Go away," Faith said. "I don't want my daughter upset any more than she already has been. Deputy Gibson, isn't it plain Mrs. Sheldon's grief is causing her to labor under a false assumption?"

Lorraine tore her eyes away from Caitlin and fixed them on the deputy with a desperate intensity. "No, wait. I demand some kind of action. Surely, you can order Mrs. Carson to have blood tests, or DNA tests, or something. All you have is her word against mine.

Caitlin is my granddaughter. I know it. I feel it in my heart and soul.''

''I will do no such thing.'' Faith no longer had to fight to keep the tremor from her voice. She was suddenly forged of rock and steel. She could never allow that to happen.

Lorraine's eyes narrowed. ''Why should you object if you've nothing to fear?''

''I refuse to discuss your unfounded accusations any further. I want you off my property. At once.'' Rock and steel. She clung to the image to keep her inner terror at bay.

''Deputy—'' Lorraine's voice had grown shrill once more.

''I don't have the authority, ma'am,'' Deputy Gibson responded patiently. ''All I can do is report back to the sheriff, and he'll contact the Indiana state police. If they see any reason to reactivate the case they'll let us know.''

''That's all?'' Lorraine was incredulous. ''Why, by tomorrow morning Mrs. Carson could be on her way out of the country with the child.''

Deputy Gibson looked around at the flower beds, the greenhouse, the well-tended lawn and garden. ''I don't think that's likely, ma'am. I suggest you and your husband do as Mrs. Carson asks and leave. We don't want this to get unfriendly.''

''I'll do no such thing. Not until I get some satisfaction. I'll find someone with the authority to make Mrs. Carson comply. My husband is a very wealthy man, Deputy. We have friends in very high places. They know how I've suffered these past months. They'll see to it we get the answers we need.''

''You do what you think you have to, ma'am. I don't have any jurisdiction in a civil case, and until I receive an order from someone who does, I'm going to be on my way. Go back to your motel. Get out of the sun and get some rest.'' It was an order, politely stated. He touched his finger to his hat brim once more. ''I'll be in touch.''

He got in his cruiser and drove away leaving the others standing as though they'd been rooted in place. Lorraine was still crying, and now Caitlin was sniffling. ''I'm thirsty,'' she whimpered.

Faith picked her up and cradled her in her arms. ''Please go. All of you.''

''I meant what I said,'' Lorraine repeated as her husband put his hand under her elbow, urging her toward their car. ''I won't rest until I have absolute proof that Caitlin is not my grandchild.''

''Is that a threat?''

''If you chose to interpret it that way. We can do it the hard way, lawyers and lawsuits and more visits by the likes of Deputy Gibson. Or we can settle the question in a matter of days. I'm willing to pay for any tests necessary for you to prove to me that Caitlin is your child.''

''Don't do it, Faith,'' Beth said. Her voice was tight with strain, but steady and her speech was clear. ''You don't have to prove anything to her.''

Lorraine waited for a full minute while Faith

searched her brain frantically for some way out of the trap she'd fallen into. She couldn't say yes to the tests and silence would condemn her, just as surely.

Triumph was evident in the older woman's eyes. "Our lawyers will be in touch. That is unless the sheriff decides to take matters into his own hands first."

"We're staying at the Lebanon Inn in Carrington," Harold said. Carrington was the county seat, about twenty miles north of Bartonsville. "If you want to discuss this further we'll be there." He looked as if he wanted to say more, but did not. He took Lorraine's arm and helped her into the passenger seat of the Lexus, then got behind the wheel.

A minute later they were gone. Faith was shaking so hard she thought her legs might give way and she would find herself sitting on the ground. She didn't look at Hugh and Beth. She couldn't. She walked to the pump and set Caitlin on her feet. She began working the handle.

What was going to happen to her and Caitlin now? How long could she fight off Lorraine and Harold Sheldon?

She dropped to her knees to offer the ladle of cold, spring water to Caitlin. She took a big drink, water dribbling down her chin. She wiped it away with her bandaged hand and gave Faith a big, wet smile. "Good, Mommy. But I still need a cookie."

Caitlin. Her love. Her reason for living. Tears pricked behind her eyelids and she blinked them away. She felt Hugh's presence behind her, warm and strong and solid. She no longer considered him her enemy, but could she trust him enough to make him her ally? Her husband? If she told him her secret could they somehow find a solution that would allow her to keep her daughter? Or would she only be giving him the weapon he needed to take Caitlin away?

CHAPTER FOURTEEN

FOR THE NEXT FEW DAYS Faith waited for something, anything, to happen. But she heard nothing from Harold and Lorraine Sheldon, or Deputy Gibson. Hugh, also, had taken pains not to be alone with her, although there had been times, even amid the noise and crowds of Bartonsville's Fourth of July celebration they all attended, that he could have taken her aside. Did he regret the kisses they had shared? The offer of a partnership, a marriage, that he had made? She thanked God for the reprieve from the Sheldons, but could not bring herself to feel the same relief about Hugh.

One thing had changed over the holiday weekend. Beth had come into the butterfly house. It wasn't Kevin, or Hugh, who accompanied her, but Caitlin.

Faith looked up at the sound of the air lock opening and saw her daughter leading Beth by the hand. It was late in the afternoon, and the butterflies were everywhere, darting and flitting among the plants, sunning on the rocks of the waterfall, sipping delicately at the feeders.

"See. Pretty," Caitlin said, tugging Beth toward a

trio of black-and-gold Australian skippers congregated on a purple African milkweed flower.

"I thought you were swimming with Jack, Guy and Kevin?" Faith said summoning a smile that she hoped showed none of her inner turmoil. Both Caitlin and Beth were wearing Patriot T-shirts over their bathing suits, and matching hot-pink flip-flops that Beth had found at the Volunteer Fireman's flea market booth the day before.

"She was missing you, so I brought her here to find you." Beth's smile looked as strained as Faith's felt.

"Don't touch the butterflies," Caitlin cautioned shaking a grubby finger.

"Don't worry," Beth said with a quivering laugh. "I won't touch."

"Are you all right?" Faith was torn between pride in Beth's courage and the ever-present trepidation that each step forward she took could trigger her memory.

"Caitlin doesn't understand phobias. She insisted I see all the pretty butterflies." Her voice was bright, but her eyes were large and apprehensive.

"You can leave her with me," Faith said. "You don't have to stay."

"No. I want to. I told Kevin it was long past time for me to face this." She let Caitlin tug her along the path to the big waterfall then sat down beside her on the rock ledge bordering the pool. "It is pretty."

"I think so." Faith sat on the bench across the path and waited. She'd turned on the fans to move the warm air and it stirred Beth's silvery hair. She pushed it back off her cheek. Her hair had grown longer since she'd arrived at Painted Lady Farm. It was almost the same length as Caitlin's now.

Caitlin slipped off her sandals and dabbled a toe in the water, watching for Faith's reaction from the corner of her eye. Her daughter hadn't asked permission, but Faith let the infraction pass unremarked. It was very warm, after all. Now both feet were in the water. "No splashing," Caitlin said, to show she knew the rules even when she was bending one of them. "'Flies don't like to get their wings wet."

Beth watched an orange-and-black giant African swallowtail float majestically by. She looked down at the top of Caitlin's shining head, then shifted her gaze to Faith. "Nothing," she said. "Nothing but butterflies. I thought...I thought maybe something would come back."

"Do you still have the dream?" Faith asked softly. She was on dangerous ground when she talked with Beth about the past, more so since Deputy Gibson's visit.

"No. No more butterflies and blood on the snow. But...I dream of her." She dropped her eyes to her hands. "I hear a baby crying and I keep looking but I don't find her."

Water flew from the pool to cover them both. Caitlin's dabbling had grown more energetic as they'd talked and finally her feet had broken the surface of the water. "Caitlin!"

Beth jumped to her feet, the back of her shirt soaking wet. "Yikes," she said shaking her head to get rid of the droplets in her hair. "That's cold."

"And that's a no-no," Faith said, scooping Caitlin into her arms, relieved that the conversation had been interrupted.

"Sorry," Caitlin said, but she didn't look sorry. Butterflies were on the move throughout the habitat. All those sunning on the waterfall had flown to safety, disturbing others at their rest, causing traffic jams on the feeding trays. Caitlin flapped her arms. "I fly, too."

"You're flying inside for a nap," Faith said.

"I'll stay out here and watch the greenhouse until she's settled."

"You don't have to do that."

"Yes, I do. I have a lot to think about," Beth said, watching a quartet of elegant and sophisticated-looking black-and-white tree nymphs as they glided by in formation.

Faith's throat was tight. What if she told Beth the truth? Between them could they come to some arrangement that would allow her to keep Caitlin? It seemed as the days passed the little girl brought them closer together, but she also kept them apart. Perhaps she would have found the courage if the Sheldons had not brought with them the danger of the authorities reopening the investigation into the baby's disappearance. With that threat hanging over her head, Faith could not vanquish her own fears and tell Beth the truth.

"I don't think we'll be very busy this evening,"

Faith said. "There's the chicken barbeque in town, and the fireworks coming up. Everyone else is down by the pond. Why don't you go join them? If a car turns in the lane we can see it from there."

A huge, ghostly cecropia moth brushed her forearm as it whispered past and Beth shivered. "Maybe you're right."

"I'm not sleepy," Caitlin insisted, hanging heavily on Faith's arms because she wanted to be let down to walk.

If she put Caitlin down for a nap now she would be able to stay awake for Bartonsville's fireworks display, the finale of the weekend-long community celebration, which was scheduled for dusk. "I want down," she repeated stubbornly, and Faith relented. When her daughter was in this mood she fought sleep like a ninja warrior.

"Okay, back to the pond." Maybe if she sat with her in the covered glider Caitlin would fall asleep on her own. The three of them left the habitat and walked through the greenhouse into the late afternoon. Kevin was coming toward them.

"I've been looking for you," he said, his brown eyes searching Beth's face. He had known where she was and was concerned about the outcome.

"I went to see the butterflies," Beth told him, and linked her arm through his.

"DO YOU THINK they're sleeping together?" Peg asked an hour later as she followed Faith along the meadow path on the regular monitoring walk for the

Ohio Department of Natural Resources. Once a week she followed the same path through her meadow and counted all the butterflies she saw within eight feet on either side. The sun was getting low in the sky and the butterflies were beginning to find their way to favorite nighttime resting places so she was getting a good count. They had left Steve fishing for bluegills in the pond while Kevin and Beth played catch with Jack and Guy under the trees. Caitlin had fallen asleep in the glider on the dock, as Faith had thought she might, and Hugh had promised to keep an eye on her.

"I suppose they could be." Faith pointed out five bright-yellow common sulfurs feeding on a stand of purple clover. Peg penciled the sighting into the log. "If it's gone that far I hope she doesn't get hurt any more than she's already been."

"I think it's more likely Kevin who'll be hurt when she and Hugh go back to Texas."

Faith had been thinking of that day, too. When would it come? How would she feel?

And she would be alone again.

"At least the Sheldons haven't been around the past few days."

"It's like waiting for the other shoe to drop," Faith admitted.

Peg gave an exaggerated shiver. "I know what you mean. She's up to something, I can feel it in my bones."

"She's searching for her grandchild. I don't think there is any more determined creature on earth,"

Faith didn't want to think about Lorraine Sheldon anymore that day. "Look, there's a pair of painted ladies. And the red admiral I've been seeing the past couple of weeks."

"Where?"

Faith pointed out the black-and-orange-red butterfly swaying gently on a tall milkweed pod. "They're territorial. That's his favorite perch."

"Except for the monarchs and the painted ladies they all look alike to me." Peg lifted her hand and shielded her eyes from the sun. "Is it just me or are the kids being awfully quiet all of a sudden? I think I should go see if the boys have Kevin and Beth hogtied to a tree. It's too quiet over there."

The boys didn't have Beth and Kevin hog-tied to a tree. In fact, the entire group was gathered around something on the coarse sand at the shallow end of the pond, including the two men.

Hugh held Caitlin, still sleeping, cradled against his shoulder. He looked at Faith and smiled, and her heart flipped. He had promised Faith he wouldn't leave her daughter's side, and he'd kept that promise, even though he was now standing no more than ten yards from where she had been sleeping. The boys and Kevin were hunkered down on the balls of their feet engaged in an animated discussion.

"What did you find?" Peg called out.

"A turtle," Jack hollered back, as if they were standing in the middle of the cornfield instead of fifty feet away.

The sound of his voice woke Caitlin and she lifted

her head from Hugh's shoulders and gave him one of her glorious smiles.

"What's that?" she asked, instantly wide-awake. She wound her arms around his neck and looked down at the ground. The simple trusting gesture sent heat through Faith, making her intensely aware of how strong and solid and loving Hugh Damon could be.

"Come see," Guy said, hunkered down on the balls of his feet like Kevin.

"If it's a snapping turtle I don't want to see it," Peg informed them.

"Hey, do you think I'd be in this position if it was a snapping turtle," Kevin asked. Beth laughed and the sound was so infectious that Peg and Faith laughed, too.

"It's a box turtle, but a big one," Steve said. "No wonder Hugh and I keep getting the worms stolen off our hooks when we're fishing."

Peg and Faith came close enough to look down at the big turtle, seemingly unperturbed by all the attention as it attempted to amble back into the water. Caitlin had wriggled out of Hugh's arms, but she didn't come directly to Faith, instead she moved cautiously closer to get a better look. Beth reached out and laid her hands on Caitlin's shoulders. The sun shone like spun gold in their hair.

It seemed to Faith that Caitlin and Beth grew more alike physically as each day passed. Or was it only that she was finally admitting to herself how similar they were?

"Stinky," Caitlin pronounced, wrinkling her snub nose. "Take it away."

"I think I will go put it in the creek," Kevin said. "Let him hunt for frogs and minnows like a real turtle. He's getting too big and fat stealing night-crawlers off our hooks in the pond."

"We'll go, too." The boys were already jumping up and down in anticipation of a trek through the meadow to the creek.

"I'm staying here," Beth said. She smiled at Kevin. "It's hot. I'll fix lemonade for you so it's cold when you get back."

"Thanks. I could kiss you for that."

"Later."

Kevin picked up the turtle, which immediately withdrew head and feet into its shell, and headed off to the creek with his noisy minions in tow.

"I'm going to make use of the glider now that Caitlin's not using it for her nap," Peg announced, handing Faith her monitoring log.

"C'mon, Hugh," Steve urged. "Our competition for the bluegills is out of the picture. Let's see if we can hook a couple."

"Sounds like a good idea." Hugh grinned.

"Cookie time," Caitlin said pointedly.

"You just had—" Faith paused as a familiar car pulled into the parking area by the greenhouse.

Peg groaned. "I spoke too soon. It's that devil woman back again." It was indeed Lorraine Sheldon who got out of the car. She was alone and Faith knew with cold certainty that whatever it was the woman had to say she didn't want to hear.

"Who?" Caitlin craned her neck to see who Peg was talking about. "Bad lady."

"Oh, dear," Peg said, pursing her lips to stop a smile from forming. "Where did she pick that up?"

"Hello, Caitlin," Lorraine said, dropping to her knees, heedless of her pale linen slacks. "How are you? Have you been swimming in the pond?"

"Yes," Caitlin said, not looking directly at Lorraine.

"I have a very big pool at my house. It's far away but maybe some day you could come there and visit and we could swim in it."

Caitlin shook her head. "Bad lady. Don't like you."

"Steve, I think we should take Caitlin inside for her snack," Peg interrupted.

"Yes, please," Faith said. Blessed Peg, always there when she needed her. Steve lifted Caitlin into his arms and without another word they left.

Lorraine rose to her feet. "You've turned her against me."

"No," Faith said. "I don't want her upset by you. You're a stranger to her, and a frightening one at the moment."

"And you intend to keep it that way."

"There's no reason she should encourage a friendship between you and her daughter," Beth said. She'd lost all the sparkle she'd had moments before.

Hugh said nothing but took a step closer to his

sister, laying his big hands on her shoulders. The underlying implication was not lost on Jamie's mother. Her defiance left her for a moment. Her lips trembled and she held out a shaking hand. "Beth, don't you want to know what happened to your baby?" she asked. She looked older, less polished, less assured. It was hard for Faith to keep all her barriers in place when twinges of empathy kept sneaking up on her. Lorraine Sheldon was a mother who had lost her son. And her grandchild. She was in pain.

Pain that Faith held the key to alleviating, but dared not use.

"You know the answer to that question. How many times must I repeat it? What did you really come for, Lorraine?" Beth's voice was tremulous, but she didn't falter. It seemed as though she was gaining courage as Faith was losing hers.

"I wanted to give you one last chance to cooperate. For Caitlin's sake. For all your sakes."

"No," Faith said. "I will not give in to your threats. I will not submit myself or my daughter to medical tests, or any other notion that comes into your head."

Lorraine took a deep breath. Her nostrils flared a little as she exhaled. "Very well. You leave me no alternative. I'm going to contact the appropriate authorities in both Ohio and Indiana and ask them to reopen Beth's case. I'm also filing suit in civil court to force you to prove beyond any reasonable doubt that Caitlin is not my grandchild."

"No." Beth's denial was instant and torn from her heart. "You can't. Where's Harold? Does he know you're doing this?"

"My husband had to fly back to Boston on a business matter. But I don't need his permission to do this, Beth. I have means and resources of my own. Friends in high places who know that finding my grandchild is the most important thing in the world to me. They have agreed to help get your case re-opened and then you'll have to cooperate."

She looked at Faith and her eyes were hard. "All of you."

THEY ATTENDED the fireworks display at the town park for the boys' sake. Caitlin had fallen asleep in Faith's arms on the way home and was now tucked away in bed. Peg and Steve and the boys had gone home. Hugh had said good-night and returned to the cabin, Beth and Kevin had gone off together. The holiday was over. Fast-gathering clouds had moved in to block the moon and the smell of rain was heavy on the air. Faith hoped it wouldn't rain too much. Steve had wheat to combine in the coming days, and any delays now would damage the quality of the crop.

She slipped the baby monitor inside the pocket of her dress and stepped out under the trees. She heard footsteps on the gravel and moved deeper into the shadows of the big maple, her heart beating just a little too fast. There was little crime around Bartonsville, but she didn't want to encounter a stranger wandering in her yard in the middle of the night.

"It's me, Faith." Hugh's low voice came to her ears a moment before he stepped into the beam of the security light. "Beth left her CD player here this afternoon. She just called on her cell phone and asked if I would pick it up for her."

Was he having as much trouble falling asleep as she had? Is that why he was awake to answer the phone so late at night? "I saw it earlier on the picnic table. I put it in the greenhouse for safekeeping. I'll go get it."

"It can wait until morning if it's in a dry spot."

"It's not a problem. It will only take a moment to fetch it."

"I didn't mean to startle you."

"You didn't startle me. I just stepped outside for a breath of fresh air before I went to bed." She'd been out in the fresh air all day, and he knew it. Tonight the air was heavy with rain and the scent of new mown grass, making it hard to breathe.

"I'll come with you." He moved to her side as she walked toward the greenhouse, waited as she fumbled with the key and opened the lock. He leaned forward, his arm brushing hers, and pulled open the heavy door panel for her.

"Thank you."

She walked into the semidarkness. "Here it is," she said finding the small, flat oval of the CD player and headphones by touch more than sight.

"Thanks." He seemed to find conversation as difficult as she did. She wished he had never offered her a proposal that had started a chain reaction of impossible wants and wishes inside her. "I'll let you get to bed."

Bed. She would never share a bed with a man again. With this man. The thought saddened her.

"Would you like to see the butterfly house by moonlight?" she asked, because she couldn't just let him walk away into the night.

"The moon isn't shining. In fact I think it's starting to rain," he said. She could barely see the smile that curved the corner of his mouth, but she could hear it in his voice.

"The security light performs the same service as the moon. It's just not as…romantic." There was no other word to finish the sentence. She hurried on. "You've never seen my night-blooming flowers. Peg calls it my moon garden."

He laid the CD player back down on the counter. "Show me your moon garden, Faith."

The air inside the butterfly house was warmer and heavier than outside, although not by many degrees. The scents of night-blooming jasmine and the pale, saucer-size globes of moonflowers perfumed the air. Chopin played softly in the background. She had forgotten to turn off the sound system when she'd closed up, it seemed. The gentle puff of air from the door stirred tendrils of her hair that had escaped from her combs.

One of the huge cecropia moths she'd raised sailed by in the dimness. Smaller moths, lunas and sphinx moths fluttered about the white blossoms enjoying the night.

They moved farther into the habitat, as silent as the winged occupants and stood beside the waterfall. The sound of moving water and the Chopin was counterpointed by the patter of raindrops on the glass roof.

"It's very different in here at night."

Faith nodded although she wasn't certain he could see the movement. "I come here sometimes when Caitlin's asleep just to sit and watch—" And dream a little, she'd almost said aloud.

"Beth told me she came inside with Caitlin before Lorraine Sheldon showed up this afternoon."

"Yes, but she didn't remember anything more." She wished she had been able to hold her tongue but the words had come spilling out.

"I didn't mention it to try to pry information from you, Faith."

She pushed her hands into the pockets of her dress to still their sudden trembling. "I haven't any to give you." She sighed. She couldn't help it. It would always be this way between them. United in silence, but for different reasons. "You're asking because you want to protect Beth."

"I want to protect all of you." He moved a step closer. Faith could feel the heat of his hard, sleek body through the thin fabric of her sundress. Was he going to kiss her again?

She wondered what it would be like to lift her hair from the nape of her neck and have Hugh lower the zipper of her dress. To let the straps slide from her shoulders, to turn and be held in his arms, taken into his bed. She knew, now, that the touch of his lips was as warm and firm as she'd imagined it to be.

"I've found you a lawyer, Faith. She's a friend of a friend. An expert in family law and custody battles. I want you to contact her first thing tomorrow morning."

She blinked in surprise. It was not what she had expected to hear him say. "A lawyer?" She hadn't taken that step herself, although Steve and Peg had urged her to do so. She knew she was hiding her head in the sand, but she couldn't help herself. It was like tempting fate to seek legal representation before she needed to. But, of course, after Lorraine's visit that afternoon she knew she could procrastinate no longer. "I...thank you. I'll consider it."

"Not consider it, Faith," he said exasperation edging his words. "You'll do it."

Her chin came up. "I will make my own decision on the matter." She couldn't give in to the powerful longing to let herself be protected by this man.

"You need to do it for Caitlin's sake."

"It's not in Beth's best interest for you to offer me a lawyer whose services you might need for yourself and your sister."

"Your having expert representation is in all our interests." He reached out and put his hand on her shoulder. "Take my advice on this, Faith, if that's the only thing you let me offer you."

"That's all I *can* accept from you."

He was silent for a moment and then he let his breath out in a low whistle. "Still, I'm going to ask for one thing more," he said. He was so near that if she leaned forward her breasts would brush against his chest.

"I...I have nothing else to give," she whispered. She could not give him her heart. She couldn't accept trust and give only silence in return. But the effort to hold herself aloof left her shaking inside and out.

"All I ask is this." He lowered his head, blocking out the moths, the raindrops drumming on the roof, the light filtering through the tree fern beside the waterfall.

She closed her eyes and waited for what she both dreaded and craved. She opened her mouth beneath the pressure of his. She wound her arms around his neck, let the small distance between them dissolve away. She remembered, after so many days and nights of feeling nothing at all, what it was to be a woman loved. The sudden hardening of her nipples beneath the thin lace of her bra, the slow, hot pooling of sensation deep inside her, the sudden overwhelming need for more.

He made a low, rough sound deep in his throat and smoothed his hands down her back, pressing to bring their lower bodies together. She felt his arousal against her belly, hard and insistent. Faith was dizzy. Would it be so wrong to let him make love to her amid the heavy warmth and heady scents of the butterfly house? They could give each other pleasure and comfort and for a little while, at least, forget the problems that awaited them beyond the glass walls.

Hugh lifted his head and broke the kiss so suddenly Faith felt as though her soul had been wrenched from her body.

"Hugh?"

He rested his forehead against hers. "This is going to get out of hand in another minute."

"I don't care," she whispered, obeying age-old feminine urging, not her brain. She swayed toward him once again.

The muscles in his arms knotted but he tightened his grip only fractionally. "You do care."

He was right, of course. God help them; their situation was complicated enough without adding unprotected sex to the equation. "I'm sorry," she whispered. Sorry for so many things, she meant to say, but not for the kiss. But she hesitated too long and the moment passed.

Hugh touched her swollen lips with the tip of his finger. He looked at her for a long, long moment and then said, "I'm falling in love with you, Faith. I have been, in bits and pieces, since we first met, I think."

She shook her head and the words she spoke seemed sharp and jagged to her ears, as sharp and jagged as the pain they caused her. "Don't you see that's why it will never work out between us, Hugh? Because that's all we can offer each other. Just bits and pieces of our hearts."

CHAPTER FIFTEEN

"IF YOU'RE A GOOD GIRL and stay right here on your swing, I promise Kevin and I will take you for ice cream at the Dairy Barn after you eat your dinner, okay?"

"Okay." Caitlin didn't look as if she planned to stay on her swing for very long, though. Even in the few weeks that she and Hugh had been living at Painted Lady Farm, Beth had noticed changes in Caitlin's behavior. She was growing more independent each day. Just a couple of mornings ago Faith had left her sleeping in her bed while she opened the screened panels on the butterfly house, a job that took maybe five minutes at most. But when she came back to the house Caitlin had awakened and come downstairs to fix herself breakfast. It had taken Faith and Beth—and Addy—fifteen minutes to clean up the spilled milk and cereal. Faith had said she didn't know whether to be angry or scared or proud that Caitlin could get the cereal out of the cupboard, a bowl and spoon from the dishwasher, and the milk out of the refrigerator all by herself. Beth suspected she was mostly proud, even if it was an awful mess to mop up.

Beth counted six cars in the parking lot by the barn. There were two or three women looking over the merchandise in the greenhouse, and a couple of bored-looking, middle-aged men watching as Steve Baden maneuvered a big, dual-wheeled, tractor out of the barn and down the lane to one of the fields that bordered the creek. She gave him a big wave as he rolled by, and he returned it with a wave and a friendly smile of his own. She wondered if he was going to bale hay today. Kevin helped some of the farmers around Bartonsville do that when he wasn't working his summer construction job.

She gave Caitlin one more push on her swing. "I'd better go see if I can help your mommy in the greenhouse," she told the little girl who was leaning precariously far back in the swing, watching the pattern of light and shadow in the leaves overhead. "You stay right here with Addy until Dana or I come back, okay?"

"Okay," Caitlin said, looking at her upside down from the swing.

Steve had dropped Dana off at the greenhouse just as Beth was setting out to walk down the lane from the cabin. Beth liked the teenager. She was bright and quick, and her smile was the friendliest Beth had ever encountered. She was a real help to Faith. Beth hoped she was, too, even if she didn't enter the butterfly house any more often than she had to.

The women who had been shopping in the gift aisle joined the two men outside, showing off their purchases. They all climbed into a big car and drove slowly up the lane to the road. Faith came to the doorway of the greenhouse and Beth waved.

"I'll be back in a minute, Kitty Cat," she repeated over her shoulder. "Stay right where you are."

"It's going to be a scorcher this morning," Faith said, fanning herself with her hand.

"Ninety degrees every day this week with a chance of thunderstorms in the afternoons."

Faith laughed, a warm rich sound that Beth loved to hear, but seldom did these days. "You're turning into a real country girl, listening to the weather report first thing every morning."

"I know. Who'd a' thunk it?" Beth laughed, too. "I'll water the herbs," she offered. "That way I can help keep an eye on Caitlin and you and Dana can do the tours of the butterfly house."

"Thanks, Beth," Faith said. She smiled but it didn't reach her eyes. They were sad and guarded. Beth would have blamed it all on the threats Lorraine Sheldon had made the week before, except Hugh wore the same expression these days. She wished Faith and her brother could find the same kind of happiness she was experiencing with Kevin, but so far it hadn't happened, and that made Beth sad, too.

"Glad to do it." And she was. She liked working with the plants, if not yet with the butterflies. She'd always figured she'd live in the city all her life. Now she wasn't so sure. Now she wanted a house with a garden and a yard where she could grow her own flowers and vegetables and herbs.

Maybe even a house in the country. In a little farming town. In Ohio...

Beth realized she'd been standing in the sun, staring at nothing in particular, for longer than a natural break in the conversation would warrant.

But it didn't matter because Faith was staring at something, too, and from the look on her face it didn't involve daydreams of houses and gardens and red-headed husbands to take care of them. The sound of a car approaching registered at the same time Beth saw dismay, and a flash of stark terror, sweep across Faith's expressive face.

Beth turned as quickly as she could manage, expecting to see Lorraine Sheldon's Lexus. But it was a county sheriff's cruiser coming down the lane. Thirty seconds later the patrol car pulled to a halt beside them and Deputy Gibson climbed from behind the wheel, an ominous and official-looking envelope in his hand.

"Good morning, Mrs. Carson," he said politely. "Miss Harden." He wasn't smiling and his expression was solemn.

"Good morning, Deputy." Faith's tone was even and equally polite, but she was rubbing her palm up and down her arm as though the steamy July morning had suddenly turned cold.

"I'm sorry to do this but I have the duty to serve you with this summons to civil court." He proffered the envelope, and Faith took it, breaking the seal with a fingernail. Her hand was shaking but that was the only sign of the inner turmoil she must be experiencing.

She scanned the pages and looked at Beth. "Lorraine and Harold are suing me to gain custody of Caitlin on their late son's behalf. The suit claims that Caitlin is their grandchild."

She should have been expecting this. She knew that Hugh had given Faith the name of a lawyer, but she didn't know if Faith had made an appointment to see the woman yet. She'd told herself it wasn't any of her business, but of course, it was and she should have asked Faith about it.

"What about me?" Beth heard herself ask the deputy in a voice that was almost as calm as Faith's, although inside she was shaking. She looked down at his empty hands. "Are they suing me, too?"

"I have no knowledge of that," the deputy said.

"Beth," Faith said gently. "Harold and Lorraine are claiming that you are Caitlin's mother. But that you are physically and emotionally unable to seek custody of her for yourself."

"That's not true." Beth couldn't help herself, the words came out high and breathless, making her sound just as weak and unstable as Lorraine and Harold claimed.

"That's for the court to decide, ma'am. I'll be going now. I'm sorry as I can be about all this, Mrs. Carson."

"You're only doing your job, Deputy."

From the corner of her eyes Beth saw another car turn down the lane. She shouldn't be surprised. It was July. People all over the country were on vacation. It was Faith's busiest season, but she wished the new visitors would turn around and drive away again. That everyone here today would go away and leave them alone to deal with this.

"I can give you some good news, Mrs. Carson." Deputy Gibson's expression softened a little around the edges. "The Indiana State Police informed our office yesterday that they see no grounds to reopen the case of Miss Harden's baby's disappearance with only the Sheldons' claims to go on. In light of that finding, our office has declined to look into the matter any further. I'm on my way to deliver that news to the Sheldons."

"Thank you." There was no relief in Faith's tone.

Beth didn't feel any, either, although she supposed she should. What good did it do to have one sword removed from over your head, when there was another one there?

"Good day." He got back into the car and left.

A couple of Faith's customers eyed the departing cruiser curiously but soon went back to perusing the shelves in the shop.

"I hope to God we never see that man again," Faith said in a voice so low that only Beth could hear. She straightened her spine just a little and smiled at the middle-aged couple and three small children, obviously their grandchildren, who got out of the car. "Hello," she said as brightly as though nothing at all in the world was wrong. "Welcome to Painted Lady Farm."

The rest of the afternoon passed by in kind of a blur for Beth. She watered plants, restocked shelves, ate lunch with Dana and Caitlin chattering away about what rides they were going to go on and what food they were going to eat at the upcoming county fair.

Beth did her best to enter into the spirit of their conversation, stoutly defending her choice of funnel cake over cinnamon candy apples as the very best food there was.

Storm clouds gathered on the horizon. Caitlin grew hot and fussy, begging to go swimming in the pond and becoming weepy when she lost her beloved Barbie for the third time that day. As the clouds thickened the butterflies grew less active, coming to rest on leaves and ledges, content to wait until morning for the sun to shine again.

The last customers pulled away as thunder rumbled low in the distance. Beth came out of the greenhouse after a fruitless search for Caitlin's lost doll, just as Steve drove into the barnyard on the tractor. He parked it in the barn and walked over to where Faith and Dana and Caitlin had joined Beth. He traded observations on the state of the weather, both he and Faith agreeing it would be just garden variety summer thunderstorms brewing, quick to blow through, but welcome, before he and Dana drove off in his pickup.

"Steve's going to hang up the Closed sign," Faith said, rubbing the back of her neck with her hand. Caitlin was holding on to her hand, her face tear-streaked. "And I'm going to take Caitlin in for a short nap."

"No nap," Caitlin whined. "I'm not sleepy. I want Barbie to go swimming with me."

"No swimming. It's going to rain," Faith said. She sounded tired. She looked frayed and distracted suddenly, and Beth realized what an effort it must have taken for her to appear upbeat and welcoming all afternoon long.

"Why don't you lie down with her?" Beth suggested. "I can lock up the cash drawer and close the screen panels before I go back to the cabin."

"You don't have to do that." The words were automatic, good manners, nothing more.

"I know I don't have to. I want to. Please, Faith. Let me help you."

She nodded, as though her mind were on other matters, and Beth knew what those matters were. The summons was sitting on the counter in Faith's kitchen. Beth had seen it when she took Caitlin inside to get a drink of juice a couple of hours ago. She'd been tempted to read it, to see her name spelled out in black and white, as a woman who was so fragile and unstable she couldn't be trusted with custody of her own child—if that child turned out to be Caitlin.

It was all so complicated. She wished Hugh were here to help her work through it. She wished Kevin were with her for the same reason.

Faith picked Caitlin up, holding her close as she walked slowly into the house without looking back.

As the door swung shut behind her, a van pulled

into the yard. Four adults and three children piled out. "We've been driving around for half an hour looking for this place," a large, red-faced man informed Beth. "We're on our way back to Michigan. We came to see the butterflies."

"I'm sorry, we're closed," Beth said. Another low rumble of thunder off in the west underscored her words. "Butterflies don't fly much when it's cloudy."

"We really would like to see them," the older of the two women replied. A family group on vacation Beth guessed, parents, kids, and grandma and grandpa.

At that moment the sun broke from the clouds and a large patch of blue sky grew with it. "Look," one of the children said, pointing up. "The sun's shining now."

Beth added up the admission charge for seven people and made her decision. There might as well be some extra money in the cash drawer to make this awful day a little less awful. And she had nothing else to do until Hugh or Kevin came home except fuss about what the Sheldons were trying to do to Faith. "All right," she said. "None of our interpretive guides are here right now, but I can let you go through the butterfly house on your own if you are careful to follow our rules."

It was over an hour later before the van and its occupants left. Beth was hot and sticky and sorry she'd given in to their demands. Not that they'd been loud, or obnoxious or misbehaved, but the humidity had been climbing steadily the whole time they were inside until the building felt like a sauna.

Beth locked the cash drawer and hid it between the two bags of mulch the way Faith had showed her, closed the screen panels and locked the greenhouse door. It was after five, the storm clouds had regrouped, and thunder sounded all around her.

She trudged across the yard and started up the lane, her leg aching more with each step. The barometer was falling in advance of the storm and she felt it in her bones. Oddly enough the ache now made her realize that it hadn't bothered her for days. She was getting stronger here at Painted Lady Farm. In body and in spirit. Lorraine and Harold Sheldon would learn that to their dismay, once she talked to Hugh and figured out how they would be able to help Faith fight the suit.

She did intend to help Faith. Caitlin was not her baby. She would know that, she repeated over and over in her mind, with each step she took. A mother would know her own child.

She caught a glimpse of Hugh's Blazer turning onto the road that ran along the edge of the farm before it disappeared down the rise. If she quickened her pace she'd arrive at the cabin just about the same time he did.

"Beth!" She spun on her heel. The note of anxiety in Faith's voice was impossible to ignore. "Beth, are you still here?"

"A vanload of people wanted to see the butterflies. I let them in...."

Faith brushed aside her explanation. "Is Caitlin with you?" she asked hopefully, hurrying across the front yard.

Beth shook her head. "No." Her throat closed and she couldn't say more. The terrified look on Faith's face was frightening her.

"Oh, God. I woke up and she was gone. I can't find her."

Beth felt goose bumps rise on her skin. Faith's eyes were big and dark with fear. "She's not in the house. I looked everywhere. I had such a headache. I lay down beside her and fell asleep. She must have gotten outside somehow."

"I didn't see her when I was in the greenhouse." Beth was looking, too, scanning the yard and the fields while she spoke, just as Faith was. The corn was high now, almost as tall as she was. If Caitlin had wandered into the cornfield it would be hard to find her. It might be impossible. Beth shuddered, refusing to imagine anything more.

Addy came around the side of the house and stood whimpering at Faith's heels, sensing her mistress's distress. "The pond," she said in a terrified whisper. "She wanted to go swimming. Oh, dear Lord, what if she's fallen in the pond?"

Hugh's Blazer pulled to a halt in front of the cabin. Beth was torn between following Faith as she ran toward the pond, Addy barking frantically beside her, or running toward the cabin to enlist her brother's help.

Her faith and trust in her brother won over the urge

to follow Faith. "Hugh! Hugh!" she called, jogging as quickly as she dared over the rough ground. He lifted one long arm in a wave and disappeared from view. Surely, he didn't think she was running and yelling for him in ninety-degree weather because she had nothing better to do? "Hugh, it's Caitlin."

She stopped a moment to catch her breath. She could see Faith running toward the deck that jutted out over the deepest part of the pond.

She looked as lost and frightened as Beth herself had for so many days and weeks. She needed a friend to comfort her, to help her in her frantic search. Once more Beth turned back toward the cabin. And what she saw made tears of relief fill her eyes.

Hugh was walking toward her, Caitlin balanced high on his shoulders, laughing, her little fingers clutched tight in his hair.

"Faith! Faith!" Beth hollered into the wind. She began jogging toward the pond, forgetting the heat and fatigue. "Faith! Look!" This time Faith heard her above the rising wind and the thunder. "It's Caitlin. Hugh found her."

Faith put her hand to her mouth as though to hold back a sob. Then she took two steps forward and sank to the ground.

HER LEGS SIMPLY refused to carry her any farther. Faith dropped to her knees and struggled to hold back tears. The surge of relief left her weak and trembling. Caitlin was safe. She wasn't going to find her floating facedown in the pond. Addy jumped onto her lap and licked her face. She closed her arms around the little dog and held her close, letting the panic drain from her.

Beth was talking animatedly to her brother. He bent slightly, nodding once or twice as she talked. Faith knew she was telling him of the day's events, of Caitlin going missing. Was it only five minutes ago? It seemed like five hours. She had never known such a hollow, empty feeling, not even when Mark had died. Not even when she'd lost the child they had made together.

That baby had been just a promise. Caitlin was flesh and blood.

"Caitlin." She held out her arms. She still didn't trust her wobbly legs to hold her weight.

Hugh swung Caitlin down from his broad shoulders and set her on the ground. Her daughter flew into her arms. "I went for a walk," she said proudly. "You were asleep."

"You shouldn't have done that, Kitty Cat," Faith scolded, but her heart wasn't in it. Later, when she wasn't so emotional they would discuss leaving the house on her own. Not now. Now she just wanted to hold her daughter and reassure herself she was safe and sound.

"Hugh find Barbie," Caitlin insisted. "I went to get Hugh."

He dropped to one knee beside Faith. It was the closest they had been in days. Faith took a breath and filled her nostrils with the spice of his aftershave and the scent of his skin. "I'll help you look for

Barbie, but you mustn't frighten your mommy that way any more. Promise.''

Caitlin narrowed her eyes and tilted her head, gauging the seriousness of his words. Hugh didn't blink, look for look. After a moment she nodded. ''Okay. I come with Mommy next time.''

Hugh shifted his gaze and his eyes held Faith's for a moment. They both knew she wouldn't be coming to the cabin, with or without Caitlin. It was Faith who looked away first.

Hugh stood up and reached down. ''C'mon, Kitty Cat. We'd better get inside and look for Barbie. It's going to come down in buckets in a few more minutes.''

Caitlin giggled. ''Like my sand bucket?''

''Even bigger,'' Hugh said, nodding solemnly.

''It doesn't rain buckets.''

''You're right,'' he said, lifting her high over his head so that she squealed with delight. ''My mistake. It's going to rain cats and dogs.''

Caitlin laughed even harder. Hugh settled her in the crook of his arm and reached down to offer Faith his hand. She steeled herself and let him help her stand. He let go of her hand immediately and Faith wished he hadn't. ''I can't believe she walked all the way to the cabins by herself,'' she said to hide the awkwardness of the moment.

''She was sitting on the step waiting for me. She said she came looking for me to help her find her lost Barbie.''

''She couldn't have been there more than a minute

or two,'' Beth said. Faith felt the shaking begin again. Even a minute or two was long enough for her to wander out onto the road, or into the pond. The new spurt of fear must have shown on her face. ''She's fine, Faith,'' Beth said, as though their positions were reversed, and for the moment they were. ''Put it out of your mind.'' There was a world of experience contained in the words.

''I'll try.''

So that was what Beth had been living with these past thirty months. The utter terror of not knowing where her child was. What had happened to her. When, or if, she would ever see her again. Faith's taste of that darkness had been mercifully brief. She hoped and prayed she'd never feel it again.

But she also knew she was going to have to tell Beth the truth about Caitlin's birth. That realization had come to her with blinding certainty when she saw Hugh walking toward her with her daughter safely perched on his broad shoulders. She had it in her power to ease some of the heartache that Beth felt.

Telling Beth everything that had happened that icy November day was the right thing to do. Hugh had known that from the beginning, had done his best to make her see it.

But where was she going to find the courage to speak the words aloud?

CHAPTER SIXTEEN

"HUGH LOOKED so right with Caitlin in his arms," Beth said. They were sitting outside the Golden Sheaf, waiting for the rainstorm to pass. The rain was coming down in buckets as her brother had told Caitlin it would, but according to Kevin, it wouldn't last long. "He loves her. I could see it in his eyes. He loves Faith, too. But I don't think she's in love with him."

"How can you tell?" Kevin had his knee propped against the steering wheel. His eyes were closed, his head resting against the back of the seat. Only their hands were touching, but that was enough contact to make Beth feel all warm inside.

"I don't know." She thought about it some more. "Maybe I'm wrong. Maybe it's not that she doesn't love him. It's that she can't let herself love him."

Kevin's hand tightened a little on hers. He opened his eyes and turned his head toward her. "Do you have a theory as to why?"

Beth sighed. "Caitlin, of course. She's afraid to love anyone who might take Caitlin away from her. Not that Hugh ever would. He doesn't think Caitlin is my daughter. He told me that and I believe him."

Her brain may have short-circuited the connection that would let her recognize her child on some instinctive level when she found her. But Hugh had had no such injury. If Caitlin was of his blood he would have told her so.

"Would you take Caitlin away from Faith?"

She looked out the rain-streaked car window. She wished she hadn't started this conversation. Her mouth was suddenly dry, and her heart had begun to race, not from passion, but from fear. Kevin had been so wonderful to her these past weeks. But she knew he wanted to take their relationship to another level. And not just a sexual one. Kevin wasn't that kind of guy.

"I think Caitlin's the sweetest little girl in the world."

"But...?"

"But I don't feel anything more special than that for her. I don't feel in my heart that she's mine." She'd told him everything else, but she couldn't tell him that she was afraid to let herself believe Caitlin was hers. Because if she did, circumstances might combine to give Caitlin to her. And she couldn't trust herself to raise a child on her own. Tears pricked behind her eyelids. She couldn't stop them. "The rain's letting up," she said hurriedly. The heavy downpour had given them the illusion of privacy. Now the sky was starting to clear, reminding her that the outside world would reappear at any moment. "Let's go inside and order. I promised we'd bring food back for supper. I'm starving. I'll bet you are, too.'' Hugh and Faith hadn't been thrilled by her offer when Kevin showed up a few minutes after Hugh had brought Caitlin back from her wanderings, but she'd made it anyway. Maybe if they spent a little time together things would be better between them.

Kevin made no move to exit the car. ''We need to talk, Beth. I need to know where you stand on this lawsuit the Sheldons are bringing against Faith.'' She had told him about Deputy Gibson's visit on the drive into town.

''I want Jamie's parents gone from my life. From Faith's life,'' she said, pulling her hand free from his. ''I'm not so damn fragile and unstable that I—''

''Couldn't take care of a child of your own?'' He reached out and tugged her hand back into his. Lightning flashed overhead, but it was nothing compared with the jolt of yearning that exploded inside Beth. Red-headed boys like Kevin, a little girl who looked like her to love and cherish. A dream she didn't deserve? Or her future?

''Kevin, please. Don't go there.''

''I need to go there,'' he said softly, but firmly. ''I want kids, someday, Beth. A whole houseful of kids.'' He lifted her hand to his mouth and brushed his lips across her knuckles, mindful of the diners in the Golden Sheaf who could see into the car. ''I want to make those kids and raise those kids with you. I love you, Beth. I want to marry you.''

''THE RAIN'S starting to let up,'' Faith said. She was standing in the breakfast alcove in her kitchen, watching as the fast-moving summer storm raced off across the fields. "Beth and Kevin will be back soon with the food. I'd better set the table. Would you like to eat in the dining room?"

She didn't turn to look at him as she spoke. Hugh had never been in her dining room. He hadn't even been inside her house since the first days after he'd arrived at Painted Lady Farm. "This is fine," he said, indicating the breakfast nook where he knew Faith and Caitlin ate most of their meals.

Caitlin was already seated at her little table, eating Froot Loops and jelly toast, with the faithful Addy standing watch at her side. Her long walk to the cabins had left her too hungry to wait for Beth and Kevin to return, she'd insisted. And from the way she was devouring cereal and toast Hugh had to believe she was telling the truth.

The silence lengthened. If he didn't do something soon, the distance between them would be too wide to ever breach. He took a step toward her, but she sensed his movement and turned, putting the table and chairs between them.

The large envelope containing the Sheldons' suit lay on the table. He touched it with the tip of his finger. "Did you take my advice and see the lawyer I recommended?" It wasn't what he wanted to say, or do. He wanted to take her in his arms and hold her close against his heart.

"She's on vacation. I have an appointment on

Thursday. It's the first day she'll be back in the office.''

"She's very good, Faith. She'll fight for you."

"Then perhaps you should retain her for yourself. To protect Beth's interests."

"I'll protect Beth," he said hearing the gruffness in his own voice. Could he protect his sister? Not from the legalities, but from all the lies that were piling up on each other? His uncertainty must have shown briefly on his face.

"How will you protect her from the pain of learning you've lied to her?" A last flicker of lightning on the horizon punctuated her words. The thunder that followed was low and far away, felt more than heard.

"She never needs to know."

Faith shook her head. She glanced at Caitlin, head bent over her cereal, absorbed in separating all the pink Froot Loops into one part of the bowl. "I can't let you do that. You'll hate yourself for it," she said very quietly. "She needs to know. I'm going to tell her."

"Faith—" He didn't know what to say next. He didn't want to say anything. He just wanted to comfort her.

"When Caitlin was lost…" She swallowed hard and pressed her fingers to her lips to still their trembling. "When I couldn't find her and I didn't know if she'd wandered off into a cornfield, or drowned in the pond, or been taken away by someone who had come to see the butterflies, I realized that I might never see her alive again. Before today, I thought I knew what sorrow was. But this was something more. Something much worse. I realized it's not knowing that withers your soul and leaves you only half alive. I care for Beth. I want her to be free of that terrible weight.''

Hugh had to swallow hard before he could speak. She was trusting him with her most closely guarded secret. "You're telling me that Caitlin is Beth's child.''

She nodded. Her hands clamped around the top of one of the high-backed kitchen chairs, until the knuckles whitened. "Yes. I delivered her in the shelter in the park. Jamie panicked and drove away with Beth, leaving the baby in my arms. I read about the accident later. I'd thought they'd both died. I thought God had given me a miracle. I kept her for my own.'' Two tears ran down her cheeks. He couldn't stand it anymore. He moved to take her in his arms, but she held him off. "No, Hugh. Don't, please.''

"I love you, Faith.'' He had promised not to speak of love again, but he couldn't help himself.

"I know. And I love you.'' She smiled and the pain beneath it tore at his heart. "You said you'd fallen in love with me in bits and pieces. That's the way it was for me, too. And the last piece fell into place today when you came walking toward me with Caitlin on your shoulders.'' Once more he moved to take her in his arms, but she stepped out of his reach. "I love you, Hugh. But you'll never hear me say it again.''

"Why?"

"Because after today, after I tell Beth the truth, your commitment will be to her. As mine will be to Caitlin. No love can survive that kind of conflicted loyalty."

The kitchen chair between them was the kind of tangible barrier he could deal with. He sidestepped it so quickly she couldn't move farther away and took her in his arms. "My loyalty isn't divided. It's to you, to all of you. We'll stand together against the Sheldons. I told you that before."

She swayed toward him for an instant, and in those few heartbeats he rejoiced because he thought he had won. But then she stiffened and pushed lightly against his chest with both hands. "You don't know what Beth will say or do when I tell her the truth. You can't promise me you'll never regret the words you've just spoken, or that I'll regret what I've confided to you."

"I—"

She touched her fingertip to his lips. "And I won't let you lie again."

The familiar sound of Kevin's rattletrap pulling into the yard came through the open screen door. Caitlin's head popped up. "Beth's back," she announced loudly, bouncing to her feet. "She's going to bring ice cream."

Faith dashed away the residue of her tears with the back of her hand. "Please, Hugh. Let me do this my own way. I want the timing to be right. I… It may take me a day or two to get up my courage."

He nodded, there was nothing else he could do.

"I need a moment to get myself together. Beth knows where everything is."

"We'll manage."

"Thanks." She left the room still wearing that sad little smile that tore at his heart.

"Hi, Beth." Caitlin pounced the moment Beth opened the screen. "Where's my ice cream?" she asked. Beth was standing just inside the door, empty-handed. And alone.

"I'm sorry, Kitty Cat. I forgot it." She looked down at her empty hands. She raised stricken eyes to his. "And your supper. I forgot that, too."

"I want ice cream," Caitlin pouted. "I'm telling my mommy. I want ice cream." She bounded away to find Faith.

"Oh, dear, now she's mad at me, too."

Hugh realized he had heard Kevin's Buick turn around and drive away as he talked to Faith. He looked closely at Beth's face. Were those raindrops or tears on her cheeks? She had gone to get food for all of them and returned empty-handed. Kevin had driven off as though the devil were on his tail. "What's wrong, Beth? Did you and Kevin have a fight?"

She gave a harsh little laugh, her mouth twisted into a mocking grin. "Worse than a fight. He asked me to marry him."

"You don't look like a newly engaged woman."

"I'm not engaged. I told him I couldn't marry him."

She looked so young and so lost standing there. But even though she was young in years, she was old in disappointment and heartache. He loved her so, and Faith was right. He had only made her pain worse by telling her he didn't believe Caitlin was her child. "Do you love Kevin?" he asked.

"Yes, but that's not enough." Her tone was tear-filled, but firm.

"Why? He knows about the baby. He obviously loves you enough that it makes no difference to him."

"It makes a difference to me. Don't you see, Hugh? Kevin wants a family someday. He loves kids. He's good with them. And I—I can't trust myself. I can't take the risk of having a baby until I know what happened to my little girl." Tears were running freely down her cheeks now, and she did nothing to wipe them away.

Hugh hated seeing her in such pain. He would do anything to take the pain away. But only Faith could do that.

"I can't marry Kevin until I know that I did no harm to my child." She wrapped her arms around her stomach, swaying a little, holding in her misery. "I can't remember." Her eyes flickered past him to the doorway where Faith stood, a still-pouting Caitlin in her arms.

Hugh sought her gaze. "It's time, Faith," he said.

She searched his face for a long, long moment, then closed her eyes, nodding slowly.

"It's time." Involuntarily her arms tightened

around the little girl. Tears glistened in her eyes but she blinked hard, holding them back. She looked past him to Beth. "You don't have to wonder what happened that day any more, Beth. I can tell you everything you want to know. You see, Beth, my daughter is your daughter, too."

Sometimes when you're given what you thought you wanted most, it turned out not to be the best thing after all. Beth laid a small bouquet of cornflowers, Queen Anne's lace and little yellow wildflowers whose name she didn't know, in front of Mark Carson's stone.

Caitlin had been told this man was her father. She pointed to his picture on the mantel in Faith's living room and called him Daddy. But what of Jamie, whose grave was in a Boston cemetery that Beth had never visited? Should Caitlin be told of him someday?

"And what about me?" Beth closed her mouth with a snap. She was talking out loud to herself again, something she hadn't done in a while. *What should Faith tell her about me?*

Faith had answered one question for her three nights ago, but in answering one, she had created so many more.

And knowing that Caitlin was her baby, alive and safe and happy, hadn't made everything right for Faith and Hugh. They tiptoed around each other as though they were walking on eggshells.

Hugh tiptoed around her, too, because she had

taken her frustration and unhappiness out on him when they were alone. He had lied to her about Caitlin, she had stormed in the privacy of their cabin. He had never done that before. Maybe she wouldn't have been so blindsided by Faith's confession if he had told her what he'd really believed.

It had been so overwhelming. She had not let herself believe that Caitlin was her daughter, because she'd never felt a mother's love for the little girl.

Faith hadn't changed the way she acted toward Beth. She didn't forbid Caitlin to spend time with her. But everything was different. In those first sweet moments she'd indulged her most private fantasy of sweeping her lost child into her arms and never letting her go. She hadn't acted on that fantasy, but Faith had read it in her eyes.

Until last night. Beth had been playing a matching game of shapes and colors with Caitlin on the picnic table as Faith closed up the butterfly house. Hugh was jogging. He wouldn't come back until dark, she knew, and then he would go straight to his room, avoiding being alone with her.

Caitlin was ready for bed. Beth had given her her bath for the first time. Her fine, silvery hair was in pigtails. She was wearing a sleeveless, petal-pink nightgown with ducklings and bunnies sprinkled over it, and her little bare feet peeked out from under the hem. Beth thought to herself, *Now I can go shopping for Caitlin and buy frilly pink nightgowns and even fuzzy bunny slipper to match if I want to. I'm her mother.*

Caitlin was jabbering away a mile a minute about how Addy was going to be in real trouble if she didn't quit chasing skunks. "Skunks," Caitlin informed her knowledgeably, "smell the worstest of anything in the whole world." She clamped her hand over her nose and squinched up her eyes. "P U," she said, fanning the air in front of her face.

"Caitlin, it's time for bed," Faith said coming through the gate. She didn't betray any of the pain she was surely feeling at the sight of Caitlin almost sitting in Beth's lap.

"Nope," Caitlin said, picking up a yellow square and placing it on the matching shape on the game board. "I stay with Beth."

"It's late, Kitty Cat. You'll be sleepy in the morning if you don't come to bed now." Faith sidestepped the child's demand. She didn't look directly at Beth anymore. It was as if she couldn't bear to see the same love she felt for Caitlin in Beth's eyes.

"Then sleep over with Beth." Caitlin hopped up and threw her arms around Beth's neck. It was so spontaneous, so right feeling that Beth had hugged her back, never wanting to let her go.

"It's all right. I'll take her to the cabin for a while."

"Sleep over," Caitlin insisted.

Caitlin slept over at Peg's house. She'd even stayed all night with Dana once or twice. Surely, it would be all right for her to stay at the cabin only a couple of hundred yards away. "Would it be all right if she stayed with me?" Beth asked. Faith's gaze settled on a spot just past her left ear, or so it seemed. She looked fragile, as though the sadness was growing so heavy within her that she could barely stand up under its weight any longer. Beth wanted to reassure Faith, but the expression "little pitchers have big ears" wasn't just some old-fashioned saying anymore. Caitlin was so quick and smart. She had already picked up on some of the tension swirling between the three grown-ups. Beth didn't want her to become aware of any more.

"All right, but you must put your game away and go potty." Faith's voice broke a little on the words. Beth wanted to put her arm around Faith and tell her everything would be all right. And it would be, but for the moment, just this one night, she had wanted to savor the wonder of her child sleeping in her arms.

Hugh was back from his run when they walked into the cabin. He had frowned when she told him with false brightness that Caitlin was going to sleep over. "She's not used to being away from her mother," he'd said carefully.

"I'm her mother," she'd shot back. Couldn't he let her live out this one small dream?

"I know you are." He'd turned away and gone to sit on the back stoop, looking out over the fields as the lights came on in Faith's house.

She had taken Caitlin into her bedroom and let her bounce on the bed, play with the stuffed animals she'd picked up at the Fourth of July flea market, and then curl up beside her and fall asleep.

Lying there beside her sleeping child she had tried

to come up with a way to solve this mess. But she was so distracted by the sound of Caitlin's breathing, the sweetness of her skin, she couldn't make her mind work. She gathered Caitlin's little body into her arms, snuggled close and closed her eyes.

When she woke it was full dark. Hugh was standing in the doorway, silhouetted against the light from the main room. He was still fully dressed, and Beth suspected he hadn't been able to sleep. Caitlin was sitting up in bed beside her, rubbing her eyes, sobbing.

"I heard her crying," he said quietly.

"What's wrong, Kitty Cat?" Beth asked hugging her close. "Did you have a bad dream?"

Caitlin snuggled against her, but didn't stop crying. "Bad lady got me. I'm scared. I want my mommy."

"I'm your mommy," Beth whispered, but the words were almost inaudible. She knew why she couldn't speak more loudly, or more convincingly. Because it was no longer the truth. She looked up and saw Hugh watching her. She swung her legs over the side of the bed and stood up, lifting Caitlin into her arms, walking carefully so that her weak leg didn't betray her.

Beth knew what she must do. It might not have been the decision she would have made three years ago, if Jamie had not forced her to do something else. But it was the right one to make now. "She had a bad dream and she wants her mommy.'' Her voice threatened to crack but she willed it firm. ''If you loan me the keys to the Blazer I'll take her back to Faith.''

CHAPTER SEVENTEEN

TEARS STILL welled in her eyes when Beth thought back to the moment she'd returned her child to the woman who'd raised her.

She'd made her decision, and she'd made her plans. Caitlin's nightmare about the "bad lady" reminded her that Lorraine and Harold must still be dealt with. But above all else she needed to talk to Kevin. He had told her when she realized she was strong enough to handle being his wife and the mother of his children he would be waiting.

She was strong enough. She had proven that to herself when she'd strapped Caitlin into the passenger seat of the Blazer and driven her back to the only mother she had ever known.

She needed to make things right with Kevin.

And her brother. For the past couple of minutes she had watched Hugh climb the hill toward her. He hadn't gone to the site today because he was worried about her, she knew. She had left the cabin before he was awake, not because she was still angry with him for lying to her, but because she needed time to make her plans.

That planning was done now and she was almost

as anxious to make amends with Hugh as she was Kevin.

"You've been up here a long time," he said, as he came toward her, hands in the back pocket of his jeans. "I thought I'd check and see if you were okay." He stayed a step or two away, uncertain of his welcome.

"I'm fine." She patted the stone bench she sat on. It was marble like the oldest headstones, rough with lichen and cool to the touch even though it was a warm afternoon. "I've had a lot to think about."

Hugh took her invitation as the peace offering she intended it to be and sat down beside her. He took off his sunglasses, blinking a little at the brightness. "Including what happened last night?"

She nodded. "I did the right thing," she said softly but with all the conviction she felt.

Hugh rested his forearms on his knees and let his sunglasses dangle from his fingertips. "I know you did." He was silent a moment. "I'm sorry I didn't tell you my suspicions about Caitlin from the beginning. I don't have any excuse except I love you and I didn't want to see you hurt again."

"I think what made me so angry is that you didn't think I could handle it." She blinked back tears. "You've always had faith in me, Hugh. Every day since I woke up after the accident, every step of the way."

"I won't underestimate you again." He reached over and covered her hand with his. "I promise, Beth. Never again."

She launched herself into his arms. "I love you, Hugh."

"I love you, Beth."

She let herself relax against his chest for a minute, then pushed herself upright, wiping away a tear that had somehow sneaked past her resolve not to cry.

"You're going to be fine," Hugh said quietly.

She smiled again. "I know. And I'm going to make it right for all of us."

"How do you intend to do that?"

She'd gone over and over it in her mind so the words just tumbled out. "I'm going back to the cabin to make some calls. Then I'm going to track down Kevin…and make my peace with him. If everything turns out the way I want it to I'll have Lorraine and Harold Sheldon back here in a couple of hours."

"What are you going to do then?"

"What's best for Caitlin. What's best for me." She hoped it was what would be best for Faith and Hugh, also. "I don't have time to explain the whole thing right now. But will you go down to the farm and warn Faith they'll be coming?" He frowned slightly but she didn't let his reluctance to be alone with Faith sway her from doing what she knew she had to. "I—I really want to find Kevin." She reached out and squeezed his hand. "Trust me, Hugh?"

"I trust you." His gaze was direct and unwavering. He reached in the pocket of his jeans and pulled out the keys to the Blazer. "I'm right behind you no matter what it is you have to do."

SHE TURNED into the junior high school just as summer school classes were letting out. She'd been so caught up in her own affairs, she'd forgotten Kevin was substituting for one of the other teachers this week. She'd driven past Peg and Steve's farm to see if he was baling hay, his parents' house, the contractor's where he helped out, looking for his car, before she remembered what he'd told her.

She drove the Blazer up behind Kevin's car and let the engine idle. She tapped her fingers on the steering wheel in cadence with her pounding heart. Now that she was here she was getting nervous. What if he'd changed his mind in the days they'd been apart? What if he'd realized he was taking on way more than he was comfortable carrying? What if—

"Hi, Beth."

She hadn't realized she'd closed her eyes until she heard his voice at her elbow. He was standing at the open window, wearing a green shirt that looked terrific on him.

"I've come back," she said quietly. "I...I've got my head on straight."

He skirted the hood of the truck and opened the door, climbing in beside her. "I've been waiting. And it's been the longest three days of my life."

She rushed into her speech before he could say anything else. "I...I don't know if I'm ready for marriage just yet. Maybe in a year or two. I want to get my degree—"

He smiled and held up a restraining hand. "I can wait. But I have to tell you we can't move in together. It's in my contract. No living in sin for Bartonsville Junior High science teachers.'' She knew he wasn't serious, but it was a reminder they would be living in a small town where everybody knew each other's business.

She leaned over and gave him a quick peck on the cheek. "But we can have great sex in the back of your car.''

He sucked in his breath and pulled her into his arms. "I love you, Beth.''

"I love you. And that's why I'm asking you not to follow me home.''

He kissed her quick and hard and then settled back against the passenger door, putting some distance between them. There were still students coming and going from the school building, and they would be quick to note the two of them sitting in the Blazer.

"Why not? I'm not sure, but I think we just got engaged, or almost anyway. Aren't I supposed to ask your brother's permission or something?''

"I think you're supposed to ask him first.''

He grinned, that sexy, wonderful grin she remembered from the very first time she met him. "Better late than never.''

"Kevin, there's something I have to tell you.''

"That Caitlin is your daughter.''

She supposed it should have surprised her that he knew, but it didn't. "You guessed, too?''

"She looks just like you. At least to me.''

She wasn't going to cry. She had made her decision. "She was born in the little park. Faith came along and delivered her. Then Jamie panicked and drove away leaving her behind with Faith."

"That's why that place bothers you so."

"Some unjumbled part of my brain remembered it, I guess." She sat quietly for a moment. No other memories came to her, and she realized they probably never would. She could live with the blank spots though, now that she knew what had happened. "I've made up my mind what I want to do about Caitlin's future, Kevin."

"Tell me." No long, drawn-out speeches or cautions from Kevin. She hadn't thought it was possible to love him more than she had a few minutes ago, but she did.

"I called the Sheldons. I told them to be at Painted Lady Farm in an hour. I don't want any more hard feelings. I want Lorraine to be at peace, too. She's not a bad woman, really. But if this doesn't work, if Lorraine and Harold don't agree to what I'm proposing, then I don't—"

"You don't want me to be involved. Is that it? Beth, I'm going to be your husband. And in less than a couple years, too. I want to be involved."

The certainty in his voice sent a thrill through her, but she did her best to ignore it. They had the rest of their lives to spend together. For the moment she had to stay focused. "I don't want to risk it. The Sheldons are already suing Faith. After today they'll probably sue me. Or worse, call in the police again. You might have to testify. You—"

"Might be tempted to lie under oath? I'll take the risk. We're a couple now. A team. And what involves you and Caitlin involves me."

He would be Caitlin's stepfather, a wonderful stepfather, if she claimed her daughter. But she wasn't going to claim Caitlin, and he deserved to be there when she told the others.

"I just wanted you to be safe if my plan doesn't work out." Her voice trembled in spite of her best efforts to keep it under control.

His smile was back and she felt as if the sun had come out from behind a dark cloud. "Don't worry. I don't think I'll ever have to contemplate perjury. My money's on you to KO the Sheldons in the first round. I wouldn't miss this fight for anything."

IF SHE COULD HAVE her dearest wish come true it would be for her life to stay as it was at this moment, Faith thought. The day was perfect. Warm, but not too hot. The sky was filled with clouds as white and puffy as the cotton candy the vendors would be selling at the county fair next week.

Caitlin was sitting at her little table behind the counter in the greenhouse, coloring a picture of a roly-poly puppy a bright magenta, chatting away to faithful Addy and two of her nearly naked Barbies. Occasionally she asked Hugh's opinion of a good color for the puppy's tail or dish.

He leaned his hip against the counter and pretended to study his choices.

Faith knew that there was something important he

wanted to tell her, otherwise he wouldn't have come to the greenhouse, but for the moment she didn't care what it was. She only wanted to see him with her daughter, and wonder for a moment what might have happened between them if she had never met Jamie and Beth.

She had just finished showing a vanload of seniors through the habitat and they were taking their time leaving the greenhouse. The ladies of the group looked through the gifts on display, cooed at Caitlin and petted Addy. It was almost twenty minutes later before the van pulled out of the driveway.

"Is there something you wanted to see me about?" she asked coming to stand by him at the counter. There were no more cars in the parking lot or pulling into the lane. Business had been steady all day and she was a little surprised by the sudden lull.

"There is," Hugh said quietly, dropping to the balls of his feet to add a couple of dancing butterflies to Caitlin's picture with a few deft strokes.

"Pretty," Caitlin said, holding up the coloring book for Faith to see. "Thanks, Hugh."

"You're welcome, Kitty Cat." He stood up. "I put the Closed sign out before I came down here."

"Why?" Faith felt her pulse begin to race.

"Beth asked me to."

She looked around. "Is she back? I've been worried about her. She's been gone all day."

"She's fine. She's the reason I'm here. She's contacting Harold and Lorraine, Faith. She wants them to meet us here. That's why I put the Closed sign out. I don't think we'll want customers around.''

''What is she going to tell them?'' She was going to side with Jamie's parents. She wanted Caitlin for herself. Faith felt the color drain from her face. She had feared this would happen ever since she'd told Beth the truth. For a few hours last night, after Beth had brought Caitlin home to her the fear had lessened, but now it was back full strength.

''It's going to be all—'' Hugh never had a chance to finish what he had been going to say. The Blazer turned into the lane and directly behind it was the Sheldons' Lexus.

''They're here. I—''

''Damn, they must have come the moment Beth called them. We didn't expect them for another hour or so.''

''I don't want to talk to them.'' She wasn't ready for another confrontation. She wasn't even scheduled to meet with the lawyer until the next day.

''Beth wants this all out in the open and settled.''

''I'm not ready for this.'' She tried to keep her voice level, ordinary for Caitlin's sake. She looked down. Caitlin was still absorbed in her coloring, her fair head bent over the page.

''Trust me, Faith. Trust Beth. She's made all the right choices the past few days.'' Hugh's voice was ordinary too, but when she looked into his eyes she saw the love he held for her.

Trust me. Faith closed her eyes against the surge of longing that almost sent her into his arms. Not now. Not yet, she told herself. She let the meaning of his words sink into her mind and her heart, let them comfort her. What he said was true. "She has come far since the day you brought her here, hasn't she?" She took a deep breath, let it out with a little whoosh. "I trust her. I trust you." It was the closest she could let herself come to telling him she loved him.

"I'll be there for both of you."

Faith turned to the doorway of the greenhouse as the Sheldons and Beth and Kevin entered. "Hello," she said, to Lorraine and Harold. "I believe Beth has brought us all here to tell us something important."

"I have," she said, looking pale but composed.

Caitlin had raised her head, checking out the group. She frowned at Harold and Lorraine but favored Kevin with one of her huge smiles. "Hi, Kevin."

"Hi, yourself," Kevin said. "I haven't seen the butterflies for a long time. Will you show me around?"

Faith gave Kevin a grateful smile. She didn't want Caitlin to witness what was about to be said. Caitlin took Kevin's hand and went into the habitat. The door closed behind them leaving the five adults standing in charged silence.

Beth folded her hands in front of her. Her knuckles were white beneath the skin, but she showed no other outward sign of nerves. She gave Faith a quick, encouraging nod. "I suppose I should start at the beginning.'' She turned to Harold and Lorraine. ''Caitlin is my baby.''

Lorraine gasped and dropped her face into her hands. ''I knew it,'' she said. ''I knew it.'' Harold put his arms around her shoulders, a smile on his face, but his eyes somber and watchful.

''I was in labor and we were lost. We stopped at that little park down the road from here. It was icy and cold, and I was scared to death. So was Jamie. I know all this because Faith told me. She delivered my baby.''

''And then she kept her!'' Lorraine burst out.

Faith wanted to cry out and defend herself. Hugh rested his hand, very lightly, on her hip. It was a simple gesture, but as meaningful as if he had taken her into his arms. She felt his strength and she stayed silent, allowing Beth to handle the situation in her own way.

''Yes, and I thank God she did. If she hadn't kept her, Caitlin would have died in that accident. We had no safety seat, nothing to protect her.''

''This is the proof we need to have her prosecuted. To get Caitlin back for you,'' Lorraine whispered.

''No,'' Beth said emphatically. ''That's only part of the story. I didn't give Caitlin to Faith. Faith kept her because Jamie panicked and drove away without her.''

''No.'' Lorraine lifted her face to Harold. ''That's not true. Our Jamie wouldn't do that.'' She turned beseeching eyes to Beth. ''You don't remember. You have only this woman's word for what happened that day, and the last thing she wants is for you to claim Caitlin as your own.''

"I may not remember," Beth said softly, but firmly. "But I know that's what happened. Jamie thought it would be faster if we traveled alone. He put me in the car and then he..." She faltered for a moment and lifted her hand to her mouth to stop her lips from trembling.

Faith stiffened. She wanted to go to Beth and comfort her. She remembered the look of anguish on her face that day, would never forget it. She hadn't wanted to leave her child behind. She had had no choice. Behind her she felt Hugh's hand tighten slightly. He knew what her impulse had been, was urging her not to act on it. Beth needed to handle this on her own.

"He asked Faith to keep her until we could come back for her and then...he drove away and left Faith standing in the storm holding our baby. That's why I don't like the park. That's why I never want to go there."

"It was November. There was ice and a storm, why do you dream of butterflies?" Harold asked.

"I was wearing a sweatshirt decorated with butterflies," Faith explained. "Beth focused on it so intently while she was delivering Caitlin that the images must have been so deeply imprinted that even the trauma she suffered couldn't entirely destroy them."

"So when Hugh learned about the butterflies he

started looking for the baby again. That's how he found you?''

''Yes.'' Faith looked at Harold and saw the sorrow of a lost child tempered by the realization that his grandchild was alive and well.

''No wonder the investigator we hired kept coming up blank. He didn't have the key to the puzzle.''

''We'll hire lawyers for you.'' Lorraine's expression showed no such bittersweet happiness, only a single-minded determination to prevail at any cost. She wiped away her tears with a manicured hand, heedless of what it was doing to her makeup. ''You must fight for custody.''

Beth took a deep breath. ''*We* won't hire a lawyer, Lorraine. *I* won't, either, unless you force me to. Faith has a lawyer. A very good lawyer.'' She tilted her head and gave Faith and Hugh a faint smile. Faith smiled back. They were united where Caitlin's future was concerned. Beth stood a little taller, lifted her chin as though ready to do battle for her child. ''She'll advise her on the best way to make everything legal. You see, I won't be seeking custody of Caitlin.'' She didn't falter. ''I gave birth to Caitlin, but I'm not her mother. Faith is.''

''You must fight for custody. Caitlin is all we have left.'' Lorraine looked from Beth to Faith, then frantically to her husband. ''She won't let us see her. You know in Ohio grandparents have no visitation rights. We must find some way—''

''That's enough, Lorraine.'' Harold gave her a gentle shake. ''We are not going to do anything more, do you understand? We will abide by whatever decision Beth and Faith make. I have lost my son. I may never hear that adorable child call me Grandpa, but by God, I will not live the rest of my days referred to as the husband of the Bad Lady.''

He took a step toward Beth and held out his hand. ''My wife and I would like very much to have some part in Caitlin's life. You have my word that there will be no more talk of police investigation or custody battles.''

Beth ignored his outstretched hand, instead she rose on tiptoe and gave him a kiss on the cheek. ''Jamie was trying to bring me back to Faith and the baby when he died. I believe that with all my heart. He was afraid. That's why he drove away. But we were coming back.''

''I know you were.'' His voice broke and he cleared his throat. ''I know.''

The air lock door opened and Caitlin bounced through two steps ahead of Kevin. She spun in a half circle, presenting her backside. ''No butterflies,'' she said proudly. ''Kevin hasn't got any on him, either.''

He went to Beth and took her in his arms. ''Are you okay?''

''I'm fine,'' she said, ''just fine.'' There were tears in her eyes but she was smiling.

''Mommy.'' Caitlin wrapped herself around Faith's legs and sent her a beseeching look. ''I'm starving,'' she moaned, eyes shut as though in abject misery. ''Cookie. I need a cookie.'' She was bent so far backward that her hair brushed the ground. Faith detached her clinging hands and held her so that she didn't topple over. Caitlin opened her eyes and stared at Lorraine. "Bad Lady, go away. Don't like you."

Lorraine's tears dried instantly. She dabbed at her eyes with Harold's handkerchief. "I'm not a bad lady, Caitlin."

"You make my mommy cry."

"She won't do it again," Harold said, going stiffly to one knee to be closer to Caitlin's height. She straightened up and turned around, her hands still in Faith's. "Are you a bad man?"

"No." Harold's eyes glistened but his voice was composed and friendly. "I'm a good man and so is my wife."

"Her?" Caitlin looked skeptical.

"Yes, her."

Caitlin looked him over from head to foot. "Do you have cookies?" she asked.

"Do you know something? I do have cookies. In my car. I hoped we might share them. Would you like to have some with me?"

He looked to Faith for permission. Once more she felt the pressure of Hugh's hand on her hip. Caitlin looked up at her. "Okay, Mommy?"

"Okay."

Harold dropped his head for a moment. "Thank you," he said when he'd composed himself.

Caitlin held out her hand as Harold rose stiffly to his feet. "My mommy says it's okay. What kind of cookies?"

"They're Oreos. My favorite."

"Me, too."

"I knew a little boy once who loved Oreo cookies."

"Boys stink," Caitlin said succinctly. She walked over to Lorraine, hand and hand with Harold. Faith had let her child go to Jamie's father without a single qualm because Hugh had been right. She could share Caitlin's love. Hugh had shown her that about herself as well. She turned to him, and he smiled, once more reading her mind.

"It's the right thing for all of us," he said very softly, for her ears alone.

"I know." She didn't add *I love you*. She didn't have to. He knew that as well.

Caitlin stopped in front of Lorraine and eyed her up and down. "She's not bad?"

Harold looked at his wife, reached up to wipe a tear from her cheek. "No, she's not bad at all."

Caitlin held out her hand. "Then you can have a cookie, too."

EPILOGUE

"HI THERE, beautiful ladies. Want a ride?" Hugh pulled the Blazer alongside Faith and Caitlin. She was pulling her daughter in her wagon down the gentle slope of the lane. Addy danced around her feet barking, but when Hugh spoke she stopped and wagged her tail. Caitlin was wearing a hooded purple jacket, and her nose was pink.

"No thanks, we'll walk." Faith's nose was pink, too, she suspected. It was unseasonably cold for the middle of October, and according to the weatherman there was no warm up in sight.

"I'm cold," Caitlin muttered. "Want to ride with Hugh."

"It's only a little farther. We'll have cookies and hot cocoa later to warm you up."

"Okay." Caitlin perked up at little at the promise of her favorite snack.

"What's going on at the cabin?" Hugh asked.

"Beth and Kevin are arguing over drapes," Faith informed him, rolling her eyes heavenward. "Beth found these fiberglass drapes at the church rummage sale. They're covered with ferns and cabbage roses. Vintage fifties. Truly awful. She's wild about them and insists Kevin hang them in his bedroom. Caitlin and I left them to argue by themselves.'' Kevin had become Faith's tenant the week before. The cabin was winterized and with the addition of two new baseboard heaters it would be comfortable in even the coldest weather. Kevin and Beth could have their privacy, but still maintain the proprieties until their wedding, now tentatively set for late spring. But Faith suspected that if Kevin had his way it would be much sooner.

Beth was enrolling in Wright State University in Dayton, a forty-five minute drive north on the interstate. She was considering a major in psychology, saying she'd undergone enough therapy in the past three years to qualify her for a degree already. Attending a few classes during the winter quarter would ease her back into academic life.

She had even reestablished contact with her father and stepmother in Boston, at least through e-mail. Trace Harden deserved to be told his granddaughter was alive, Beth told Faith, but a timetable for introducing him into Caitlin's life hadn't been set.

Hugh parked the Blazer behind Faith's van and met them in front of the greenhouse, now closed for the season. Steve and Hugh had helped drain the waterfalls and move the big tree ferns and other tropical plants into the chrysalis room where it would be easier to keep them alive over the winter.

She was back at work at the hospital. The news of her marriage to Hugh the second week in August was no longer the main topic of conversation around the nurses' desk, and she was glad for that. She smiled to herself. She had the feeling that something else about her life would soon take its place.

Hugh had met some of her friends and co-workers, who thought him wonderful. He'd gone to church with her and Caitlin, and to the Bartonsville football homecoming game with Steve. They'd been invited to Sunday dinner with Kevin's parents. He seemed to like life in small-town Ohio and had decided to stay on with the Cincinnati engineering firm. His next assignment was rebuilding a hundred-year-old bridge over the Ohio River, a project far more to his liking than constructing a shopping mall.

She had everything she had ever wanted from life, and more. She placed her hand on her still-flat stomach. She wasn't certain, hadn't taken a test or gone to the doctor. But she was sure she was pregnant. She felt her color rise and hoped the chill in the air would hide her blush.

Another love. Another child. Miracles both.

Caitlin climbed out of the wagon and ran to Hugh. "I need my Barbie," she said breathlessly as he lifted her high above his head. "She's in the greenhouse."

"I don't think so, Kitty Cat," Faith said. "You haven't played there in days."

"She has so many dolls I'm surprised she even notices when one is missing." Hugh rubbed noses with Caitlin to show he was only teasing.

"Believe me, she notices." Tonight when they were alone in her bed—their bed—she would tell him about the baby. She wondered what he would say. Would he think it was too soon? She watched her husband, Caitlin secure in his arms, as he carried her to the greenhouse, and her worries dissipated like mist in the sunlight.

No, he would not think it too soon to add to their family. Because they were a family. An unorthodox one to be sure. Beth and Kevin would always be part of Caitlin's life. Faith accepted that. Their children would grow up side by side.

The lawyers were still deciding on the best course of action to legitimize Faith's custody of Caitlin. It was an unusual case they all agreed, each step must be carefully evaluated before being taken. But in the end they had no doubt Caitlin would be Faith's legally and forever.

And there was also Harold and Lorraine to deal with. They had returned to Boston at the beginning of October, but planned to be in Ohio for Thanksgiving.

"We might as well invite them to Thanksgiving dinner," Peg had said upon hearing the news. She'd been wearing an old sweatshirt of Steve's stretched over her belly. "They are Caitlin's grandparents, after all. And every kid deserves grandparents. Especially rich grandparents." She grinned at Faith.

"I hadn't thought of that," she said.

"Well, I have."

So the invitation had gone out, with Beth's approval, and Kevin had volunteered to winterize one of the smaller cabins for them to stay in.

Hugh had the door to the greenhouse open. He stepped inside and put Caitlin down so she could search her table and sandbox for the lost doll. Faith and Addy followed them inside.

He was standing before the monarch cage, watching something. Caitlin had found her Barbie beneath a sand bucket and was busy cleaning her up with a piece of paper towel she'd pulled off the role Faith kept under the counter. She moved to Hugh's side, and he reached out to put his arm around her waist. "What are you looking at?"

He pointed to the back of the cage. Two monarchs were perched on a wilting milkweed plant, slowing fanning their wings. "I didn't think you planned on hatching any more this year."

"I didn't. Obviously I overlooked a couple of chrysalides when we turned the last batch free." Monarchs were a migratory species. The last generation hatched each summer carried the instinct to make the long, dangerous journey to their winter breeding grounds in Mexico. Faith had released her butterflies a week before the current cold snap.

"These guys won't have a chance if you turn them loose now. It's supposed to get below freezing for the next three nights," Hugh said.

"I know. It's a shame. They'll feel the pull to fly south, but instead they'll have to live out their lives here." She could provide them with nectar substitute and the greenhouse would stay warm enough to keep them from freezing. Still, it was too bad they couldn't join the others on their journey.

Hugh turned her to face him. "What if we took them someplace warm and let them go? Aren't monarchs able to find their way back to where they came from no matter where you turn them loose?"

"We'd have to drive a couple of hundred miles to do that." Instinct would lead the butterflies unerringly back to their breeding ground, and their offspring would return to Bartonsville to begin the cycle again next spring.

"Actually, I was thinking of more than a couple of hundred miles." He was watching her closely, and as it always did, his nearness and the intensity of his eyes short-circuited her thought processes. It took a moment for the meaning behind his words to register. "How about a quick honeymoon in Texas? I need to get rid of my stuff. Besides, we've been married almost two months. It's time we had a few days to ourselves, damn it."

"Uh-oh. Bad word, Hugh." Caitlin's clear voice came from behind them.

Hugh's eyes widened in surprise. "Caught again," he said.

"She has ears like a bat," Faith said.

"I'll try to remember."

She looked over her shoulder at the two orange-and-black butterflies. Mark had loved them so. She did, too. Raising them was part of her life now. And she did want some time alone with her new husband. The house was big, Beth's room was at the other end of the hall, but still— "I'm not scheduled to work again until next week. I suppose I can ask Peg to watch Caitlin and Addy.''

''She doesn't need another dog and a not quite three-year-old underfoot. We could ask Beth to keep Caitlin.''

She swiveled her head to meet his eyes once more. He was waiting for her to answer, waiting to see if she was really at peace with Beth's involvement in Caitlin's life.

She smiled. ''I think that would be okay. She's so much stronger. And she has Kevin to back her up. I think they'll do fine.''

He pulled her close for a quick hard kiss. ''Turning these fellows loose where they have a chance to make it home is my way of saying thanks for their bringing me here to fall in love with you.''

''And I with you.''

Her heart felt as light and free as the butterflies they would be sending to find their home beneath the warm Mexican sun. She tightened her arms around his neck and kissed him back.

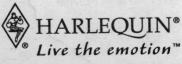

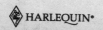

Corruption, power and commitment...

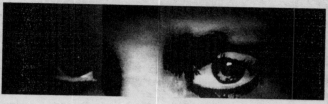

TAKING THE HEAT

A gritty story in which single mom and prison guard Gabrielle Hadley becomes involved with prison inmate Randall Tucker. When Randall escapes, she follows him—and soon the guard becomes the prisoner's captive... and more.

"Talented, versatile Brenda Novak dishes up a new treat with every page!"

—USA TODAY bestselling author Merline Lovelace

brenda novak

Available wherever books are sold in February 2003.

HARLEQUIN®

Makes any time special ®

If you enjoyed what you just read,
then we've got an offer you can't resist!

Take 2 bestselling love stories FREE!
Plus get a FREE surprise gift!

Clip this page and mail it to Harlequin Reader Service®

IN U.S.A.
3010 Walden Ave.
P.O. Box 1867
Buffalo, N.Y. 14240-1867

IN CANADA
P.O. Box 609
Fort Erie, Ontario
L2A 5X3

YES! Please send me 2 free Harlequin Superromance® novels and my free surprise gift. After receiving them, if I don't wish to receive anymore, I can return the shipping statement marked cancel. If I don't cancel, I will receive 6 brand-new novels every month, before they're available in stores. In the U.S.A., bill me at the bargain price of $4.47 plus 25¢ shipping and handling per book and applicable sales tax, if any*. In Canada, bill me at the bargain price of $4.99 plus 25¢ shipping and handling per book and applicable taxes**. That's the complete price, and a savings of at least 10% off the cover prices—what a great deal! I understand that accepting the 2 free books and gift places me under no obligation ever to buy any books. I can always return a shipment and cancel at any time. Even if I never buy another book from Harlequin, the 2 free books and gift are mine to keep forever.

135 HDN DNT3
336 HDN DNT4

Name	(PLEASE PRINT)	
Address	Apt.#	
City	State/Prov.	Zip/Postal Code

* Terms and prices subject to change without notice. Sales tax applicable in N.Y.
** Canadian residents will be charged applicable provincial taxes and GST.
   All orders subject to approval. Offer limited to one per household and not valid to current Harlequin Superromance® subscribers.
® is a registered trademark of Harlequin Enterprises Limited.

SUP02   ©1998 Harlequin Enterprises Limited